C. L. PATTISON

The
House
mate

HEADLINE

First published in 2019 by
HEADLINE PUBLISHING GROUP

1

Cataloguing in Publication Data is available from the British Library

ISBN 978 1 4722 6199 1

Typeset in Sabon LT Pro by EM&EN
Printed and bound in Great Britain by Clays Ltd, Elcograf S.p.A.

Headline's policy is to use papers that are natural, renewable and recyclable
products and made from wood grown in well-managed forests and other
controlled sources. The logging and manufacturing processes are expected
to conform to the environmental regulations of the country of origin.

HEADLINE PUBLISHING GROUP
An Hachette UK Company
Carmelite House
50 Victoria Embankment
London EC4Y 0DZ

www.headline.co.uk
www.hachette.co.uk

The Housemate

I can't remember what brought me down there, to the scrubby patch of woodland on the edge of the Common. Was it the way the light was filtering through the trees, or was it the sound of laughter? It doesn't much matter either way.

When I ventured into the woods, what I saw made my stomach lurch in shock, like the feeling when you miscount going upstairs in the dark and climb a step that isn't there. In that moment, everything around me seemed surreal, supersaturated – the brittle blue of the sky, the luminous green of the moss, the wicked little breeze lacing its way up along my arms and legs, lifting, ever so slightly, the ends of my hair.

I hid behind a tree and watched her with the enemy, listened to the soft laughter that rose like an arpeggio, as my brain struggled to comprehend the depth of her betrayal. My first instinct was to run, but then I felt rage, like a wave, begin deep behind my ribcage and grow, filling every artery and vein, until my eyeballs swelled with it. I wanted to plunge my fingernails into her face, to pull open the seams of her pretty smile and cut angry, crescent-shaped lines into her cheeks. I wanted her to scream, to writhe, to bleed. I wanted her pain to last forever. And in the end I got my way; I usually do.

It took planning and a certain amount of guile, but when it came to it, she was like a lamb to the slaughter. Right up to the end, she didn't suspect a thing. And just like that, the bitter taste in my mouth was replaced by a sudden, soaring rush of joy.

1

Megan

I saw it first. The small, cream-coloured postcard, bottom row, second from the left. There was nothing remotely attention-grabbing about it, the characters hastily formed, the descriptors spare, the punctuation lacking – the work, it seemed to me, of someone in a hurry. Easy enough to overlook among the many and varied enticements in the convenience store window: bicycles for sale, childminding services, an unplanned litter of guinea pigs, free to a good home.

I rubbed the smeared glass with my elbow and leaned forward for a closer look. As I read the words on the post-card, I felt a rush of light-headedness that made my palms tingle and my heart beat faster. I knew we'd been right to set our sights high, to hold out for something that ticked every box on our wish list. Now, at last, it seemed our patience had been rewarded.

Eager to share the good news with Chloe, I went to the open door of the shop and looked around until I spotted her, standing at the till. As she half-turned to hook her bulging canvas tote over her shoulder, I waved to catch her eye and made a beckoning gesture with my hand.

'I think our prayers have been answered,' I said, as she walked towards me. Without further explanation, I took her by the arm and led her to the window. 'Read that,' I said, rapping on the glass with a knuckle.

She leaned forward, letting her shopping bag slide down her arm to the ground. '*Bellevue Rise*?' she said, arching her eyebrows. 'That's up by the cemetery, isn't it?'

I nodded. 'Yep.'

'Didn't we agree it had to be a ten-minute walk to the nearest station, *max*?'

'It's sixteen minutes to the overground,' I replied. 'Fourteen if you're walking briskly. Hardly a deal-breaker.'

Chloe stuck out her bottom lip and exhaled a puff of air as she tried to dislodge the strands of honey-coloured hair that had fallen into her eyes. 'No, I don't suppose it is,' she admitted. She turned back to the postcard and continued reading. 'Shit,' she muttered under her breath a moment later.

'What?' I asked, unable to keep the impatience out of my voice.

'This place is fully furnished. I thought we were sick of living with other people's dodgy taste in interior design.'

'Let's not judge it before we've even seen it. For all we know, it could be straight out of the pages of *Ideal Home*.'

She made a face. 'Unlikely.'

Sensing her reluctance, I clasped my hands pleadingly.

'Come on, Chloe, it's a whole house, with a garden and an eat-in kitchen and two double bedrooms. It'll be a million times better than those pokey flats we've been looking at.'

Her eyes slid wistfully back to the shop window. 'It *would* be lovely to have a proper house and I could probably put up with the walk to the station. But aren't we both ignoring the elephant in the room here?'

I looked down at the pavement and nudged an ancient piece of chewing gum with the toe of my shoe. 'I assume you're talking about the rent?'

Chloe rolled her eyes. 'Of course I'm talking about the rent; it's way more than we can afford, especially when you factor in the cost of commuting.'

'I bet I can get the price down,' I said confidently. 'Remember those gorgeous handwoven throws I bought in Marrakesh? *Seventy-five per cent* discount, thank you very much.'

Chloe smiled, remembering the two weeks we'd spent in Morocco – just one of many fun holidays we'd had together. 'Yeah, but that was less to do with your negotiating skills and more to do with the fact the stallholder fancied you,' she beamed. 'And anyway, they *expect* you to haggle. That's why everything in that souk was vastly overpriced to begin with.'

I scowled melodramatically. 'Rain on my parade, why don't you?' Reaching into my jacket pocket, I pulled out my mobile phone and waved it in front of her face. 'So what do you reckon? Shall I contact the landlord and arrange a viewing asap? This one isn't going to hang around for long.'

Chloe shrugged. 'Why not . . . what have we got to lose?'

It had been six weeks since Chloe and I had embarked on our quest for the perfect property. We met twelve years ago at an Argentine tango taster class in our first week at university. The tango soon fell by the wayside, but we formed an unshakeable friendship that had outlasted numerous boyfriends, Chloe's year abroad in Prague, my six-month Southeast Asia trip, and more changes of address than either of us cared to remember. Even though we'd lived at least a hundred miles apart for most of our friendship, we'd been there for each other through good times and bad. When I was unexpectedly crippled by a violent bout of gastroenteritis, Chloe made the four-hour round trip by public transport to my sickbed, armed with essential oils, homemade lemonade and her Netflix password. And when *she* discovered her boyfriend of three years was cheating on her with his financial advisor, I organised a surprise spa weekend for us. Not only did this provide my best friend with a much-needed distraction, I also used the time to talk her out of reporting her boyfriend's hook-up to the FCA for professional misconduct, thus saving her a lot of time, energy and potential embarrassment.

It's strange, really, because, on the face of it, we're polar opposites. Chloe's a stage designer for an up-and-coming theatre company in London. She's creative, spontaneous and highly sensitive; she wears her heart on her sleeve and always sees the best in people. My background's in science. I'm a pharmacist; I'm calmer than Chloe and more circumspect. I love being organised and the reassurance of a perfectly-put-together plan. Our friendship shouldn't work, but for some inexplicable reason, it does. The Japanese have a special word for it – *kenzoku*. Literally translated, it means 'family'. It's the deepest sort of connection there is, deeper than soulmates even – almost like you've known each other in a past life.

Until recently, I was based on the south coast, locuming at various GP surgeries . . . fairly tedious stuff, but the money was good. I'd wanted to move to London for a while – not just for my career, but also to be closer to Chloe, and three months ago, I landed a job at one of the top London teaching hospitals. Since then, I had been living in temporary hospital accommodation, but with the tenancy on Chloe's flat share coming to an end, we'd decided to get a place together, just the two of us. Unfortunately, the task was proving rather more difficult than we'd anticipated. We'd both spent hour upon hour scouring the internet for suitable prospects, but the rental market in London was brutal and, with so many tenants bidding for a limited number of properties, we had suffered numerous disappointments. It really would be an incredible stroke of luck if a humble card in a shop window turned out to be our saviour.

2

Chloe

The sun was setting by the time we arrived at Bellevue Rise. A last faint gauze of light hung over number 46 – a Victorian end-of-terrace in a street that seemed narrower than it actually was because of the cars parked nose-to-tail along its length. We came straight from work, both of us swapping our heels for sensible flats in anticipation of the walk from the station, which, as Megan had predicted, took sixteen minutes precisely. When we arrived, we stood on the pavement for a few moments, looking up at the red-brick property, with its handsome bay windows, each assembling our own first impressions. There was a small front garden, surrounded on three sides by a low box hedge badly in need of pruning. Flanking the central path were two large rose bushes in full bloom, their petals a pretty, faded pink.

Before we had a chance to ring the bell, the front door swung open and a stale smell of old dinners gusted out from the interior, reminding me of the nursing home where

I'd worked for less-than-minimum wage the summer I took my A levels. The landlord looked to be in his mid-sixties; his face was long and stern and there were deep furrows bracketing his mouth. He didn't introduce himself, and simply offered a firm hand to each of us in turn, his demeanor suggesting he had more important things to do. Without preamble, he led us into a narrow hall, its walls lined with a haphazard collection of botanical prints.

'We'll start in here,' he said, thrusting open a panelled door. Megan followed him in, but I lingered on the threshold, taking in the scene that lay before me. It was a sitting room, high ceilinged and generously proportioned. All around it pieces of furniture stood in elegant poses, high-backed chairs with elaborately curved legs, rickety side tables, a louche chaise longue, baring its faded striped chest to the ceiling. A handsome fireplace yawned from the far wall, a shrunken arrangement of dried flowers clamped between its cast-iron jaws.

'This is a nice big room,' Megan remarked.

'It was two rooms originally, but they've been knocked through,' the landlord explained.

I stepped into the room, noting the absence of any personal items – books, coffee cups, remote controls. 'Have the previous tenants moved out already?' I enquired.

'There *were* no previous tenants,' the landlord replied. 'This was my sister's house. She died last year, probate has only just gone through.' He ran a hand through his silvery hair. 'My wife thinks I should sell it, but the property market's pretty flat at the moment, so I've decided to hang on to it, at least for a year or two.'

Megan prodded the arm of a wingback chair. 'There's rather a lot of furniture in here,' she said, getting straight to the point, like she always did. 'Would you consider putting some of the larger pieces into storage?'

The landlord shook his head. 'I haven't got time for all that. You either take it as seen, or not at all.'

'I think it's wonderful,' I said, my gaze drawn to the grandfather clock that loomed at the far end of the room, its throaty tick punctuating the silence. 'I feel as if I'm on a film set.'

The landlord smiled thinly and turned towards the door, drawing the sitting room inspection to an abrupt close. We followed him down the hallway to a modest kitchen with dated wall units and a scuffed slate floor. There was just room at one end for a farmhouse table with painted legs and five mismatching dining chairs.

'I know it doesn't look much, but you've got everything you need,' he said, as he moved around the room, pulling open doors. 'Combination boiler, fridge-freezer, washing machine, dishwasher . . .' He went over to the back door, jangling coins in his trouser pockets, as he peered out through the glass into the gathering dusk. 'As you can see, the garden's a decent size and there's a perfectly serviceable mower in the shed. It's electric, not petrol, easy enough to use. There's a nice little patio just outside the door here. I've had it pressure washed; the sandstone paving's come up really nicely.'

'I like the pergola,' Megan said, pointing towards the sturdy timber structure that sat on an elevated platform at the far end of the garden. It was smothered in plant life, the exact species indistinguishable in the diminishing light.

'Yes, it's beautiful in the spring; the clematis is spectacular. My sister used to love sitting out there.' He gave a strangled smile and jerked his head ceilingwards. 'The bedrooms are upstairs if you want to take a look. I'll stay down here if you don't mind. The stairs are quite steep and I'm waiting for a knee replacement.'

The master bedroom, with its grand bay overlooking the street, was less extravagantly furnished than the sitting room directly beneath it. Centre stage was a large brass bedstead and Megan immediately flung herself down on the mattress and spread her arms wide.

'What's it like?' I asked her.

'Not bad; it's a bit on the firm side, but nothing a memory foam topper won't fix.'

I went over to a whitewashed armoire, tracing its delicate curlicued edges with a fingertip. 'This is really pretty; the landlord's sister certainly had a good eye.'

'Hmm, it's a bit fussy for my taste,' Megan said, rising from the mattress. 'Come on, let's check out the other room.'

The second bedroom didn't have the elegant feel of the first, or the ornate original ceiling rose, but to me it felt much cosier. In one corner, a mahogany wardrobe sheltered an army of arthritic wire hangers and next to it sat a dressing table and a chintz-skirted stool. A newish double divan was pushed up against the opposite wall, where a William Morris paper of golden lilies appeared to be losing its grip.

'You can have the bigger bedroom, if you like,' I said, taking in the view of the back garden from the sash window. 'I much prefer this one.'

'You've decided you want to move in already?' Megan said, her voice swerving upwards in surprise. 'Don't you need some time to think about it?'

I shook my head emphatically. 'What's there to think about? We won't find anything better than this. OK, the furniture's not what we would've chosen and the location's a bit further out than we wanted, but it's still the best thing we've seen by a mile.'

'*Yessss*!' Megan said, punching the air triumphantly. 'I just knew Bellevue Rise was going to be the one.'

I couldn't help smiling. Megan was right to have a good feeling about this place; I often think she's more intuitive than she gives herself credit for. I tilted my head towards the door. 'Let's have a quick look at the bathroom, shall we? Then we can go downstairs and start turning the thumbscrews on the landlord.'

The bathroom held few surprises. There was a modern over-bath shower, but everything else was old and tired. A tarnished mirror hung above the watermarked sink and the black and white lino floor was curling at the edges.

'At least it's *got* an upstairs bathroom,' I remarked as

we went back out on to the landing. 'So many of these Victorian houses don't.'

Just then, I spotted a stripped pine door to my left that I hadn't noticed before. It didn't match the other doors and it was set at an unusual angle, as though it wasn't an original feature, but merely an afterthought. 'I wonder what's in here,' I murmured.

'Probably just the airing cupboard,' said Megan, who was already halfway down the stairs, keen to kick-start negotiations.

Curious, I twisted the ceramic doorknob. The door opened with a loud creak. 'Wow,' I said, exhaling a loud breath when I saw what lay on the other side. 'I wasn't expecting this.'

Megan stopped and looked over her shoulder. 'What is it?'

'Come and see for yourself.' I took a couple of steps into the room. It was small, little more than a box room, and contained an old-fashioned bureau with a drop-down leaf lined in green leather, a battered Lloyd Loom chair and a single low bookcase. The walls were tongue-and-groove beneath a low dado rail and painted a soothing shade of green.

Megan appeared at my side. 'I don't remember it saying anything about a study in the advert,' she said, looking around the room in wonderment.

'No, but what a fantastic bonus,' I said, imagining the possibilities. 'Just think, we'll be able to use this when we're working from home, instead of cluttering up the kitchen table with our laptops.'

'But I never work from home,' Megan pointed out, not unreasonably.

'Oh well, you can always come in here when you're doing your online dating. I'm sure you could use some privacy while you're sending your topless selfies,' I said, nudging her playfully in the ribs.

'Cheeky mare,' she retorted.

'Only teasing, hon,' I said, hooking an arm around her neck. 'You know I love you really.' I dropped my voice to a whisper. 'Seriously, Meg, we *have* to knock the landlord down on the rent; I think I'll die if we don't get this house.'

Megan nodded in agreement. 'Leave it to me.'

We found the landlord still in the kitchen, fiddling with something under the sink.

'Had a good look, have you?' he said, pushing down hard on his thighs as he eased himself up.

'Yes,' Megan said. 'And we'd like to make an offer.'

The landlord held up his hands like a policeman directing traffic. 'Oh no, I'm not accepting any offers. I've done my research, I know what places go for round here and I think the rent is more than reasonable.'

I felt a childish stab of disappointment.

'Um, OK,' said Megan, her confidence clearly wavering. 'The rent might be reasonable, but unfortunately we just can't afford it. Surely there's a little bit of wiggle room?'

The landlord sighed wearily. 'Sorry, the answer's still

no. You're not the only people interested. I've got two more viewings booked for tomorrow.'

I gave an audible groan. 'But we'd be model tenants. We've both got good jobs and can provide you with excellent references.'

'That's all very well, but references aren't going to pay the mortgage.'

I caught my bottom lip in my teeth and flashed a panicky look at Megan.

'*Please*,' said Megan. 'We really love this place.'

We stood in silence, nobody willing to break the deadlock. Then the landlord tucked his chin in to his neck, as if he was gathering his thoughts. 'There is another option,' he said.

I looked at him expectantly. 'Yes?'

'The study,' he went on. 'I know it's small – most of it was sacrificed when my sister put in the upstairs bathroom – but it could be converted to a third bedroom. I'd be happy to remove the existing furniture and put in a single bed and a chest of drawers. I might even be able to squeeze in a wardrobe.'

Megan frowned, as if she didn't understand where he was going with this. 'And then what?'

He threw his hands in the air in an impatient gesture. 'And then you'd have to find a third person to share with you. Given the size of the room, they'd have to pay less rent than you two, that's only fair.'

Relief surfed through me but then, to my dismay, Megan started shaking her head.

'I'm sorry, but that's not going to work,' she said. 'We've both had a gut full of sharing with other people. We want—'

She stopped mid-sentence, silenced by the arm I'd just flung across her sternum.

'I think that sounds like an excellent idea,' I said smartly. Ignoring Megan's sharp intake of breath, I offered my hand to the landlord. 'We've got a deal; when can we sign the contract?'

3

Megan

It was two weeks since we'd moved in to Bellevue Rise and the place was already beginning to feel like home. Before we turned our attention to looking for a housemate, we decided to spend a little time getting Number 46 just the way we wanted it, even if it did mean we had to cover the entire rent in the meantime. The gloomy hallway was practically unrecognisable. The botanical prints had been replaced by a series of cheerful abstracts that Chloe had liberated from the theatre's props room, along with an Oriental carpet runner and a pair of matching Art Deco-style lampshades. The sitting room had been brought to life with brand-new cushions, over-sized table lamps and my beautiful Moroccan throws, and upstairs, the dreary brocade curtains in the bedrooms had been swapped for pretty voiles we bought at a knockdown price in the market down the road. True to his word, the landlord had remodelled the old study and, while there was no escaping its challenging dimensions, it was now a neat and functional single bedroom with a modicum of storage.

A few days ago we'd posted an advert on a 'spare room' website. Thanks to the comparatively low rent we were asking, we'd received a healthy number of enquiries – which, after much animated discussion, Chloe and I had whittled down to a shortlist of six. We interviewed the first candidate yesterday and I can sum up the experience in one word: *awkward*. She wasn't unpleasant exactly; it's just that we had absolutely nothing in common. Chloe and I aren't fussy; we're not expecting to find a friend for life. We just want someone with similar interests, someone who's sociable and easy to live with. Someone normal. Needless to say, both of us were hoping today's candidate would be an improvement.

'What's her name again?' Chloe asked as we tidied up the sitting room in advance of her arrival.

I refolded a throw and draped it over the arm of the sofa. 'Samantha Charlesworth; she's thirty-two and self-employed. Her email didn't give much else away.'

Chloe glanced at the grandfather clock. 'She's due in fifteen minutes, just time to stick the kettle on.'

I winced, recalling yesterday's torturous encounter. 'Is it too early for something stronger?'

Chloe gave a mild shrug. 'Quarter to six; nearly G and T time.'

'Perfect,' I said. 'Make mine a large one. Plenty of ice, please.'

*

I was surprised when, a mere five minutes later, the door-bell's weedy chimes sounded. Tossing down the cushion I was plumping, I hurried out into the hall. When I opened the front door, standing on the doorstep was a tall, slender woman with a strong nose and a big mouth that was slightly parted to reveal an attractive overbite. She was stylishly dressed in black cigarette trousers, skyscraper wedges and a coral-coloured poncho.

'Sorry, I know I'm early,' the woman said, running a hand through her hair, causing the eclectic row of silver bracelets on her wrist to jangle. 'I had no idea the trains south of the river were so efficient; I thought it would take me a lot longer to get here.'

'Hi,' I said, stepping back from the door. 'I'm Megan and I guess you must be Samantha.'

'Yes,' the woman replied with a smile. 'But everyone calls me Sammi.'

I heard Chloe's footsteps behind me. 'Hi, Sammi, I'm Chloe, come on in,' she called out over my shoulder.

As Sammi stepped over the threshold, Chloe gestured to the bottle of Hendrick's in her hand. 'Meg and I were just about to have a drink. Care to join us?'

Sammi gave the faintest incline of her head. 'Thank you, that would be lovely; it's been a *very* long day at the office.' She was well spoken enough, but I thought I detected a faint Estuary twang.

'What is it you do exactly?' I enquired as I closed the door behind her.

Sammi's hazel eyes flickered over my body briefly,

before her gaze returned to my face. 'I'm a freelance fashion journalist. I mainly work from home, but I'm doing some shifts at *Marie Claire* this week.'

I must admit I was impressed. So, apparently, was Chloe. 'Wow, that must be amazing. Do you get to go to all the shows?' she asked eagerly.

'Some of them; I covered Milan last year and I'm in the process of setting up some post-show interviews with up-and-coming designers at London Fashion Week.'

Even more impressive. 'Sounds like a fun way to earn a living,' I remarked.

'I know,' she replied, putting her hands to her cheeks coquettishly. 'I've been doing this job for more than ten years and I'm still pinching myself. What do you do, Megan?'

'I'm a pharmacist; I work in a hospital.'

'How wonderful; I imagine a job like that gives you a lot of satisfaction,' she said silkily. 'And I bet you meet all sorts of interesting people.'

I threw a hand in the air in a polite display of modesty. 'It has its rewards.'

'Right then, Sammi, why don't I show you round while Megan pours the drinks?' Chloe said, thrusting the Hendrick's into my hands. 'Her gin and tonics are way better than mine.'

Sammi's face split in a wide smile. 'Sounds like a plan.'

4

Chloe

The tour of the house took longer than I expected. Our guest was enthusiastic and talkative, full of compliments about the quirky furniture, the clever styling, the period features. As I took her from room to room, I found myself warming to her more and more. Despite her confident manner and well-groomed appearance, it seemed to me that there was something wild and elemental lurking just below Sammi's glossy exterior. Her whole being seemed to bristle with energy as if she might glow with the force of her own coiled energy if we turned off the lights.

'I was just about to send out a search party,' Megan said wryly as we concluded our tour in the sitting room.

'Sorry, it's totally my fault,' said Sammi. 'I just can't get enough of this place. I made Chloe show me every last nook and cranny.' She made an expressive gesture with her French-manicured hands. 'But I see you saved the best till last. This room is absolutely stunning. I love the bay window and that fireplace is to die for.'

'You approve of our humble abode then?' Megan asked.

'I love it,' Sammi said, as her restless eyes continued to roam the room. 'You two are so lucky to live here.'

Megan scooped up a bulbous gin glass from the nearest side table and handed it to Sammi. 'What about the room, though? It's pretty small; I know I wouldn't be able to fit all *my* stuff in there.'

Sammi shrugged. 'Honestly, it's not a problem; I travel pretty light.'

'I bet you've got heaps of clothes, though,' I said.

'Not really,' Sammi murmured, taking a sip of her drink.

'So where are you living at the moment?' Megan asked.

'A flat share on the District Line,' she replied, rather vaguely. 'But I'm ready for a change of scene. I don't want to sound harsh, but the people I live with are starting to get on my nerves.'

I nodded in empathy. 'Megan and I have had our share of irritating housemates over the past few years.' I sat down on the sofa and gestured for Sammi to do likewise. 'Please, make yourself comfortable. We've got a few questions to ask you, if that's OK.'

'Of course,' she said, sinking elegantly into the nearest chair. 'Ask me anything you like.'

'We'll start with an easy one,' said Megan as she joined me on the sofa. 'What do you like to do in your spare time?'

Sammi crossed one leg over the other and laced her

fingers around her knee. If she was nervous, it didn't show. 'Let's see now . . . I go to the gym a couple of times a week and I enjoy reading – nothing very highbrow, just whatever's in the bestseller lists. But my big passion is cooking. A few years ago, I spent the summer in Tuscany and learned how to make authentic Italian food – not the fancy stuff, just honest, rustic home cooking, the sort of food real Italians eat.'

I smacked my lips together. 'I love Italian. Unfortunately, it doesn't love my waistline quite so much.'

Sammi's eyelashes fluttered. 'I know the feeling.'

I found that hard to believe; Sammi didn't look as if she had an ounce of spare flesh on her.

'OK, question number two – and sorry if this sounds a bit nosey – but do you have a partner? It doesn't matter either way, it's just so we know if we should expect any overnight guests.'

Sammi shook her head. 'My last serious relationship ended last year. How about you two?'

'I'm single,' said Megan glumly. 'But not for the want of trying.'

Sammi raised a quizzical eyebrow. 'Online dating?'

'Guilty as charged.'

'In that case you'll have to give me some tips. I must admit I've only dipped my toe in the water, but so far all I've caught are sharks and tiddlers. Honestly, I sometimes wonder where all the decent men in London are hiding.'

Megan made a sympathetic moue. 'I keep asking Chloe's

boyfriend to fix me up with one of his friends, but he claims they're all gay or married.'

'How long have you and your boyfriend been together?' Sammi asked me.

'Not long; we're just coming up to our six-month anniversary,' I replied, feeling myself smile, the way I always did whenever I talked about Tom.

'How did you guys meet?'

'At work. I'm a stage designer at a theatre in Pimlico and Tom's a freelance sound engineer. He worked on one of our productions at the beginning of the year, but now he's got a contract with a film company in Soho.'

'You two sound like a real pair of high fliers.'

I swirled the ice cubes around my glass. 'We just love what we do, I think that's the most important thing.'

'Tom's such a sweetheart,' Megan said. 'I reckon he's the best thing that ever happened to Chloe – apart from me, of course.'

Sammi smiled. 'Are you two super close then?'

'Yeah, Chloe knows me inside out and back to front.'

I nodded vigorously. 'We're more like sisters than friends.'

'How lovely,' Sammi said, brushing a stray hair from her poncho. 'Is there anything else you'd like to ask me?'

I let out a long sigh. I wasn't sure these questions served any useful purpose; either you gelled with someone or you didn't. 'I don't know about anyone else, but I've had enough of this stupid interrogation,' I said. 'Personally, I'd rather hear some gossip from the catwalks.'

Sammi's tawny eyes glowed like copper. 'So where would you like me to start?'

Darkness was falling by the time Sammi departed. My inhibitions loosened after a couple of gin and tonics, I hugged her on the doorstep and promised to be in touch soon. I stood in the doorway and watched her as she walked to the end of the road, her sheet of chocolate hair shining under the street lights.

'I think that went really well, don't you?' I said, as I returned to the sitting room.

Megan nodded thoughtfully. 'Yeah, she's all right, and I think she was quite taken with the house.'

I sat down on the sofa and hugged a cushion to my chest. 'I think Sammi would make a *great* housemate; in fact, I reckon we'd be hard pushed to find anyone better.'

Megan looked at me strangely. 'How can you say that when we've only interviewed two people so far?'

'I don't know, there's something about her . . . it's hard to put into words; it just seems like she'd be a good fit.'

'I don't think we should make any hasty decisions,' said Megan, practical as ever. 'Perhaps Sammi only looks good in comparison to yesterday's candidate – and the only way we can eliminate that bias is to meet the other four contenders.'

I shook my head in amusement. 'You always analyse things in such a scientific way, Meg.'

'Do I?' she said, frowning.

'Yes – *you* think with your head, I think with my heart. That's why we make a good team.'

Megan went quiet and began pulling at her bottom lip, the way she always did when she was thinking. 'Don't you think Sammi's rather polished?' she said at length.

'Well, she does work in fashion.'

'I wasn't talking about her appearance.'

'So what *were* you talking about?'

'The way she had all the right answers on the tip of her tongue. I thought she seemed a bit . . . I don't know . . . *rehearsed*.'

'Perhaps she's done so many house-sharing interviews over the years she's got her technique down,' I suggested. 'We shouldn't let it count against her.'

Megan made a mumbling sound.

'So shall we offer her the room then?' I said pushily.

Megan sighed. 'Well . . . OK, if you really want to; I suppose it'll save us the hassle of interviewing all the others.' She raised her glass in the air. 'Here's to finding our new housemate.'

I smiled; I hadn't expected Megan to give in so easily. I tapped my glass against hers. 'To our new housemate.'

5

Eleven, twelve, thirteen . . .

I'm staring at the lounge wall, counting the birds. It's such pretty wallpaper; it has a blue background and there are tree branches all over it. Sitting on the branches are multi-coloured birds: big ones, small ones, some are even spreading their wings as if they're about to fly away. But my favourites are the teeny ones with the long pointy beaks. Dad says they're called hummingbirds and they can fly right, left, up, down, backwards and even upside down. How cool is that?

Dad's not here; he won't be back from work till six-fifteen. He's a surveyor, although I'm not exactly sure what that is. I think it must be a good job, though, because he has a beautiful brown leather briefcase (that I like to sniff when no one's looking because it smells so lovely!) and inside it are lots of maps and drawings and other important-looking bits of paper.

Mum's lying down on the sofa. She has a nap most afternoons after I get home from school. I don't know why she's always so tired; she doesn't exactly do much since she gave up her job at the bank. Her hair's fanned out across a cushion and she's snoring really loudly – so loudly I keep losing count of the birds. I'd much rather be upstairs in my bedroom, making friendship bracelets with the kit I got for Christmas (I've made twelve bracelets so far, but I don't have anyone to give them to just yet). Mum won't let me go upstairs, though; she says I have to stay down here, so she can keep an eye on me. Or maybe it's so I can keep an eye on her. I can't remember. I'm not even allowed to watch TV because Mum says the noise will wake her up. Usually I read a book, but I've run out of books. I get them from the library and I gobble them up really quickly. That's why I'm counting birds; there's nothing else to do.

I hope Mum wakes up soon because I'm dying for the loo; I have been for the past half an hour. I look over at the door to check it's definitely shut. It is. The handle makes a big squeak when you press down on it and I know that if I try to open it I'll wake Mum up and then there'll be All Hell To Pay. I bite down on my lip so hard I taste blood and carry on counting.

Fourteen, fifteen, sixteen, seventeen . . .

Hmmm, I might have counted that big green one twice.

Eighteen, nineteen . . .

I don't think I can hold on much longer, even though I'm trying my hardest. I snake my hand under my navy blue uniform skirt and press it between my legs. I want to pee so bad it hurts. I turn away from the wall and look out of the window, hoping I'll see something to take my mind off it. It looks as if my luck's in because there's Mrs Dobson going for a walk with her golden Labrador. I watch them for a little while, all the time thinking how much *I'd* like to have a dog (a sister would be better, but a dog's the next best thing). It would be my best friend and we'd go everywhere together. It would sleep in my room at night, and in the morning it would jump on my bed for cuddles. But then Mrs Dobson's Lab cocks its leg against a tree and starts to do a big long wee. Oh no . . . now I want to go even more! I look away quickly and my eyes settle on Mum's cheese plant standing in the corner of the room. She got it as a leaving present when she left the bank and it's grown really big, so big she had to buy a new pot for it last weekend. Then, just like that, I know what I have to do.

Ever so quietly, I get up from my chair and start creeping over to the cheese plant. The carpet's thick and fluffy and my plimsolls don't make a sound when I walk on it. When I get to the plant, I turn around, lift up my skirt, pull down my pants and stick my bum right out, so it's over the edge of the pot. As I let go, I feel so much better that I almost sigh out loud, but I manage to stop myself in time. I take care to pee very slowly, so it has time to sink into the soil, instead of running over the top and on to the carpet (it's lucky I've got strong thighs from gym club!).

I'm still peeing when there's a loud noise from out in the hallway. It sounds like stuff being pushed through the letterbox, probably one of those free newspapers or a brochure from the estate agents. Straight away, I freeze; my heart feels like one of those clockwork mice that spin around. I look over at Mum just as her eyelids pop open.

For a moment she stares at me and her dark eyes look like ink blots. Then her face twists as she realises why I'm standing there with my pants down and my bum up in the air. In a flash, she's up off the sofa and stomping across the room. I think I know what's coming next.

'You dirty little bitch,' she roars. 'What the hell do you think you're doing?'

She grabs the collar of my white school shirt and pulls me towards her. My pants are still round my ankles and I almost trip and bash my head on the sharp corner of the sideboard. But I'm not worried about that; I'm too busy thinking *I hope she doesn't tear my shirt* – because if she does, I'm going to have to go through the laundry basket and find a dirty one to wear to school tomorrow because there are no clean ones left.

Mum's got hold of both my shoulders now and she's shaking me so hard I can feel my brains rattling inside my skull. 'You're no better than an animal!' she screams, her words coming out all bunched up. 'I said you belong in the gutter and now you've proved me right.' Her hand flies up in the air, then it comes back down towards me and I shrink as I feel the whack on the back of my thighs. Mum's hand is big and hard and it hurts like anything. I know there'll be a red mark there next time I look at it and by the time I wake up tomorrow it will have turned into a bruise. When Mum's finished with me, I crumple to the floor. I can tell I'm crying because there's wet on my cheeks, but I'm not making a sound. What's the point when no one can hear me?

6

Megan

I surveyed the half-dozen cardboard boxes and two large suitcases that were lined up in the hallway. 'Where's the rest?' I asked Sammi as she returned from paying the black cab driver.

'That's the lot,' she replied, reaching past me to hook her expensive-looking patent leather handbag over the newel post at the foot of the stairs.

'Seriously, that's your entire life – right there?'

'I told you I travelled light,' she replied coolly.

I shook my head in disbelief. 'I had to hire a man and a van when I moved in.'

'I had to hire *two* men,' said Chloe, as she emerged from the kitchen. She flipped the tea towel she was carrying over her shoulder and went to hug Sammi. 'Welcome to your new home; we're so glad you said yes.'

'Believe me, I didn't have to think about it for a second,' Sammi said, smiling, as they broke apart.

I stepped forward to give Sammi a kiss. 'It was great

that you could move in so quickly,' I said, as her cheek brushed mine like a cool breath. 'Your old landlord must've been a bit cross that you only gave two weeks' notice.'

She smiled creamily. 'I paid him for the whole month, so he's got nothing to be cross about.'

'Still, it's a shame that you had to fork out for *two* lots of rent,' Chloe murmured. 'We would've held the room for you for a couple more weeks.'

'I don't mind, it was worth it. Like I said, I was keen to move on.'

'Oh well, his loss is our gain,' I said, bending down to pick up the largest of the boxes. 'We'll give you a hand taking your stuff upstairs, but then we'll have to leave you to it. We've got tickets for a photographic exhibition at the Barbican; then we're meeting some friends for lunch. Sorry about that.'

Sammi pushed her hair back off her forehead. Her eyebrows were thick, almost lush, and they balanced the tense, defiant line of her jaw. I found myself thinking how attractive she was – not beautiful exactly, but certainly striking.

'Why would you be sorry?' she asked.

Chloe cast a curious glance at her. 'Because we're leaving you alone on your first day in the house.'

She took a soft intake of breath, as if understanding had suddenly dawned. 'Please, don't give it another thought; I've been looking after myself for years.'

'Well, if you need anything while we're out, you can always call or text us,' I told her. 'You've got both our numbers.'

She grasped the handle of a suitcase and began heaving it towards the stairs. 'That's kind of you, but I'm sure I'll manage.'

It had just gone six-thirty when Chloe and I returned to Bellevue Rise. We were accompanied by Chloe's boyfriend Tom, who had joined us for lunch and a mooch round Covent Garden. As we stepped through the front door, we were greeted by the mouth-watering aroma of garlic and roasting meat. We followed it to the kitchen where we found Sammi standing at the hob in Chloe's Cath Kidston apron, cheeks pink from the heat of the oven. She was stirring something in a huge cast-iron saucepan, while the extractor fan whirred noisily above her head.

I raised my hand in greeting. 'Hey, how's it going? Sorry we're back so late.'

'No problem, I've been busy making myself at home,' Sammi replied. 'I finished all my unpacking, so I thought I'd crack on with dinner. How was the exhibition?'

'Really good, it was a 1960s retrospective. You should go; I'm sure you'd find it interesting from a fashion point of view,' said Chloe, as she took Tom's arm and drew him forward. 'Sammi, I'd like you to meet my boyfriend, Tom. Tom, this is Sammi.'

They exchanged hellos and Tom sauntered over to the hob to inspect the contents of the saucepan. 'That smells amazing,' he said, using his hand to waft the savoury steam up towards his nose. 'What are you making?'

'Chicken *cacciatore*, roasted aubergines and Parmesan potatoes.'

'Sammi's an expert in Italian cuisine,' Chloe told him. 'She might let you lick the saucepan if you ask her nicely.'

'I can do better than that,' Sammi said. 'I've made enough food for everyone; I thought it would be nice if we all ate dinner together on my first evening.'

My eyes widened in appreciation. 'Wow, Sammi, you didn't have to go to all that trouble.'

She balanced her wooden spoon carefully across the top of the saucepan. 'It's no trouble; I enjoy cooking for other people.'

'I can't wait to taste it,' Tom said, rubbing his hands together. 'How long have we got – enough time for me to pick up some wine from the off-licence?'

'It'll be ready in fifteen minutes, give or take.'

'Perfect. What would everyone prefer – red or white?'

'Red would go better with the food,' said Sammi, hooking her long hair behind her ears.

'Red it is, then.'

'I think I'll grab a quick shower while you're doing that,' Chloe said, thrusting her front door key into Tom's hand. 'Then I'll come down and lay the table.'

'And I *must* change out of these shoes,' I said, following Chloe towards the door. 'My feet have been killing me since London Bridge.'

When we got upstairs, Chloe made straight for the bathroom, but I hesitated on the landing, noticing that Sammi's bedroom door was slightly ajar. Keen to see what my new housemate had done with the tiny space, I nudged the door with my foot. I was expecting to be greeted by a colourful and lavishly accessorised boudoir; what I got instead was an exercise in minimalism. The walls were bare, not a single picture or photograph was in sight and there were no fripperies or decorative embellishments of any kind; even the duvet cover was plain white. The handful of personal items that *were* on display – a laptop, a jewellery box and a stack of magazines – were neatly arranged on the low bookcase that now doubled as a bedside table. The whole room felt temporary, somehow, like theatrical scenery from one of Chloe's productions that had been assembled for a specific purpose and could be shifted at any moment.

Intrigued, I stepped into the room. In the background, I heard the groan of ancient plumbing as the shower came on. I felt a prick of guilt, knowing that Chloe would take a dim view of my snooping. I went over to the room's newly acquired wardrobe and opened the single door. Inside, Sammi's clothes had been arranged with military precision, trousers at one end, skirts and dresses at the other, everything draped perfectly over pretty padded hangers. On the floor of the wardrobe, shoeboxes were stacked three high and each had a Polaroid photo of the contents attached with gaffer tape. I shook my head, marvelling at Sammi's organisational abilities, which rivalled even my own. With an envious sigh, I closed the wardrobe door and turned back towards the landing. Just then, an unexpected flash of colour caught my eye . . . the corner of a bright orange book, poking out from under the bed. The room was so immaculate, I thought it must have fallen there by accident while Sammi was unpacking. Almost without thinking, I bent down to pick it up. It was surprisingly heavy and on the front the words 'Photo Album' were embossed in narrow black letters. It looked well used; the front cover was covered in grubby fingermarks and the corners had softened with age. Unable to stop myself, I flipped the cover. The album fell open randomly somewhere in the middle and I found myself looking at a photograph of a young girl with long dark hair and protruding front teeth. She was sitting on a woman's knee in what appeared to be the living room of a house. The woman was holding the girl tightly around the waist – almost *too* tightly, it seemed to me. Glancing at the transparent pocket on the opposite page, I was surprised to see that, rather than a photograph, it contained a folded-up page, apparently torn from a newspaper. The paper looked soft as if it had been folded and unfolded numerous times. Frowning, I turned over the page. I managed to catch a glimpse of an official-looking letter bearing an elaborate crest when I heard a sharp voice from the landing.

'What are you doing?'

I looked up. Sammi was standing in the doorway, still wearing her apron, which now bore a large, tomato-coloured stain. She looked so different; her face was pinched, her eyes brimming with anger. It was as if for a second a window had flown open and I had caught a glimpse of something beyond the glossy façade. A spider of anxiety crawled up the back of my neck.

'Shit, Sammi . . . I'm really sorry,' I stuttered, unable to understand why I hadn't heard her coming up the stairs. 'The door was open; I just wanted to see what you'd done with the room.' I snapped the album shut and held it out to her. 'I noticed this lying under the bed and I thought it must have fallen there by accident; I was just about to put it on the bookshelf for you.' My voice faded; even to my own ears it sounded like a lame excuse.

Sammi's mouth twisted into a hard grin of contempt. 'But you just couldn't resist having a quick nosey first,' she said, snatching the album from my hands and hugging it to her chest possessively. I felt my cheeks flushing scarlet, like the shame-fever of a child who's been caught in some terrible act.

'It just fell open; I really didn't mean to pry,' I said, the words withering on my tongue, desiccated by Sammi's accusatory face. In a clumsy, tentative way, not knowing what else to do, I put my hand on her arm, whereupon she recoiled as if I'd given her an electric shock.

At that moment, the bathroom door opened and Chloe appeared on the landing dressed only in a towel. She stopped dead when she saw us standing together in Sammi's room. 'Is everything all right?' she asked.

Sammi turned and tossed the album down on the narrow single bed. When she turned back a split second later, I was surprised to see that her look of fury had gone and in its place was a placid, almost blank expression. 'Sure,' she replied smoothly. 'I just came up to ask if you two are OK with nuts; I've made a chocolate and hazelnut *semifreddo* for dessert.'

Chloe's eyes rolled heavenwards. 'Mmm, nuts and chocolate . . . two of my favourite things.'

'Mine too,' I said quietly.

Sammi's eyebrows clenched. 'Goodness, you two really are separated at birth; you even have the same taste in food.' I wasn't sure if I was imagining it, but I thought I could detect a faint undertow of sarcasm in her voice. She turned on her heel and walked the few paces to the top of the stairs, leaving her precious album lying on the bed. 'Don't worry about laying the table,' she told Chloe amiably as she passed her on the landing. 'It's taken care of already.'

By the time I returned, somewhat sheepishly, to the kitchen with Chloe, Tom was back from the off-licence. We found him ferrying a series of steaming serving bowls to the kitchen table, which had been beautifully laid with stiff linen napkins and cut-crystal wine glasses, both of which we'd inherited from the landlord's sister. A large vase of pink roses, presumably picked from the front garden, formed a heady centrepiece.

'This is such a treat,' said Chloe, pulling out a dining chair.

'Yes, it's very sweet of you, Sammi,' I said, feeling bad about what had just happened and acutely aware that I had some serious making-up to do. 'It should be me and Chloe making *you* a meal on your first night.'

'Like I said before, it's really no trouble,' Sammi said breezily as she joined us at the table. 'Don't stand on ceremony, everyone . . . please, dig in.'

Tom began unscrewing the top from a bottle of Merlot. 'Did you used to cook for your old flatmates?'

'I did when I first moved in, but after a while I stopped.'

'Oh?' said Tom, as he moved around the table, filling wine glasses. 'Why's that?'

Sammi's nostrils flared almost imperceptibly. 'To be perfectly honest with you, we fell out.'

Chloe frowned as she reached across me for the aubergines. 'What happened?'

Sammi began helping herself to a healthy portion of Parmesan potatoes. 'At first, they all seemed really nice, but after a while I started to feel they had it in for me.'

'What did they do to make you think that?' I asked her.

Sammi's fork hovered momentarily over a casserole dish, before she drove it into a piece of chicken. 'Honestly, guys, it's such a boring story and really not worth retelling,' she said.

I wanted to press her for more details, to ask her what her flatmates had done that was so awful – but, given what had just happened between us, I didn't want to risk incurring her wrath again.

'Well, I don't think you'll have any problems with Chloe and Megan,' Tom said. 'They're both pretty respectful of other people's feelings.'

I cringed inwardly. My behaviour upstairs had hardly been a good indicator of my *respect for others*. At least Sammi had had the decency not to say anything to Chloe; I was grateful to her for that. I glanced over at Sammi, but her eyes were locked on Tom.

'Anyway, that's enough about me,' she said, dabbing her mouth delicately with the corner of her napkin. 'I want to hear all about your work, Tom. Chloe tells me you're working for a film company at the moment, it sounds fascinating . . .'

I was quiet during dinner. I still felt awkward about the photo album and I knew I should never have ventured into Sammi's room without her permission. I expected the atmosphere between us to be frosty but, to her credit, Sammi betrayed no hint of censure. It was almost as if nothing had happened. She even complimented me on the earrings I was wearing and asked me to send her a link to the website where I'd bought them – and, as the evening wore on and the wine flowed, I found myself slowly relaxing. The food was delicious and Sammi was clearly an accomplished cook. Her *cacciatore* was melt-in-the-mouth and the decadent dessert was practically restaurant quality. The minute everyone had finished eating, she jumped up and began gathering up the dirty dishes from the table.

'*We'll* clear up, Sammi, it's the least we can do,' I told her firmly as I prised a stack of bowls from her hands. 'Why don't you go through to the sitting room? I'll bring you a coffee, if you like, and we'll come and join you when we're done here.'

'Actually, I think I'll have a bath if you don't mind,' said Sammi, rising from the table. 'I'll probably head straight to bed after that; I'm feeling really tired all of a sudden.'

'Of course,' said Chloe. 'There should be plenty of hot water left.' I thought she sounded a little disappointed at the prospect of Sammi's early departure. I must admit that I was disappointed too; I'd been looking forward to finding out more about our new housemate.

'Are you OK for towels?' I asked, conscious of Sammi's meagre luggage and keen to portray myself in a more positive light. 'You're welcome to borrow one of mine.'

Sammi shook her head. 'I'm good, but it's kind of you to offer, Megan.'

'I guess we'll see you in the morning then. Thanks again for dinner; it really was delicious.'

She gave a small, spiky smile, then she slipped from the room.

Even with three of us, it took ages to clear up. Sammi's meal had been a triumph, but she had used a bewildering number of saucepans, utensils and ovenware in the process. Afterwards, we retired to the sitting room where Tom and Chloe promptly became engrossed in the latest episode of a crime drama they were addicted to. Struggling to pick up the thread of the show mid-season, I reached for my phone. My first port of call was Facebook, where I shared several photos I'd taken earlier on at the exhibition. In between uploads, my eyes kept flicking to the other two, who were curled up together on the sofa. Chloe's head was resting peacefully on Tom's broad chest. His arm was draped across her shoulders and he was plucking absent-mindedly at the ends of her hair. I found myself thinking what a great couple they made; it was wonderful to see Chloe so happy and settled. I turned my attention back to Facebook and impulsively searched for a name: *Samantha Charlesworth*. A handful of results came up, but none was a match. I tried again: *Sammi Charlesworth*. Still nothing. I performed the same searches on Twitter. Zilch. Ditto Instagram. I was just about to try a generic Google search when the crime show went to an ad break.

Chloe looked over at me. 'Don't tell me you're cruising Tinder again.'

'No, I am *not*,' I retorted. 'I was just seeing if I could find Sammi on Facebook; I wanted to send her a friend request.'

'Good idea, I'll do the same.'

'You can't, she not's on there.'

Chloe's eyes flitted back to the TV. 'That's a shame.'

'She's not on Twitter or Instagram either. Don't you think that's weird . . . a journalist with no social media presence?'

Tom stretched his arms above his head and gave a massive yawn. 'Perhaps she uses an alias, loads of people do.'

'Hmmm, maybe.'

'I bet she's on LinkedIn . . . here, give me that,' Chloe

said, reaching over to grab the phone from my hands. She began punching keys at lightning speed. A few seconds later, she turned the screen towards me. 'See, I was right . . .'

I peered hard at the screen. A picture of Sammi stared back at me. Her glossy hair was twisted into an elaborate chignon and she was wearing subtle lipstick and an eye-catching statement necklace. Her expression was friendly but distant. I took the phone from Chloe's outstretched hand and began scrolling down. A brief CV followed the photo, together with half a dozen glowing endorsements from past employers.

'She looks gorgeous in that picture, doesn't she?' Chloe said.

'Yep, she certainly scrubs up well.' I dropped my phone in my lap and stared at the TV, but my mind was elsewhere. 'What did *you* make of Sammi, Tom?' I said after a few moments.

'She's a good-looking girl, there's no doubt about it.'

Chloe elbowed her boyfriend in the ribs. 'What about her *personality*?'

Tom smiled and kissed the top of Chloe's head. 'She seems very nice – and she's clearly intelligent; I think you two have made a good choice.'

I took a deep breath in through my nose. 'Let's hope you're right.'

7

Today is the first day of the summer holidays – and if that's not exciting enough, it also happens to be my eleventh birthday. I didn't wake up until eight-thirty, which is quite late for me. The house is quiet and still and there's a ray of sunlight on my pillow, so I lie there for a while like a cat on a car bonnet, enjoying its warmth.

A few weeks ago, Dad asked me if I wanted a birthday party. I knew he didn't mean the usual sort of party, in our front room, with cake and balloons and pass the parcel, because no one ever comes to our house, except the postman and the Jehovah's Witnesses, and they're not allowed *inside*. He was talking about a party at McDonald's, or the bowling alley, or one of those places that other kids go. I would've said yes, but I didn't think anybody would come, except for Liam, of course. I'm not sad enough to have a party for two people, so I told him I'd rather go to the zoo instead. I think I've been to the zoo before, but it was so long ago I don't remember it, so this is kinda like my first time, which makes it extra special. The only thing that would make it even more special is if it was just me and

44

Dad going, instead of me, Dad and *Mum*. When Mum and Dad are together, it's like there's no one else in the room, even if the other person in the room does happen to be celebrating their birthday. I think Dad must really love Mum because he treats her like a china doll, which might break into a million pieces if you play with her too roughly. Mum treats Dad like . . . well, she's a bit nicer to him than she is to me. But only a bit.

Eventually, I get out of bed and creep out on to the landing. Mum and Dad's bedroom door is shut tight, which means they're still asleep. I go to the bathroom for a wee, remembering not to flush or I'll be in BIG trouble, then I tiptoe down the stairs.

In the kitchen, all the dirty dishes from yesterday are piled up on the draining board. The dishwasher's broken; it has been for ages. The bin's full too – so full the lid won't close properly and it smells like something died in there. I don't know why the house is always such a mess, especially when Mum doesn't have anything else to do. When I have my own house, it's always going to be clean and tidy and there'll be one of those air freshener plug-in things in every room.

I'm starting to feel hungry, so I make myself some Coco Pops (thank God for cereal . . . sometimes I have it for breakfast *and* dinner!) and carry my bowl through to the living room. I switch on the TV, taking care to turn the volume right down, the way I've been told to, and flick through the channels until I find a cartoon.

By the time Dad appears in his pyjamas, I've already

spent a whole hour and twenty-nine minutes of my birthday on my own. Despite his lie-in, Dad looks tired and there are big creases under his eyes. 'Morning, Birthday Girl,' he says. 'Sorry I slept in; Mum and I had a bit of a late one last night.' He strokes my head with one of his giant hands and I close my eyes, wanting the moment to last forever. But it doesn't. 'Mum and I haven't had time to get you a present,' Dad tells me. 'But we'll stop at the shops on the way to the zoo and buy you something nice – how about that?'

I force myself to smile, but there's a scratchy feeling at the back of my throat. 'What time are we leaving for the zoo?' I ask, because it's quite a long drive and I'm worried that the day's slipping away.

'Let's see how Mum's feeling first,' Dad says as he shuffles towards the kitchen.

Seeing as I don't have any presents to open, I decide I might as well go upstairs and get dressed. I wanted to wear my red dress, the one with the bows on the front, but when I check I see that it's still in the laundry basket. I work out that it's been there for sixteen weeks and two days. I know this because the last time I wore it was when we went to visit Grandma over Easter. It didn't go very well. Grandma doesn't like Mum and she's not very good at hiding it (not like me – I'm excellent at pretending to feel one way when really I'm feeling quite different!). We only stayed for two hours, then Dad said we'd better be getting back. As Mum was marching off down the driveway, Grandma pulled Dad's arm on the doorstep and hissed into his ear: 'I've told you before – *she's* not welcome here.' I think she meant Mum. Or maybe she meant me; I hope not.

Anyway, back to my birthday outfit. In the end, I choose my blue pleated skirt and a green T-shirt that always reminds me of our next-door neighbour's parrot. It escaped once – the parrot, I mean, not the T-shirt – and it was me who spotted it, two whole days later, in the cherry blossom tree in our back garden. Dad threw a tea towel over the parrot and picked it up and took it back home. Our next-door neighbour was so pleased he gave me a bag of treacle toffee. That was one of the best days of my life.

My blue pleated skirt's all creased, but I'd better not try ironing it myself because last time I did that I burned a hole in my school skirt and Mum went MENTAL. Speaking of Mum, she's up at last; I can hear her moving around on the landing. I hold my breath as she walks past my bedroom door, praying she won't come in. Luckily, she doesn't. I get dressed quickly, then I go to the bathroom for a wash. While I'm cleaning my teeth, I hear Mum shouting at Dad. Her voice travels all the way up the stairs. I put my fingers in my ears because I don't want to hear her; it must be awful to be so angry before the day's even begun. I wish Dad would stand up for himself – stand up for both of us – but he never does. I think he must be scared of Mum too.

The shouting goes on for quite a while, so I stay upstairs, where it's safe. Eventually Dad comes into my bedroom. He looks worn out, just like I do after gym club. He tells me we're not going to the zoo after all because

Mum's not well and we have to stay at home and look after her. I nod, my chin wobbling as I fight to hold back tears. But there's good news as well, Dad says, as he chucks a pile of takeaway menus on my bed: I can choose whatever I like for lunch.

By the time the food arrives, Mum's gone back to bed, so it's just Dad and me, which is the way I like it. Dad says he's not hungry, which is even better because it means I get a whole twelve-inch stuffed crust all to myself. I eat it greedily, pulling off a fat slice and chomping down on the crust, not caring when the cheese squirts out and dangles off the end of my chin. I know I'm being a proper pig, but I can't help it; despite the Coco Pops, my stomach feels like an empty bowl that I could fill forever. As I get stuck in to a second slice, I think to myself that maybe it hasn't been such a bad birthday after all. There have been much, much worse.

8

Chloe

'Come on, Chloe, be realistic – do you seriously think you'll pull this off?'

I balled my fists, driving my fingernails into my palms. 'Of course I do, Bryan. Why would I waste my time presenting a design concept if I didn't think it was achievable?'

I should have expected this reaction from Bryan Donohue, the theatre's production manager. Ever since he'd joined the company eighteen months ago, our relationship had been an uneasy one. Bryan's job was all about schedules, budgets, procedures – and he'd proved himself an efficient and highly focused organiser. But when it came to the bigger picture, I sometimes felt he lacked a crucial understanding of creativity, of the way the artistic mind worked. 'Of course, if you don't think you have the imagination to realise my vision . . .' I said, maintaining a steady eye contact.

'It's not that at all,' Bryan grunted back. 'I just think your design is overly ambitious.'

The gaze of everyone in the room returned to the model box that lay on the table between us. A painstakingly accurate scale model of my set design, it had taken me weeks to build – not to mention the storyboards, computer-modelled set plans and dozens of hand-drawn perspective sketches that had preceded it. I knew my concept was daring, but then, so was the script. Written by an award-winning young actress-turned-playwright with a spectacular Instagram following, *Neurosis* was a radical and thought-provoking study of mental illness, free from the usual constraints of narrative and timeline. The theatre had beat off stiff competition to secure the performance rights and, even though opening night was months away, the critics were already sharpening their pencils in readiness.

'What do *you* think, Richard?' I said, turning to the artistic director. A brilliant and thoughtful man with a long and distinguished career in contemporary theatre, Richard Westlake had been my mentor ever since I joined the theatre straight out of university, with only a degree in Stage Design and a few weeks' work experience to my name. I started out as a general dogsbody, at the beck and call of any department who needed me. But, over the years, I had worked my way up to my current position of principal stage designer. It was a job I loved and I poured my heart and soul into every production, but I had certainly expended more time, creativity and pure passion on this project than any that had gone before it.

Richard smoothed his hair, letting his hand come to rest

on the back of his neck. 'I think it's great,' he said. 'The clever use of the trap door, the frame over the stage to make the space feel claustrophobic, the giant revolving mirror, reflecting the introspective nature of the piece . . . it's original, immersive, fantastically bold. I think what you've done here is create an alternative reality, rather than just a set.'

My heart vaulted with relief. 'Thank you, Richard, I'm glad *you* share my vision,' I said pointedly.

'Bringing this production to the stage is going to take an enormous amount of dedication and hard work, from *all* of us,' Richard continued. 'But if we succeed, the publicity will be huge and we all know what that means . . .'

I nodded. 'Bums on seats.'

'This set won't be cheap,' said Bryan, tugging anxiously at the flesh of his neck. 'By my estimate, we'll be kissing goodbye to almost twenty-five per cent of the annual production budget. With figures like those we can't afford for this to be a flop.'

'In that case, we're going to have to pull out all the stops,' said Richard. 'Are you prepared to do that, Chloe?'

I placed a hand over my heart. 'I promise you, Richard, I'll do whatever it takes.'

The minute the meeting was over, I scooped up the model box and hurried back to my studio, where Jess, my endlessly patient and supremely efficient assistant, was anxiously awaiting the verdict.

'How did it go?' she asked eagerly, as I pushed aside a

heap of sketches on my desk to make room for the model box.

'Bryan thought it was far too ambitious.'

'*Idiot*,' Jess spat. 'Was he any more specific?'

'Not really.'

'No surprises there, then,' Jess said witheringly. 'It wouldn't be so bad if he gave us constructive criticism, but he just seems to rubbish our ideas for the sake of it. Perhaps he's trying to justify that whopping great salary of his.' She tossed her biro down on the desk in disgust. 'You're bloody good at your job, Chloe. Everyone here knows that – why hasn't *Bryan* managed to figure it out?'

Privately, I agreed with Jess's analysis, but professionalism prevented me from saying it out loud. I sat down at her desk and broke into a smile that I hoped wasn't too smug. 'Fortunately, Bryan's opinion didn't count for much on this occasion.'

'You mean . . .' Jess said expectantly.

'I mean that Richard *loved* it.'

Jess shrieked in delight. She, more than anyone, knew how much time and effort had gone into my design. 'Richard Westlake, I want to have your babies!' she bellowed as she beat out a drum roll on the desktop.

I snorted with laughter. 'I think Richard's husband might have something to say about that.'

'A minor detail,' Jess said, batting her hand in front of her face. 'Take it from me, Chloe, your set design's going to make *Neurosis* one of this theatre's most talked-about productions ever; the critics are going to love it.'

'Hmm, let's not count our Olivier awards just yet,' I said, staring hard at the model box on my desk. 'I still don't know if I can turn this pile of cardboard and polystyrene into a reality.'

'Oh, come on; you're not seriously doubting yourself, are you?'

I chewed on my bottom lip. 'I must admit I put on a good show in Richard's office, but deep down I was shitting myself. The technical requirements of this set are enormous. Maybe Bryan's right, maybe my concept *is* too ambitious. But I know one thing . . . I'm going to die before I prove him right.'

Jess grinned. 'And I'm going to do everything I can to help you.'

'Good, you can start by setting up a meeting with the tech crew so I can run my idea for the revolving mirror past them. It's absolutely critical to the design; if we can't get the mirror right, we may as well give up now. Check my calendar first. I know I haven't got much availability this week . . . or next week, come to think of it.'

As Jess pecked at her keyboard, I began rifling through my overflowing in-tray, frowning as I came across a quotation for a pair of custom-built French windows that was way more than I had been expecting. I made a mental note to contact the supplier later and see if I could renegotiate the price. Failing that, I would have to lower the spec on the windows. The theatre was a business, at the end of the day, and it was imperative I kept a close eye on the bottom line, even though it didn't come naturally to me. I rubbed my temples, thinking of all the tasks I still had to do that week. I knew I had to keep on top of things, because when I get stressed, a kind of fog descends on my brain – the kind that inhibits logical thought and robs me of energy. Pushing the in-tray away, I switched on my computer and started going through my lengthy list of emails.

The rest of the day passed in a whirl of activity. I had a drawn-out meeting with the theatre's head mechanist to discuss an elaborate cable system he had devised to accommodate complicated scenery changes for an upcoming musical. Afterwards, I paid a visit to the scenic artists to check on the progress of some painted backdrops I had designed for the same show. Lunch was a salad bowl at my desk while I trawled through eBay for retro fabric I needed for a mood board I was working on. The rest of the day was given over to sitting in on a final dress rehearsal for the theatre's current production, before I had to stay late to oversee some last-minute tweaks to the set.

By the time I left work, I was utterly exhausted. As I trudged home from the station, I was looking forward to catching up with Megan and telling her all about my small victory over Bryan. It wasn't until I arrived home to find the house dark and empty that I remembered she was working a late shift at the hospital. A hastily scribbled note on the kitchen table, meanwhile, revealed Sammi was at a launch party for a new range of jewellery and wouldn't be back till late. Irritated that I would be spending the evening alone and too tired to cook, I threw together some cheese and crackers and ate them in front of the TV. By ten o'clock, my eyelids were already drooping and so I headed upstairs for a quick shower before falling into bed. As I drifted off to sleep, my mind was still buzzing with ideas for the new production.

It felt as if the air was being slowly sucked out of my lungs. My mouth gaped as I scrabbled for breath, my hands clawing at the smothering duvet. Around me, the room lay in shadow, but I could feel the black smoke curling around my nostrils. I could hear the crackle of flames as they licked at the panels of my bedroom door. My heart spiralled up into my throat. I was confused, disorientated, unsure of what was happening. Only one thing was clear – I had to escape, no matter what. I threw off the duvet and rolled out of bed. Around me the room pitched and swayed like a rolling ship, making me feel dizzy. I knew instinctively I would never make it down the stairs, so I turned instead towards the window, where the soft glow of distant street lights was guiding me to safety. As I staggered towards the light, I was aware of the breathless knocking of my heart that seemed to come from somewhere outside me, as if someone were rapping at the door. Suddenly, I stumbled on something lying on the floor and my legs almost gave way, but I flung out a hand and managed to steady myself on the nearest piece of furniture. I kept moving doggedly towards the window, driven on by the roar of the flames and the sound of my own ragged breathing. It seemed to take an age, but once I got there, it was an easy matter to part the thin voile and heave the sash open. Hitching up my nightie, I threw one leg over the windowsill and braced myself for the long drop to the garden . . .

I woke with a numbness cauterising my left arm from shoulder to elbow, as if an invisible body had been pressing against it all night. I sat up, strangely feeling even more tired than when I went to bed. A soft light was filtering through the gap in the curtains and around me, the room lay in disarray. The chintz stool had been knocked over and various items from the dressing table – my hairspray, a box of tissues and all my make-up brushes – were scattered across the floor. The first thought that hurtled across my mind was that we'd been burgled. Then a movement caught my eye – the voile billowing in the breeze from the open window. Although I had only the foggiest recollection of the previous night's events, a mixture of fear and disgust, bordering on nausea, rose in my throat. I shivered with certainty. I knew what this meant: it was starting all over again.

9

Ever so carefully I unfold the top of the paper bag, remembering that it must be used another six times before it can be thrown away. It's funny, but every time I open the bag I find myself wondering what's inside. The reason it's so funny is because every single day since I started at St Swithun's, I've had the exact same thing for lunch. Two cheese and pickle sandwiches on white bread and an apple.

It's not that I don't like cheese and pickle, it's just that it would be nice to have something else for a change. Even if the sandwiches were just cut into triangles, instead of rectangles. Or if I had a pretty pink lunchbox with Disney characters on the front and a matching flask, then at least my sandwiches wouldn't get squished inside my satchel. But I mustn't grumble because there are babies in Africa who don't get any lunch at all; at least that's what Mum says.

The afternoon is warm and sunny, so I'm sitting under the big oak tree on the playing field. Usually I have lunch with Liam, who has the whitest skin I've ever seen and really bad eczema (sometimes he scratches it so hard it bleeds – *ewww!*). But Liam's off sick today, so I'm on my own. I don't really mind; Liam's not that much fun. He's a bit of a baby and he never wants to do the things I want to do, like skipping and making daisy chains. Unfortunately, I'll have to make do with him until something better comes along.

After lunch, it's English, which is one of my favourite lessons. I'm the best reader in the whole class, that's what Miss Pickering says. Miss Pickering is very kind and pretty. Once, she lent me her hankie when my nose started running and I didn't have a hankie of my own. It was a lovely hankie with a frilly edge and her initials in one corner: HJP. I asked her what the initials stood for and she told me: 'Harriet Jane Pickering'. I took the hankie home with me by accident and Miss Pickering never asked for it back. I keep it in the biscuit tin under my bed with all my other treasures.

We're reading *The Secret Garden* at the moment. Miss Pickering goes round the room so we all have a turn at reading out loud. I've read *The Secret Garden* already, but I don't mind reading it again because it's one of my favourites. I wish *I* had a secret place I could go where nobody would ever find me, but I guess I've got more chance of having egg mayo in my sandwiches tomorrow!

When the bell goes at three o'clock, I jump up quickly and run to the coat pegs on the wall before anyone else can get there. I only live a fifteen-minute walk from school, but Mum gets cross if I'm late home. As I unhook my satchel, Miss Pickering calls my name and says she needs to have a quick word. I don't know it yet, but what she tells me will change my life forever.

The next morning, I'm so excited to get to school I run the whole way there! As I sit down at my desk, I'm feeling very big and important because I'm the only kid in the classroom who knows what's about to happen. When Miss Pickering walks in with the register tucked under her arm as usual, she's not alone. Holding her hand is a girl a little bit shorter than me with a heart-shaped face and fiery hair. She isn't in school uniform like the rest of us. Instead she's wearing a navy blue and white striped dress, the bottom half of which is gathered so it poufs out; it looks as if it cost a lot of money. Instead of a satchel she's carrying a drawstring bag with her name on it in fat, stitched-on letters: ANOUK. Her blue eyes are big and round as she stares around the classroom. There are twenty-six of us and only one of her, so I expect she's feeling quite scared.

'Children, I'd like you to meet a new member of the class,' Miss Pickering says. 'This is Anouk, would everybody like to say good morning to her?'

'Good morning, Ann-oook,' we sing together.

''*Allo*,' Anouk says in such a cute voice it makes me want to cry.

'I know term began last week, but Anouk has come all the way from France; that's why she's a little bit late,' Miss Pickering tells us. Then she turns towards me. I make myself really tall by sitting up straight and sticking my chin out like a chicken . . . this is it, my big moment!

'I thought it would be a good idea if I gave one of you the very special job of looking after Anouk, just until she finds her feet.' Miss Pickering smiles at me and asks me to come to the front of the class. Out of the corner of my eye I catch Eleanor Hardy glaring at me all squinty-eyed, like a cat watching a bird; I bet she'd gobble me up if she could. I'm glad she's jealous; she's mean to me all the time. Once, she stuck strawberry Hubba Bubba in my hair on purpose and Mum had to cut it out with scissors. *And* she said I smelled funny. Miss Pickering heard her and made her say sorry; she wasn't very happy about THAT!

Miss Pickering takes Anouk's hand and puts it into my hand. It feels small and slightly damp. As I lead Anouk back to my table, I'm loving the way everyone's watching us. I point to the empty chair next to mine that Miss Pickering must have put there before she went home last night. 'Don't be scared,' I whisper to Anouk as she sits down and smooths her pretty dress over her lap. 'I'll take care of you.'

10

Megan

I felt a little frisson of excitement – or possibly just plain lust – when I spied his email in my inbox. *From: Peter Chambers. Subject: Ethics Committee.* Pete's an orthopaedic surgeon; I met him four months ago on my first day at the hospital when he visited the pharmacy with a query about an anticoagulant he'd prescribed. Our conversation was brief, but he made quite an impression on me.

Pete wasn't conventionally handsome; his features were too uneven for that. But he had a muscular physique and his eyes radiated creases all the way to his ears, which made him look as if he were smiling even when he wasn't. He had this amazing charisma too, an aura of omnipotence that I found incredibly sexy. Apparently lots of surgeons have it, although I haven't met enough of them to confirm or refute this hypothesis. After that first day in the pharmacy, we kept bumping into each other in and around the hospital. Pete always seemed rather pleased to see me – slightly flirtatious even – but the platinum band on his wedding finger was enough to kill off any romantic designs I might have had on him. I may be a prolific dater, but I also have a strict moral code – and married men are definitely off limits.

Pete and I both sat on the hospital's Ethics Committee – a multidisciplinary forum for the discussion of ethical issues affecting the delivery of patient care; in fact, Pete was the acting chair. They put out an appeal for new members soon after I joined the hospital and I thought it would be a good way to mix with colleagues from other departments, as well as forming an impressive addition to my CV. The Committee met quarterly and that afternoon I was scheduled to attend my inaugural meeting.

I clicked on the email and it sprung open.

> Hi Megan,
> Just checking to make sure you're coming to the meeting today. We don't have a pharmacist on the Committee, so your input will be most useful. I'm not sure what time you're going off shift, but some of the members usually go for a quick drink afterwards and you're more than welcome to join us.
> Pete

I hit reply.

> Really looking forward to this afternoon and happy to contribute in any way I can. The drink sounds great btw 😊
> Megan

The meeting was much more interesting than I'd anticipated. The Committee debated the eligibility of patients for renal transplants, as well as concern among hospital staff that the setting of priorities in surgical waiting lists was being influenced by pressure from the local media. I didn't have a chance to speak to Pete beforehand – he was too busy talking with one of the senior clinicians – but at the start of the meeting he made a point of welcoming me to the group and he seemed fascinated by what I had to say about toxicology in patients with chronic kidney disease. The meeting ended around five and most people rushed off straight away, leaving just a few stragglers chatting among themselves. As I returned my coffee mug to the tray, I wondered if perhaps people weren't going for drinks after all, but then Pete appeared at my elbow.

'Pub?' he said, arching his eyebrows.

I nodded. 'Lead the way.'

It was only when we were walking down the corridor that I noticed no one was following us.

'Are the others going to meet us there?' I asked him.

Pete held open the door that led out into the car park and gallantly stood aside to let me go first. Our bodies brushed as I passed him and I caught the scent of a citrusy aftershave.

'It's just us, I'm afraid. I didn't realise everyone else had other commitments. I hope you're not too disappointed.'

'Absolutely not,' I replied, suppressing a smile.

We didn't go to the Mitre, which was the nearest watering hole and a regular hangout for hospital staff. Instead,

Pete took me to the Three Kings, an upmarket gastro pub, a ten-minute walk away. Being Friday, it was fairly busy, but Pete found us a table on the mezzanine level, away from the main hubbub, where we could actually hear each other speak. He got the first round in and we exchanged hospital chitchat for a while, discussing how we thought the meeting had gone and gossiping about the new Head of Oncology, who seemed to be ruffling a few feathers.

'So how are you enjoying the job?' he asked when we were on our second round of drinks, which he had also insisted on paying for. 'This is your first hospital post, isn't it?'

I nodded. 'I'm absolutely loving it, although I am finding the shift work more demanding than I thought I would.'

'Yeah, it plays havoc with your body clock *and* your social life, but you're young enough – you'll get used to it,' he said, his blue eyes crinkling attractively. He ran his thumb over the rim of his pint glass. 'Does your other half work in medicine?'

I shook my head. 'Actually, I'm single.'

'Really? I'm surprised to hear that.'

I felt a blush blooming on my cheeks. 'I guess I just haven't met the right person. How about you? Is your wife a doctor too?'

'No, she's a solicitor.' His jaw tightened. 'But the way things are going, she won't be my wife for much longer.'

His frank admission took me by surprise. Pete and I weren't exactly friends; we hadn't known each other long enough for that, and it seemed strange that he would be taking me into his confidence, unless . . . All at once I got a fluttering sensation in my chest as if a butterfly were trapped behind my ribcage. 'Really?' I said, unsure of the correct response.

He smiled sadly. 'Fiona and I have been leading separate lives for quite a while now. We did think at one point we'd be able to work things out, but we've both realised now that we're fighting a lost cause.'

'I'm very sorry to hear that.'

'Don't be.' He looked at me and our eyes locked together. I could feel the heat emanating from his thigh where it almost touched mine.

I cleared my throat. 'Do you and Fiona have children?'

'Two – a boy and a girl; they're both at boarding school.'

'Don't you miss them?'

'Desperately. I'd much rather have them at home with us, but Fiona doesn't think it's practical with the long hours we both work. The kids love it, though, and they're both doing incredibly well academically. To be honest, it's no bad thing that they're out of the way right now when things are so tense at home between Fiona and me.' He laid both hands on the table, palms down. 'Anyway, I have no intention of boring you to death with tales of the woeful state of my marriage. Tell me more about you. Are you from London originally?'

'No, I grew up in Reigate in Surrey, mainly because it's commuting distance from Gatwick. Dad used to be a pilot for one of the big airlines and Mum was cabin crew – at least, she was until I came along. After that, she worked in a travel agent's.' I paused as I conjured up a mental image of my parents. 'Even after forty years of marriage, they're still really in love; they actually hold hands when they're out shopping together, would you believe?'

Pete smiled. 'I think that's wonderful. What about brothers and sisters?'

'One brother, younger than me; he's a pilot too.'

'So why did you decide to break with family tradition and pursue a career in pharmacy?'

'I was good at sciences and I wanted a career that involved helping people. I knew I'd never stick ten years of medical training, so pharmacy seemed like the next best thing.'

'Smart decision. Pharmacy's one of the fastest growing areas of healthcare; there are some great opportunities out there.' Pete lifted his empty pint glass. 'Same again? Or do you have to be somewhere?'

It was late by the time we pitched out of the pub, both slightly the worse for wear. As we said our goodbyes outside the Tube station, Pete asked for my number. *Where's the harm in that?* I thought to myself as I punched it into his phone.

I was grinning to myself the whole way home. I couldn't wait to tell Chloe about my evening. I'd dropped Pete's name into our conversations a few times and she knew I had a slight crush on him . . . well, quite a large crush actually. It was a couple of days since I'd seen her and I knew she'd been very busy at work. She was involved in a big project, a play about mental illness that involved all sorts of complicated stage effects, and she'd sounded quite stressed about it the last time I spoke to her. Perhaps I ought to suggest a night out together. I could even invite Sammi along. It was two weeks since she'd moved in and the incident with the photo album seemed to be water under the bridge. Certainly, neither one of us had mentioned it since. I was pretty sure she hadn't said anything to Chloe either, because if she had, Chloe would have told me.

When I got back to the house, just before eleven, the lights were still on in the kitchen. I found Sammi sitting alone at the table, drinking camomile tea.

'Hi Megan, how come you're back so late? Was there some sort of emergency at work?' she asked as I filled the kettle at the sink.

I opened a cupboard, looking for the china mug that Chloe had bought me as a moving-in present. Emblazoned across the front were the words: *World's Best Friend*, surrounded by pink hearts. It was a tongue-in-cheek thing we did, buying each other 'best friend' tat, the more saccharine the better. Then I realised Sammi was already drinking from it. I felt a jab of irritation and swallowed it quickly, telling myself not to be so juvenile; it was only a bloody mug.

'Nope,' I said, reaching for the tea bags – the regular ones, not camomile; I can't stand that stuff. 'I've been out for a couple of drinks with a colleague.'

Sammi sank her teeth into her lip as if something was troubling her. 'Oh. It's just that Chloe said you were going to go to yoga with her tonight.'

I smacked my forehead with the palm of my hand. 'Shit, I completely forgot about that. Was Chloe really pissed off?'

'I'm sure she'll forgive you. After all, that's what best friends do, isn't it?' Sammi said, reaching behind her neck and flipping her impossibly shiny hair over her shoulders, as if she were centre stage in a shampoo ad. 'She sent you a text to ask if you were running late, but you didn't reply.'

I groaned, remembering that I'd put my phone on silent for the Ethics Committee meeting and had forgotten to change the setting when we went to the pub.

'I know how much Chloe was looking forward to that. I can't believe she missed out because of me,' I muttered, unable to believe my own stupidity.

'Oh, she didn't miss out,' Sammi said. 'I went with her instead.'

I frowned. 'I didn't know you did yoga.'

'I don't. It was my first time and I have to say, I *really* enjoyed it.' I caught a spark of something in her eyes – amusement and pity fusing together. 'I've told Chloe I'll go again with her next week, if she's up for it.'

'Good idea,' I said cheerily, as if I couldn't care less. I got up from the table. 'I'd better go and apologise. Where is she – upstairs?'

Sammi yawned, revealing the moist red cavern of her

mouth. 'I'd leave it till the morning if I were you. Chloe went to bed ages ago; she'll be asleep by now.'

Ignoring her, I headed towards the stairs, pausing on the landing to see if there was any telltale sliver of light under Chloe's bedroom door, but there wasn't. I knew I'd still be asleep by the time she left for work in the morning, so I made a mental note to text her as soon as I woke up. I hated letting people down, especially my best friend.

11

The school bell rings and my heart skips. The reason I'm so happy is because, instead of hurrying home to Mum like I normally do, I'm going to Anouk's house for tea! I haven't been invited to anyone's house since Year 3, so I'm very, VERY excited. It's been fifteen days and six hours since I first met Anouk and my life has changed so much already. For one thing, I don't have to hang out with Liam any more. His whiny baby voice was getting on my nerves and looking at his crusty eczema scabs used to put me off my lunch.

Everyone at school likes Anouk because she's pretty and foreign, and because her hair is to die for. And some of that like is starting to rub off on me! The kids in my class treat me differently now. At lunch break they actually talk to me, and I'm not the last one to get picked when we choose teams in PE any more. Not *everyone*'s being nice; Eleanor Hardy's still as mean as ever. The other day she called me a stalker, just because I went with Anouk when she had to use the bathroom. What a stupid thing to say! I wouldn't be doing the job Miss Pickering gave me very well if I left Anouk on her own, even for a second, now would I?

Anouk's mum Lucy is waiting for us at the school gates. She's small and pretty like Anouk, but she doesn't have the French accent. She was born in England, she tells me, but moved to France in her twenties to work as an au pair and that's when she met Anouk's dad. But then the company that Anouk's dad works for decided to send him over to England . . . am I ever glad they did!

Anouk's house is massive. It has electric gates that swish open all by themselves and a garage that's big enough for three cars. Inside it's full of brand-new furniture and there are big vases of flowers everywhere that make the whole house smell like a garden. When Anouk said *come for tea*, I thought we'd be having beef burgers or soup, which is mostly what I have at home, but Lucy has made something called a *cass-oo-lay*. It has big fat sausages and little brown beans in a thick gravy that's better than any gravy I've ever had before. For pudding there's chocolate mousse – made from scratch, not out of a packet! I wish I could have seconds, but I say *no, thank you* when Lucy asks me because I don't want her to think I'm a greedy pig.

Lucy is ever so kind to Anouk; I love the way she calls her 'darling' and 'angel'. My mum would NEVER call me 'angel'. To her, I'm the devil. And when Anouk spills blackcurrant juice all over the table, Lucy just smiles and wipes up the mess with a cloth. I would've got a thump for that. I'd probably have to lick up the spill as well, just like I did the time I knocked over the vinegar bottle.

After tea, we go and play in Anouk's bedroom. The walls are painted pink and she has this gorgeous floaty net thing over her bed *and* her own TV. We play with her doll's house for a bit and then Anouk asks if she can plait my hair. It feels so good, sitting on her pretty, padded window seat, while she fusses over me. My hair's a bit knotty (how embarrassing!), but Anouk doesn't seem to mind. Afterwards, I give her the friendship bracelet I've made. It's pink and purple because I know they're her favourite colours.

'Best friends forever?' she asks, as I tie it on her wrist. I'm so happy I could cry. It's as if something tight and crinkly has opened up inside me, like a flower reaching for the sun. 'Best friends forever,' I say back. Then I see the time on Anouk's Cinderella alarm clock. Suddenly, I feel all breathless and light-headed, as if a big hand is squeezing my windpipe. I should have been home eighteen minutes ago. I jump up and tell Anouk I have to go.

I tell Lucy I don't mind walking because it's not very far, but she insists on taking me in her car. At least it means I get to spend another ten minutes with Anouk, but I make sure Lucy drops me at the end of our road because she mustn't see inside our house. The plan is to let myself in with the key I keep on a piece of string around my neck and sneak upstairs without Mum noticing. But she's lying in wait for me, like a crocodile at the edge of a river.

'Where have you been?' she barks, pouncing on me the minute I walk through the door.

'You know where I've been,' I tell her. 'At Anouk's house.'

'Don't get smart with me,' she says. 'You should have been back half an hour ago. I've been sick with worry.'

We both know that's not true. She'd be quite happy if I never came home again.

Then Dad's voice drifts out from the lounge. 'Leave her be, Janine, she's home now, that's all that matters.' Mum takes a step back and it looks as if, just for once, she's going to listen to Dad. I turn away from her and walk towards the stairs. Then she notices there's something different about me.

'Who did that to your hair?' she says, grabbing the end of my plait and yanking me backwards so hard I nearly fall over.

'Anouk,' I say, trying my hardest to keep the wobble out of my voice.

Mum laughs, a horrible, cold, Cruella de Vil laugh. 'Hasn't anyone ever told her you can't polish a turd?' I don't know what she means, but then a lot of what Mum says doesn't make any sense at all to me.

'I'm sick of hearing about this bloody Anouk,' she hisses, breathing her stinky breath all over my face. 'It won't last – you do know that, don't you?' She unfolds her fist and whacks me across the head with the palm of her hand and for a few seconds all I see is stars. 'Now get out of my sight,' she says, pointing up the stairs. 'I can't stand looking at you.' I don't need telling twice.

12

Chloe

Do you ever wake up in the morning and feel out of sorts right from the get-go? Well, I was having one of those days. I was still a bit annoyed about Megan standing me up yesterday. We'd been talking about doing yoga classes for ages. It was Meg's idea; she knew I'd been under a lot of pressure at work and she thought it would help me relax. I must say I'm surprised she let me down; it really wasn't like her. Still, I'm glad Sammi offered to come instead. I didn't fancy going on my own and being the only person in the class who didn't have a clue what they were doing. I enjoyed spending time with Sammi. She gives the impression of being a bit aloof but actually, once you get to know her, she's really quite sweet.

At least Megan texted me this morning to apologise; it turns out she went for drinks with one of the surgeons at work and totally forgot our yoga date. She said she'd tell me more when she saw me, but who knows when that will be. It's a funny thing, but now that we live together we seem to be talking less than we did when we lived in different counties. It can't be helped, I suppose, not when we're both spending so much time at work these days.

I felt odd and rather irritable as I got ready, even though I'd slept well; at least I think I had. I wasn't looking forward to going to work, which wasn't like me. The deadline for the completion of the *Neurosis* set was fast approaching and there was still so much to do. Once I realised the scale of the task I'd set myself, the elation I'd felt at Richard Westlake's endorsement had quickly worn off. As Bryan was fond of reminding me, expectations for this production were alarmingly high. The scriptwriter was hitting the headlines on a weekly basis, thanks to her burgeoning romance with a British director twenty years her senior. This, together with the casting of a young unknown in the lead role, had created a real buzz around the production. Tickets were selling like hot cakes and the theatre's press officer was already fielding calls from journalists. Bryan was breathing down my neck every minute of the day and I knew that if I went a penny over budget, or failed to bring any aspect of the design to fruition, he would be absolutely unbearable. I loved my job, but sometimes I felt physically sick at the prospect of everything I had to cram in to each day.

Ivor, the theatre's Construction Manager, was looking at me as if I'd just asked him to donate a kidney.

'Oh no, that'll never work,' he said, his tongue working busily between his teeth as he studied the sketch laid out on the table in front of him. 'It's going to be much easier if we revolve the stage, instead of the mirror itself.'

'But Ivor, as I keep telling you, I need the *mirror* to revolve, or the scene won't be nearly as effective.' I dug the heels of my hands into my eyes – why did I feel so goddamn tired all the time? 'Surely you guys can make it work.'

I waited, somewhat impatiently, as his brain engaged in a silent calculus. Ivor had been at the theatre so long he was practically part of the furniture. He oversaw all aspects of set building and had responsibility for our in-house team of workshop technicians, as well as any external contractors. When I first joined the theatre, he was incredibly patient with me, and generous in sharing his knowledge; I would always be grateful to him for that. He had a tendency to be a bit of an old woman, however. He was partial to shaking his head and making clucking noises, while at the same time telling me that there was simply no way my designs could be brought to life, at least not in the way I was proposing. But then he would go away and think about it for a while, before inevitably announcing that he could now see a way around a problem that, just a few short days ago, was utterly insurmountable. It was irritating, especially today when I was feeling a bit off-colour, but it was just the way Ivor worked and there was nothing I could do about it.

Finally, he spoke. 'I tell you what,' he said, giving his chin an exploratory tug. 'Leave it with me and I'll get back to you once I've had a chance to mull over the options.'

'Great, but Ivor . . .' I gave him my sweetest smile. 'Please don't take too long about it, because the clock's ticking on this one. Dress rehearsals start next month.'

He nodded as he began rolling up the sketch. 'I'll see what I can do, but I'm not making any promises,' he said, frustratingly non-committal as usual.

Back at the studio, more bad news awaited me. One of the set's key props was a chair, from which the main protagonist would deliver a number of streams-of-consciousness monologues. The chair would remain on stage for the entire performance and I wanted it to be a real statement piece – iconic and eye-catching, without being too distracting for the audience.

Somewhat limited by budgetary constraints, I'd spent hours (many of them at weekends) scouring second-hand shops and antiques markets in search of the perfect chair. Eventually, I found it on an obscure website – an oversized, baroque-inspired dining chair, fashioned entirely from clear Perspex. It had arrived that morning by courier, but as I peeled off its protective wrapping, I saw to my immense frustration that one of the Perspex arms had snapped off in transit. At first, I thought it might be salvageable, but on closer inspection it was completely beyond repair. The chair was a one-off, crafted by a design student back in the nineties. There was no chance of getting another one, so now I had to go back to the drawing board.

As I surveyed the now useless chair, my chest was drum-tight and I could feel my stomach cramping. All I wanted to do was relax with a soothing cup of peppermint tea, but there was simply no time.

Yet again, I ended up working late and when I got home I was so worn out I couldn't even be bothered to eat. Megan was out – goodness knows where, I had totally lost track of her work schedule – and Sammi was sprawled across the sofa, watching TV in her PJs and an eye-catching Missoni-print robe. It was nice to see her using the sitting room for a change; she more often than not spent evenings holed up in her tiny bedroom. She claimed to be working up there, but sometimes I did wonder if she was avoiding us. I chatted with her for a while, before making my excuses and heading off to bed. As I got undressed, a huge tiredness came over me, a kind of lethargy in the face of my ever lengthening 'to do' list. It was like being given an algebra problem when your brain's exhausted and you know there's some distant solution, but you can't summon up the energy to even have a stab at it.

I think it was around three a.m. that I heard the tread of unfamiliar footsteps coming up the stairs. I'd had a pathological fear of intruders since childhood and I was always reminding Megan to make sure she double-locked the front door when she came back from a late shift. She was as security conscious as I was, and she always did . . . but someone was definitely climbing those stairs. The footsteps stopped outside my bedroom door and a moment later I heard the sound of the doorknob shifting.

'Hello,' I said, a faint question mark hanging over the

greeting. No answer came. As the door opened, a funnel of dread opened up inside me. I felt as if I was riding a rollercoaster at the exact moment the car inched over the summit and plummeted to the ground below. The change in force had scrambled all my organs, my intestines throbbing as though my heart had tumbled there.

There was a long silence and then, to my horror, I felt the bed dip behind me and a strong pair of arms encircled me from behind. I went rigid with fear, scarcely able to believe what was happening. It was all I could do to breathe – but every time I exhaled, the arms squeezed me tighter and tighter to the point where I couldn't get enough air into my lungs. I tried screaming, but no sound came out. I tried fighting, but my limbs were gripped by a terrifying paralysis.

I don't know how long this went on for, but suddenly, without warning, I was released. In an instant, I was on my feet and moving towards the window. I glanced back towards the bed. It was empty, the pillows in disarray, the duvet lying in a tangled heap on the floor. I felt a brief moment of relief before, in the milky half-light of the breaking dawn, my eyes picked out an amorphous shape in the opposite corner of the room. Its hooded eyes were yellow, like an alligator's, and I watched as they rotated slowly, scanning, evaluating. A sneer trembled like an electrical current across the creature's top lip while, above it, crimson nostrils flared rhythmically. Suddenly, its mouth opened. A wide circle, twitching and trembling, that revealed an obscenely quivering tongue, the fleshy redness of its throat, strings of spittle strung across a dark cavity. It let out a long, slow sigh, like air that's been trapped forever, deep underground.

The next moment, the thing was lunging at me, grabbing me by the neck and slamming me against the William Morris wallpaper. I could see vile fumes rising like wood smoke from its body, curling in the air to insinuate themselves into my mouth and through the jelly of my eyes. Then its lips were pressing against mine and one of its scaly hands was snaking under my nightdress. A wave of revulsion washed over me. *Is this how my life is going to end?* I thought as my eyes burned with tears.

When I woke up, hauled into consciousness by the accusatory bleating of my alarm clock, I was, thankfully, none the worse for wear – physically, at least. Only the violet smudges under my eyes gave any hint of the night's harrowing events. As I stared at the reflection in my dressing table mirror, I knew I needed to talk to someone. Certainly not Tom. Our relationship was in its infancy; he'd be totally freaked out and I couldn't risk driving him away. There was only one person who would understand what I was going through. After all, she and I had been through this before.

13

Megan

I gazed at him as he re-entered the room after using the loo. There was a lightness in my head, a dizzy blend of disbelief and elation in the face of my own recklessness. His chest was broad and carpeted in whorls of mahogany hair, his thighs were strong and muscular from his daily cycle commute, and to top it all, he was great in the sack.

Believe me, when I got up this morning, having sex with Pete Chambers had been the furthest thing from my mind. Despite giving him my number, I hadn't heard a peep from him since our evening at the pub, nine days earlier, and I'd only glimpsed him once at work, striding down a corridor, issuing terse instructions to the harried-looking theatre nurse jogging at his side. Then, this morning, he'd phoned out of the blue to see if I was free for brunch in Clapham in an hour's time. It was a Sunday and I'd planned to spend the day catching up on household chores – mowing the back lawn, which had now reached ankle height, tidying my bedroom and doing a couple of loads of laundry –

tedious, but long overdue tasks. Plus, it was very short notice – barely enough time to wash and blow-dry my hair. Still, I told myself, it would be lovely to see him again.

Just like that night in the pub, the conversation between us was so easy, so natural. At the same time, I noticed that my breaths were shallower than usual and kept catching in my throat when I spoke. I was normally fairly circumspect with people I didn't know very well, especially men I was romantically interested in. It was a kind of self-protection mechanism, I suppose. But with Pete, I felt as if I had shed a layer of skin, as if all my normal reserve and inhibition had been stripped away. We talked about anything and everything – my trip to Australia last year to see my family, and my long-held ambition to volunteer for Médecins Sans Frontières; his passion for red wine and the plans he was making to cycle across America. When I brought up the subject of his wife, he told me about the divorce lawyer he had consulted, assuring me it was only a matter of time until the decree nisi came through. I must admit that part of me didn't want to know anything about Fiona – the woman who'd owned him for the past God knows how many years; but the other part *had* to know because, as I said before, I don't get involved with married men.

When we left the café two hours later, I think we both knew what was on the cards. I just hadn't expected it to happen right there and then. Almost before I knew what was happening, Pete's hands were either side of my head and his fingers were in my hair. I wrapped my arms wantonly around his neck, inviting him to kiss me – and he did.

His mouth was soft and full and he teased the underside of my top lip with the point of his tongue, a gesture I found almost unbearably erotic. And the fact we were kissing in the middle of the street, in broad daylight, with people milling all around us, made it all the more thrilling.

After a little while, Pete stopped kissing me, stepped back and looked at me with a hunger and a giddy slide of his eyes, before suggesting that we 'continue this somewhere more private'. I didn't need much persuading. It had to be my place, of course – we could hardly go back to his with Fiona there. Luckily, I had Number 46 all to myself. Chloe was spending the weekend at Tom's and Sammi was in France, doing research for an article she was writing for one of the Sunday supplements about daily life in a Paris atelier.

Now, as Pete sank wordlessly into bed beside me, I was looking forward to talking some more, but he fell asleep almost immediately. With a satisfied sigh, I slotted my head into his collarbone and stared at his right hand which was resting on my hip, wondering how many lives those long, strangely delicate fingers had saved. After a little while, I tilted my head upwards, admiring the unobtrusive strength of his chin and the freckles that extended, in a russet constellation, across the bridge of his nose. We'd been lying, entwined in this way, for less than twenty minutes when he suddenly jerked awake. 'What time is it?' he asked in a thick voice.

I reached for my mobile on the bedside table and held it up over both our faces. 'Two-thirty . . . shit,' he muttered, as he rolled out of bed and began foraging for his underwear, which had been kicked under the bed in the throes of our passion.

I sat up. 'Do you really have to go right this instant?'

He flung me a grimace of apology. 'I hate rushing off like this, but I've arranged to meet a friend at three. Sorry, Megan, I should've mentioned it earlier.'

I felt a lurch of disappointment; I had assumed we would be spending the rest of the day together. 'Can't you phone him and cancel?'

'Not really, we've had this in the diary for ages. He's an old mate; I can't let him down.' He pulled on his boxer shorts, then leaned over the bed and ran his finger along the curve of my cheekbone. 'We'll have to do this again.' He grinned boyishly. 'I don't just mean the sex. Perhaps I could take you for dinner next time.'

I smiled back. 'Sounds great.'

He turned away from me and I watched as he rescued his jeans from the back of a chair and pulled them on hastily. 'No need to get up,' he said, walking towards the door, T-shirt in hand. 'I can see myself out.'

I lay back down and listened to him bounding down the stairs. It was followed by the click of the latch on the front door and then I was on my own.

14

It wasn't always this way. We used to be a normal family: Mum, Dad and me. The house was clean and tidy and everything I wore smelled of fabric conditioner. We had home-cooked meals for tea and went camping in Spain in the summer holidays. Dad always had a twinkle in his eye, instead of the sad look he wears now, like someone's just given him a Chinese burn – and Mum . . . well, Mum was the way mums are supposed to be: soft, kind, smiley. But then The Bad Thing happened and everything fell apart.

I was as shocked as anyone. I had to have time off school and everything. Dad even took me to see a counsellor. I thought it would be fun talking about myself, but after a while I got the feeling the counsellor was trying to trip me up. So in the end, instead of telling the truth, I told her what I thought she wanted to hear. That way, I figured, she would say I didn't need to keep coming to see her. And guess what . . . it worked! That was the moment I realised that I'm a lot smarter than people think I am. Sometimes now, I look at myself in the mirror and I wonder why they don't see what I am; I guess most people are pretty stupid, though.

I understand why Mum and Dad went a bit crazy afterwards; anyone would if it happened to them. But I really thought that after a little while – maybe six months or so – things would get back to normal. They didn't. In fact, they just kept getting worse.

The first time Mum hit me, I couldn't believe it. Before The Bad Thing, I'd never even got a smack across the legs – not even when I pulled up all Mum's geraniums because I wanted to make my own perfume out of the petals. But now I get slaps, shoves, scratches . . . one time Mum even pulled a big clump of my hair out. And don't get me started on the names . . . Mum calls me names I've never even heard of; I don't know how she manages to come up with so many different ones! Dad pretends not to see what's going on, but he knows all right. How could he live in the house with us and *not* know?

I've learned all sorts of tricks to make things not quite so bad. At home, I make myself as small and quiet as possible; that way Mum might forget I'm there. Sometimes I even hold my breath, hoping I'll be able to disappear into one of the cracks in the wall. I get up really early too, so I can get to school before Mum wakes up. This morning I arrived before the caretaker had even unlocked the gate! I'm in the classroom now and no one else is here yet, so it's just Miss Pickering and me . . . bliss! Miss Pickering calls me her Special Little Helper and today I'm helping her put out the paint pots for art class.

'How are you getting on with Anouk?' she asks as she sets up an easel.

'Oh, Miss, Anouk's the best thing that's ever happened to me,' I say. 'We're best friends.'

Miss Pickering gives me a smile that is as bright as a falling star. 'That's wonderful news; I knew I could rely on my Special Little Helper to make the new girl feel at home. Are you looking forward to the field trip next week? I really think you're going to enjoy our visit to the seaside. We'll be looking round the castle first and then we'll have a picnic on the beach.' She scratches the side of her face as if she's about to say something she doesn't really want to. 'Which reminds me, I don't think your parents have paid for the trip yet, have they? It's not very much, we wanted to make sure everybody in the class would be able to come.'

'I did take the letter home, Miss. Dad said I could go; I don't know why he hasn't given me the money.' My bottom lip starts trembling then and something in my chest pulls tight as a stitch. Quick as a flash, sweet Miss Pickering is at my side.

'There's no need to get upset,' she says, putting her hand gently on the side of my head and pulling me towards her. I take a deep breath in, inhaling the air around her. She smells of strawberries and cream and felt-tip pen. 'If they still haven't given you the money to bring in by Tuesday, *I'll* pay for you, but you mustn't tell anyone or I'll get into trouble – all right?'

'Thank you, Miss,' I say. 'And don't worry, you can trust me. I'm ever so good at keeping secrets.'

15

Chloe

'Why are you in such a filthy mood, Chloe? You've spent most of the evening staring into space and when you do speak to me, it's only to bite my head off.'

I blinked hard. 'I've already told you; I've had a very stressful day at work.'

'So have I, but do you see me taking it out on you?'

Tom was right. It had been a mistake to meet in the pub after work when my nerves were jangling and I was ready to lash out at the nearest person who, unfortunately on this occasion, just happened to be my boyfriend. I was shattered after another terrible night's sleep and Bryan had been on my case all day because I'd gone over budget on the props for a contemporary dance production we were staging in the New Year. On top of that, Tom's relentless perkiness, and the way he kept picking at the label on his beer bottle and scattering the bits all over the table, was starting to get on my nerves.

He leaned forward and fixed me with his blue-grey

gaze. 'So listen, here's an idea – why don't we cut our losses and go back to mine? Maybe you'll cheer up once we get naked.'

I knew he was only trying to lighten the mood, but I could barely raise a smile. The plan had been for me to stay over at Tom's, but it probably wasn't a good idea. My sleep patterns were all over the place and there was no point keeping Tom up half the night.

I pushed my lime and soda to one side. 'Actually, if you don't mind, I think I'll just go home.'

Tom's face clouded with disappointment, making me feel even worse than I already did.

'Please don't take it personally, it's just that I really need a good night's sleep.' I gave an apologetic grimace. 'And I'm sorry for being such a bitch all evening; I don't know why you put up with me.'

He leaned forward and kissed the tip of my nose. 'Because I care about you, that's why.' Then his eyes narrowed. 'Are you *sure* you're all right?'

I nodded. 'Just tired, that's all, and I always sleep much better in my own bed.'

'Fair enough, but make sure you get out of the right side of bed tomorrow morning, OK?'

'I'll do my best.'

Tom lifted his beer bottle and drained the last mouthful. 'Come on then, I'll walk you to the station.'

I felt impossibly weary on the train journey home – not just physically tired, but shut down, like an overheated appliance. I didn't even have enough energy to read the newspaper that someone had left on the seat next to mine. Instead, I sat slumped in the seat with my head resting against the window, counting down the stations until it was time to get off.

It was Megan's week of day shifts and I had assumed she'd be at home, but all I found was Sammi, tapping away at her laptop on the kitchen table.

'Hey there,' she called out cheerily, as I dumped my bag in the hallway. 'I thought you were staying at Tom's tonight.'

'Last-minute change of plan,' I replied, walking into the kitchen. 'Have you seen Megan this evening?'

'No,' she replied, pushing her laptop away. 'But I know she was planning to go out straight from work . . . a retirement do for one of the anaesthetists, I think.'

'Really?' I said in surprise. Megan usually let me know if she had plans for the evening. Maybe she had and it had slipped my mind, although it wasn't like me to forget. The news felt like a kick in the teeth; I'd been relying on Meg to be there for me. And then, all at once, I couldn't see properly because the tears in my eyes were making the room wobble and shimmer.

'Chloe?' I heard Sammi say. 'What's wrong?'

'Nothing.' It was a struggle to keep my voice from quavering.

Then came the sound of chair legs scraping on the slate floor, followed a few seconds later by the gentle pressure of Sammi's hand on my shoulder.

'Why don't you come and sit down? I'll make us some camomile tea; I was about to put the kettle on anyway.'

I let Sammi steer me to a chair and tried to compose myself as she busied herself with the tea things. She peered at me anxiously as she handed me a mug. 'If you want to talk, I'm happy to listen, but if you'd rather be left alone, that's fine too; I can always finish my work upstairs.'

The trouble was, I didn't know *what* I wanted. Half of me recoiled at the thought of unburdening myself to a person I barely knew; the other half was desperate to talk to *somebody*. In Megan's absence, Sammi was probably as good as anyone because, if I didn't offload soon, I was surely only one bad night away from total meltdown. Clearing my clotted throat, I began to talk.

'When I was a kid, I started having these horrible nightmares – except that they were more than just nightmares.'

'How do you mean?' Sammi asked, looking at me curiously.

I gripped the mug of camomile tea in both hands, drawing comfort from its warmth. 'I'd physically act out whatever my mind thought was happening to me. My eyes would be open and anyone looking at me would think I was awake, but I wasn't. My mum would hear me shouting in the middle of the night and she'd come into my bedroom to find me fighting off an invisible intruder, or crawling on the floor trying to escape a poison gas attack . . . all kinds of bizarre scenarios.

'Sometimes, when I woke up I'd remember everything

that had happened, but usually I'd only have a hazy memory. I'd see the after-effects, though – a smashed mirror, books knocked off shelves; once I even sprained my wrist after I tried to punch a hole in the wall.' I glanced at Sammi, who was staring at me open-mouthed. 'I know, it sounds crazy; laughable even, but I can assure you there's nothing in the least bit funny about it when it's happening to you.'

'Of course not,' Sammi said quickly. 'I think it sounds quite horrific. Did you ever talk to anyone about it – a doctor, I mean, or some sort of therapist?'

'After it had happened a few times, my mum took me to the family GP. He called them "night terrors"; that was the first time I'd ever heard the expression. They typically occur when you're coming out of a deep sleep and your fight-or-flight response is triggered. You're not fully asleep, but you're not awake either. There's no cure as such and my GP said the best thing I could do was try not to worry too much and eventually I'd grow out of them.'

'And did you?'

'After a year or so, they did get less frequent, but they've never gone away completely.'

Sammi gave me a startled look. 'So you still get them now?'

'I haven't had one for ages. The last time was nearly ten years ago when I was at uni, in the run up to Finals. I did my best to hide it from everyone, even my closest friends; I thought I could handle it on my own. But then the matter was taken out of my hands.' I paused and sipped my tea.

'Back then, Megan and I were both living in halls. One night, I accidentally locked myself out of my room and ended up having to crash on Megan's floor. She woke up in the middle of the night to find me gone and the door to the room wide open. She eventually tracked me down to the communal kitchen. I'd climbed into a broom cupboard and I was lying on the floor, curled in a foetal position, trembling and moaning. I've no idea what threat I thought I was under; I couldn't remember any of it the next morning. Luckily, Megan realised I wasn't properly awake, even though my eyes were open.'

'That was smart of her,' Sammi said in an undertone.

'She was three years into a pharmacology degree, so she had more medical knowledge than most people – and anyway, Megan's always been a very intuitive person. Luckily, she had the good sense not to try and wake me up, which apparently is just about the worst thing you can do. Instead, she got me to my feet, took me back to her room and watched over me all night, just in case I tried to do something else stupid. I can't tell you how embarrassed I felt in the morning when Meg told me what had happened. She wasn't the least bit judgemental though, and when I told her it had been happening since I was a kid, she took it upon herself to try and help me manage my condition. She did loads of research and found out what some of the most common triggers were – stress, exhaustion, alcohol, sleeping in unfamiliar surroundings. All through my exams, she made sure I ate properly, took regular breaks from revision, went to bed early, avoided booze. It seemed to work; I really thought I'd kicked them into touch.' I heaved a great sigh. 'Until now.'

Sammi's face was etched with concern. 'You mean they've come back?'

'Yes, I'm afraid so. I'm under so much pressure at the moment. There's this huge project I've been working on . . . it could make or break my career. I really need to be on my A-game right now, but the night terrors are absolutely exhausting. The next day I'm so tired I can barely function. Then I get even more stressed and—'

'—it's just one great big vicious circle,' Sammi supplied.

I smiled, grateful for her understanding. 'It's got to the stage where I don't want to go to sleep because I'm worried about what I might do.' I gave a little shudder. 'I think I actually tried to climb out of my bedroom window the other night.'

Sammi gasped. 'Shit, Chloe, that's really scary; you could do yourself a serious injury if you fell from that window.' She frowned and began twirling a piece of her long hair around her finger. 'I bet Megan's really concerned, isn't she?'

I drew my tongue back and forth across my bottom lip. 'She doesn't know the night terrors are back. I haven't had a chance to tell her because we've hardly seen each other lately. I don't know if she's doing overtime or what.'

Sammi gave a slow, feline blink. 'I expect she's busy with her new man.'

I frowned. 'What new man?'

'That surgeon she's just started seeing.' She looked at

me steadily. 'From the sound of it, they're really into each other.'

I felt as if I'd been stung. Megan and I told each other everything – or at least we *did*. I was used to receiving blow-by-blow accounts of every date she went on. I couldn't believe she'd embarked on an actual romance – especially one with a highly desirable *surgeon* – without telling me. 'She hasn't said anything to me,' I said.

Sammi's hand flew to her mouth. 'Oops, I hope I haven't said anything I shouldn't.'

'No, no, it's fine. I'm sure she was planning to tell me at some point, but like I said, we never seem to be in the house at the same time these days.' Which was true enough – but what was wrong with a text? I frowned at Sammi. 'So when did Meg tell you about this new guy?'

'A couple of days ago; you'd already left for work and Megan and I were having breakfast in the kitchen. She kept getting text messages and every time one arrived, she'd reply to it straight away. Eventually I asked her who it was and she told me it was one of the surgeons at work – Pete, I think she said his name was.'

I was even more annoyed now. Megan had mentioned Pete a few times and I knew she liked him. Why had she confided in Sammi, a virtual stranger, and not me – her best friend?

'At first, I thought he was contacting her about some work-related thing,' Sammi went on. 'But then Megan told me they were seeing each other.' She spread her arms wide and shrugged. 'Sorry, Chloe, that's all I know.'

She reached across the table and took one of my hands in hers. It struck me as an oddly intimate gesture, but then again I had just spilled my guts to her. 'Anyway, that's enough about Megan. What are we going to do about these night terrors of yours? It's got to be worth another visit to the GP. Now that you're an adult, they can't fob you off by saying you'll grow out of it; there must be something they can do.'

'I don't know,' I said, shifting uncomfortably in my seat. 'I'd rather find a way of dealing with it myself, to be honest.'

Sammi gave my hand a gentle squeeze. 'You know, Chloe, there's nothing wrong with admitting you have a problem and seeking help for it.'

Something in her tone made me look up and I saw a shadow cross her face. It was slight – a thin, fine cloud across a spring day – but noticeable all the same. The next moment it was gone. She released my hands and cleared her throat. 'I get anxiety attacks,' she said. 'Not very often, but when I do get them, they can be quite debilitating.'

I was shocked. Sammi exuded confidence and self-belief; it was hard to imagine her exhibiting any kind of weakness or vulnerability. 'Oh,' I said, rather taken aback. 'I'm sorry to hear that. Do you know what sets them off?'

Sammi picked up her mug and blew on the hot liquid. 'Pressure at work, relationship troubles . . . the usual things. Over the years I've learned how to spot the warning signs and deal with them before they spiral into full-blown attacks.' Her eyes flickered from side to side, as if her brain was dissociating from the memory. 'The turning point came when I realised I couldn't deal with the problem by myself and asked my GP for help. He prescribed an anti-anxiety medication that worked wonders. I rarely have to take it these days, but just knowing it's there if I need it is reassuring.'

'Maybe I *should* make an appointment at the surgery then,' I said half-heartedly.

'I really think that would be a good idea.' Sammi's eyes flitted to her open laptop. 'Goodness, is that the time already? Sorry, Chloe, I really need to finish this piece before I go to bed.' She tossed her head back and laughed. 'Bloody deadlines, eh?'

'Oh God, yes, of course,' I said, feeling awful that I'd distracted Sammi from her work. 'I'm going to take a quick shower, then hit the sack, I think.' I rose to my feet and carried my mug over to the sink. As I threw the rest of my tea away and rinsed the mug under the tap, Sammi came up behind me.

'If you ever need to talk again, please remember that I'm always here for you,' she said in her quiet, cool voice.

I turned and smiled at her. 'Thanks, Sammi, I really appreciate it.'

16

Megan

I groped on the floor for my phone and checked the time: 8.22. I had been trying to get back to sleep for the past half an hour, but there was a godawful racket going on outside my bedroom window. I was feeling rather delicate after last night's retirement do. My head was thumping and my mouth was dry as a sponge left out in the sun. I hadn't intended to drink at all, but I must have had four – or possibly five – glasses of wine in the end. I'd only meant to show my face; after all, I barely knew Dr Varma. But then Pete showed up and I ended up staying the whole night. Unfortunately, we didn't get to spend much one-on-one time together. Pete wanted us to keep our relationship under wraps, just for a little while. There were people at the hospital who knew his wife and he didn't want her getting wind of our relationship because it might affect their upcoming divorce proceedings. He insisted the situation with Fiona was fairly amicable, but his feeling was that, if she found out he was seeing someone else, she might decide to play hardball. And being a solicitor her-self – albeit a probate specialist, rather than a divorce lawyer – she would know how to hit him where it hurt. But that was OK; I didn't mind waiting. Pete was worth it.

Despite my crashing headache, I couldn't help smiling to myself as I remembered the lustful looks he'd thrown my way when no one was looking, and the way he'd fur-tively squeezed my arse cheek while we were queuing at the crowded bar together. I could have lain there for hours, just thinking about him, especially as my shift didn't start till midday, but the noise outside was unrelenting. I got out of bed and peered groggily through the curtains. The source of the noise soon became clear – Sammi was mowing the tiny square of lawn at the front of the house. Why she felt the need to do it quite so early in the morning was anyone's guess.

I knew I'd never be able to get back to sleep and I was desperate for caffeine, so I got up and headed downstairs to the kitchen. Along the way, I noticed that Chloe's bed-room door was wide open and her bag had disappeared from the coat stand by the front door. She seemed to be leaving for work earlier and earlier these days. I'd been feeling a bit distant from her lately; we really needed to spend some quality time with each other. I was keen to tell her about Pete and me in person, rather than by message, and I knew she'd be hungry for every last detail.

I made a strong cup of coffee and carried it into the back garden. Chloe and I had bought a cheap bistro set for the patio and it was perfectly positioned to catch the early morning sunlight. Summer was on its last legs and it was a bit chilly to be sitting there in just my PJs, but I figured the cool air would help wake me up.

Despite the droning of the lawnmower, it was peaceful out there and I was enjoying the solitude and the heady smell of honeysuckle. I was barely halfway through my coffee when Sammi appeared at the side of the house, dragging the lawnmower behind her.

'Morning, Megan, how was the retirement party?' she trilled when she saw me sitting there.

'Good, thanks. My head's a bit sore, though; I really could've done with a lie-in.'

The barb seemed to go right over her head. 'Sounds like you had fun,' she said, walking over to me, a skein of orange electrical cable in one hand, a circuit breaker in the other. 'Was the surgeon there?'

At first, I wasn't sure what she was getting at. 'Lots of surgeons were there,' I said. 'Dr Varma was very highly regarded.'

She gave a tinkling laugh. 'No, silly, I meant did *your* surgeon go . . . Pete, isn't it?'

I was puzzled. I couldn't remember telling Sammi about Pete. Why would I do that when I hadn't even told my best friend? I must have let something slip without realising, or maybe she overheard me talking to him on the phone. 'Yeah, he was, actually, but we didn't spend that much time together. There were lots of other people I wanted to catch up with.'

'Still, as long as it's going well.' She held out the lawnmower cable and the circuit breaker. 'Do me a favour and plug this in for me, will you? I might as well do the back garden while I'm at it.'

Holding back the crotchety sigh that threatened to erupt from my mouth, I took the items from her and carried them into the kitchen. When I returned, she was over by the shed, adjusting the height on the lawnmower. Her legs were bare beneath a colourful flared skirt and I noticed she had intensely white skin, through which her veins flowed like rivers on a map.

'Ready when you are,' I called out, resuming my position on the patio. She waved at me in response and switched on the lawnmower.

I had to admit it was good of her to tackle the lawn. The grass seemed to grow virulently and neither Chloe nor I were the least bit interested in gardening. I felt slightly guilty as I watched Sammi toiling away. It was a good-sized lawn and sloped up quite steeply at the far end, by the pergola, so it wasn't a quick job.

Whenever I cut the grass, it tended to be a haphazard affair and afterwards, the lawn would be dotted with long tufts that I had missed. Sammi, by contrast, took a very methodical approach, striding purposefully up and down the lawn, creating neat stripes in her wake. As she worked, she wore a look of grim determination, lips pinched, chin stiffly set. You'd think she was embarking on a life-or-death challenge that had to be conquered, rather than carrying out a mundane domestic chore. By the time the job was finished, some twenty-five minutes later, her cheeks were pink and there was a sheen of sweat on her top lip. I found myself wondering why she hadn't removed the pretty pink cardigan she was wearing.

'You've made a really good job of that,' I called out to her. 'I'm going to make myself another coffee. Can I get you anything?'

'A glass of water would be lovely, thanks,' she replied, brushing the grass clippings from her ankles.

When I came back out, Sammi – who, I observed, still hadn't shed her cardie – was sitting in a patio chair, her head tilted up towards the sun.

'Did you see Chloe before she went to work this morning?' I asked, handing her the water.

'Only briefly, she was leaving just as I was getting up. We didn't speak much because she was in a rush; she wanted to catch the seven-forty train.'

'She doesn't usually leave that early,' I said, sipping my coffee and enjoying its bitter tang.

Sammi looked around the garden with a sweeping, hawk-like stare. 'She's working on a big project at work at the moment; I think she's quite worried about it.'

'Oh yes, the play about mental illness; she mentioned it a couple of weeks back.' I gave a little grimace. 'I think Chloe sometimes worries unnecessarily. She's super talented and I, for one, have complete confidence in her creative abilities.'

As Sammi turned to look at me, I felt the pressure of her gaze. There was something unflinching about it, a kernel of hardness. 'I don't suppose it helps that she isn't sleeping very well at the moment,' she remarked.

'Oh?' I replied, frowning. 'That's news to me.'

Sammi stretched her long legs out in front of her and I noticed a large, fading bruise on her right shin. 'Yes, we had a long chat about it last night.'

'*Did* you?' I said, studying her. 'So what did Chloe say exactly?'

'Just that she's been having these awful nightmares, where she thinks she's in some sort of danger and ends up acting out what's happening – even though it's all in her head.'

I looked at her sharply. 'The night terrors are back?' I was surprised – no, *shocked* – that Chloe hadn't shared this important information with me. I had seen how deeply the night terrors had affected her when we were at university and the thought of her going through anything like that again was almost unbearable.

'It certainly seems that way. Poor Chloe, I think she thought she'd seen the last of them when she was at uni.' Sammi flashed me a narrow smile. 'I hear you were a great support to her when she was doing her Finals.'

I shrugged. 'I just did what friends do.'

Sammi leaned towards me and lowered her voice conspiratorially, even though there was no one around to hear her. 'To be honest, Megan, I'm actually quite concerned about her.'

I turned away, my cheeks blazing with self-reproach. I hadn't been there when Chloe needed me, too caught up in my burgeoning romance with Pete. In desperation, she had turned to Sammi instead.

'I told her she ought to see a doctor; there must be something they can do. I expect *you'd* know what treatments are available, wouldn't you?' Sammi said, in a tone that sounded vaguely haranguing.

'There are various drugs that might help,' I said. 'Cognitive behavioural therapy has also proven to be quite effective; it's just a matter of trial and error really. It's possible that Chloe might be able to conquer it herself, though, just like she did when we were at uni.' I sighed, remembering what a difficult time that had been – for both of us.

Curiosity simmered in Sammi's eyes. 'Do you think Chloe's told Tom about the night terrors?'

'I've no idea. They haven't been together very long; she might not feel comfortable talking to him about it.'

'Oh, but Tom seems like the sort of man who'd be very understanding,' Sammi said with an odd little smile. 'It would be nice to get to know Tom better. We don't see him at the house very often.' She ran a hand through her long hair and shook it so the ends fell around her shoulders in a sexy, tousled heap. 'Perhaps I should speak to him myself about it.'

'I don't think that would be a good idea at all,' I said firmly. 'It's really Chloe's decision whether or not he finds out.'

I was beginning to feel uncomfortable; it was as if Sammi and I were engaged in a competition about which one of us was best equipped to tackle Chloe's problem. I rubbed my forehead and told myself to stop being so silly. I had a hangover and I was feeling oversensitive, that was all. There was nothing untoward about my housemate's motives; she was just trying to help.

'I really appreciate you letting me know about this, Sammi, but leave it with me. I'll talk to Chloe and we'll work something out between us.'

Sammi said nothing for a long while, but looked at me instead with an eerie blankness – eyes still, mouth tight shut. When she did speak, her voice sounded flat, almost robotic. 'Of course, Megan. You are Chloe's best friend, after all.'

17

It's the day of the school trip. We're going to visit a castle on top of a hill and then we'll have a picnic and play rounders on the beach. I spent ages last night deciding what to wear. Miss Pickering said shorts and T-shirt were best, but the only shorts I've got are the ones I wear for PE, so I decided to make some by cutting the legs off a pair of pyjama bottoms. One leg's a bit longer than the other one, but I don't think anyone will notice.

Dad never did pay for the trip, even though I reminded him a gazillion times. Luckily, Miss Pickering gave me the money out of her own purse, just like she promised. I took it to the school secretary and said it was from my parents, like Miss Pickering told me to. It's really not fair that she had to pay, because I bet a teacher gets paid less than a surveyor does. But I'm glad she did because otherwise I would've had to stay behind in the classroom, all on my own, and that would have been *sooo* embarrassing.

As soon as we're all here, Miss Pickering makes us line up in twos (I'm in a two with Anouk, of course!). Then Miss Pickering and our classroom assistant, Mr Wylie, take us outside to where the coach is waiting. Anouk looks gorgeous as ever in denim shorts, a cute, cap-sleeved top and a red sun hat with a frill round the edge. Her skin is golden and perfectly smooth all over, not like mine, which is the colour of skimmed milk and covered in scars from when I had chicken pox. I bet I look horrid next to her, like some kind of spiny creature, who lives on the bottom of the sea and never sees the light. I notice that Miss Pickering has a camera in a case around her neck, and as we stand in line, waiting to get on the coach, I ask her to take a photo of Anouk and me. That way I'll be able to remember this day forever.

The first half of the trip goes really well. The castle is amazing, even if half of it has crumbled away. Miss Pickering lets us explore on our own, so long as we stay in our twos. Just as Anouk and I are heading towards the moat, Elliott asks me if he and Sanjay can come with us. Imagine that . . . Elliott Parker wants to spend time with me! Before Anouk came, I don't think he'd ever spoken a single word to me – not even a 'Hi' or a 'Get out of my way'.

Once we've finished at the castle, Miss Pickering leads the way to the beach. I feel so proud as I walk along the seafront, holding Anouk's hand. I know we look completely different, but no one can ignore the way we fit together like pieces of a jigsaw puzzle. But the proud feeling quickly turns to a sick feeling – probably because it's a very warm day and I haven't had any breakfast (I wanted to, but the milk in the fridge smelled funny). As we go down some stone steps on to the beach, there's an odd feeling in my head, as if fingers are pushing and squeezing on my eyeballs. Then a blurry, dark shadow appears at the corner of my vision. I'm just wondering whether I ought to find somewhere to sit down when the world slips sideways.

When I wake up, the first person I see is Miss Pickering. She's kneeling on the sand next to me and she's fanning me with her straw hat. Right next to her is Anouk, her hair shining like a halo in the bright sunlight. Miss Pickering helps me sit up and gives me a drink of water from a plastic bottle. Over her shoulder, I see the others a bit further down the beach, playing rounders with Mr Wylie. Miss Pickering says I have to stay lying down until I feel better. She tells Anouk she can go and play rounders if she wants, but Anouk says no, she wants to be with me. I look at her and think, *This is my best friend.* Just saying those words in my head makes me feel so much better.

Later, after we've had our picnic, it's time to go back to school. Eleanor Hardy is right behind me in the queue for the coach and she doesn't even bother to whisper. 'She's such a drama queen,' I hear her say. 'I bet there's nothing wrong with her; she probably just *pretended* to faint so she could be the centre of attention. And have you seen what she's wearing? God knows where she got those horrible shorts; they look like charity shop rejects.'

As she speaks, a rush begins to well up behind my face like a sneeze; my eyes burn and my nose twitches. I can feel the pressure of my rage growing against my ribs; it tastes metallic and slightly burnt. I put my hands up to my head.

I have to, otherwise I feel as if it might pop off. At the same time, Anouk tugs at my arm. 'Just ignore her,' she says in her soft, sing-song voice. 'She doesn't know anything about anything.' And just like that I feel the rage sliding away.

After the coach drops us back at school, I'm ready to walk home like I always do, but because I fainted on the beach, the school secretary has phoned my mum and asked her to pick me up instead. I wish it was Dad coming, but that would mean he'd have to leave work early and Dad never leaves work early. I sometimes imagine him sitting in his office after everyone else has gone. He's sharpening his pencils, or making chains out of paper clips, while the cleaner pushes her mop and bucket around him – anything to delay coming home to Mum and me. I bet he gets a bad feeling in his stomach as he climbs into his big silver car and starts driving home. I've got a bad feeling now, knowing Mum will be here any minute.

It's only me and Miss Pickering left at school by the time Mum eventually shows up. She must have walked because her face is all red and she's panting like a dog who's been locked in a car with the windows shut.

This is the first time Miss Pickering and Mum have met. I hope she doesn't notice the sweaty marks under Mum's arms and the way her hair's stuck to the side of her head from where she's been lying down. Miss Pickering says that I'm all right now, but tells Mum she should keep an eye on me for the next twenty-four hours. Oh no, that's the last thing I need!

Mum nods and says all the right things, but I know she's angry by the way her mouth never slips out of its tight line. As we say goodbye to Miss Pickering and walk away, Mum's hand is on my shoulder and she's asking me if I'm OK to walk home, or if I'd rather get the bus. But I know it's all an act; as soon as we turn the corner, her voice changes, like a sudden cold wind.

'You selfish little cow,' she hisses in my ear as we walk past the newsagent's. 'What sort of child makes her sick mother walk miles to pick her up from school when she's perfectly capable of walking home herself?'

Sick? Drunk, more like! Underneath the peppermint stink of mouthwash, I can smell the wine on Mum's breath. She thinks I don't know about the drinking, but even a blind person could see it. No wonder she's always needing to lie down. If she didn't, she'd probably *fall* down.

'It wasn't me; it was the school secretary,' I tell her. Bad move. A second later, my skull is pushed into the nearest lamp post and, for the second time today, I feel like I'm about to pass out.

18

Chloe

Bile and dread inched up in my throat. Where the hell was I? It was difficult to know; there was no light in the cage and my eyes were heavy and swollen. Several minutes dragged by, each folding and contracting, one into the other. Then, slowly, *very* slowly, my senses started to return. Touch came first as I realised I was sitting on something cold and very hard. Then sight – it wasn't a cage after all, but some sort of wooden shelter with four supporting posts and windows all around. Gingerly, I felt the surface beneath me. Ah, so I was sitting on tiles; I could feel the mortar in the joins between them. As my eyes adapted to the darkness, something stirred the air around me, like a breeze on a hot day and then, just like that, I was wide awake. *Now* I knew where I was: in the kitchen at Number 46. Under the table in the kitchen, to be precise.

I gave a strangled laugh, a choke in the back of my throat; relief mixed with confusion. At least I was safe – but what on earth was I doing in the kitchen? As I crawled out from under the table, I wondered how long I'd been there. My feet were cold and my bottom felt numb from sitting on the slate floor, so I suspected it must have been some considerable time. I wrapped my arms around my body and looked around the kitchen – at the gas hob and the knives in the knife block and all the cleaning products lined up under the sink – all the things that could potentially harm me if I wasn't fully cognizant. Shaking my head at the scariness of it all, I made my way back upstairs to bed.

A kind of panic scooted through me when I looked at the clock on my bedside table and saw how late it was. Then, remembering it was Saturday, I sank gratefully back on to the pillows. I lay there for several minutes, recalling the night's disturbing events, shuddering with disgust as I wondered what phantasm, imaginary assailant, or improbable natural disaster I'd been fleeing from. Snapping myself back to the present, I threw off the duvet and went to retrieve my slippers, which were tucked under the dressing table. As I put them on, I looked into the mirror. The sight of my face nearly brought tears to my already bleary eyes. It was blotchy, lined, pixillated with stress, and my hair stood in a clown-like frizz around it. I looked like shit; I *felt* like shit too. Even though I'd just woken up I could already feel a dark, draining fatigue setting in, like a suction pump to the brain.

Then, in the reflection over my shoulder, I noticed something very odd. There was a small fireplace in my bedroom – now blocked up with a piece of white-painted MDF – and on the mantelpiece above it I kept two photographs in matching pewter frames. One was a selfie of Megan and me, on holiday in Ibiza. We're sitting on the beach, watching the sun come up. I'll never forget it; it was one of the best nights of my life. It was the other photo – a beautiful shot of my sister and me taken outside our house when we were little kids – that was the problem. And the problem was that the photo, frame and all, had gone.

I walked over to the mantelpiece and stared at the gap where the picture should have been. I could clearly see the shape of the frame in the light film of dust that coated the mantelpiece. I was flummoxed. I never moved those photographs; I had no reason to, and I distinctly remembered seeing both pictures in their usual positions yesterday evening as I got ready for bed. It fleetingly occurred to me that I might have moved the picture of my sister and me at some point during the night, but I quickly rejected the idea. My night terrors always followed a similar theme, and physically picking up an item and moving it somewhere else didn't fit my MO. Sure, I might have knocked it over as I grappled with a non-existent attacker – but if that had happened, it would be lying somewhere nearby. And it most definitely wasn't.

As I looked around to see if anything else was out of place, I felt a strange, creeping sense of unease. It seemed as if a storm was brewing, right above my head. I gripped the edge of the mantelpiece. What was happening to me? Work, relationships, a decent night's sleep . . . all of it slipping away like waves from the shore. My thoughts were snarled, but one idea kept coming back to me: had somebody been in my room during the night? I frowned and shook my head. The notion was ridiculous; there must be another explanation. I desperately needed to talk to my best friend. If anyone could make sense of this, it would be Megan, with her cool head and no-nonsense approach. Unfortunately, she was working the entire weekend. Still, at least I had Sammi. I knew she was at home; I could hear her moving around in the kitchen below me.

'It's happened again, hasn't it?' she said, as soon as she saw my face. 'The night terrors.'

'Is it that obvious?'

'Let's just say you look as if you've had a rough night.' Sammi pulled out one of the dining chairs and gestured for me to sit down. 'Do you want some tea?'

'Coffee, please – or a shot of adrenaline, whichever's easiest.'

'That bad, huh?'

'Yup.'

Sammi flashed me a sympathetic smile. 'Do you remember any of it – the nightmare, I mean?'

I ran a hand through my tousled hair, acutely aware that I must look hideous compared to Sammi, whose appearance, as always, was immaculate. 'Only bits and pieces. I think I was hiding from something – or maybe it was some*one*; I don't know. When I woke up, I was right here in the kitchen, under the table of all places.'

A look of horror flitted over Sammi's face. 'But you don't remember coming downstairs?'

'Nope.'

She shook her head in pity. 'You poor thing, I wondered why one of the chairs was knocked over when I came down this morning.'

'Was it?' I said, wincing. 'Sorry, I didn't notice.'

'There's no need to apologise.' Sammi began spooning instant coffee into a mug. 'This whole thing must be ghastly for you and I can't believe it's been happening since you were a child. How did it start? Did something happen to set it off, or did it just come out of the blue? Do you remember?'

I gave a harsh laugh. 'Oh yeah, I remember all right; it was my parents' divorce. I doted on my dad and then, literally overnight, he was gone. I don't think I'd ever felt so scared in my life. It didn't help that I kept my feelings bottled up and didn't talk to anyone about how I was feeling. I guess my brain had to find an outlet somewhere.'

Sammi had paused her coffee making and was looking at me intently. 'And that fear manifested itself in your night terrors.'

'I think so.' I looked down at the table and absent-mindedly used the end of my finger to pick up some stray salt grains that had spilled from the grinder. 'Are you close to *your* parents?'

She hesitated for a second and as I looked up I saw her expression change. Beneath the veneer of dewy foundation and neutral lip gloss, there was something else: longing, loneliness, loss . . . feelings that shifted like slides on a projector across the pale landscape of her face. 'My mother's dead and I don't have any contact with my father,' she said tonelessly.

'That must be tough for you,' I said, feeling bad that I'd asked her. 'Do you have any brothers and sisters?'

'No,' she said, flipping the switch on the kettle. 'I'm an only child.' She pinched the bridge of her nose. 'I'm sorry. I'd rather not talk about my family if you don't mind; it brings back painful memories.'

'Of course I don't mind,' I said quickly.

I got up from the table and walked over to the back door. The garden was looking particularly pretty that day. The begonias were at their blowsy best and I was pleased to see that someone had finally taken it upon themselves to mow the lawn. 'You know, Sammi, I'd like to think we're friends,' I said, as the kettle started to boil.

Behind me, Sammi cleared her throat awkwardly. 'Me too.'

'I want to say thank you for being so supportive during this past couple of weeks. It's really helped to have someone to talk to about the night terrors.'

'It's nothing, really. I just wish there was something concrete I could do to help.'

I turned around and looked her squarely in the eye. 'I want you to know that you can talk to me too . . . if you ever feel the need, that is. It sounds as if we've both been through some tough times in the past.'

She started to say something as she picked up the kettle.

As she began to pour, she was looking at me and not paying attention to what she was doing. The next moment, boiling water was spraying all over her left forearm. Shrieking in shock, she dropped the kettle on the worktop and clutched her arm.

'Quickly, get it under the cold water,' I said, rushing over to her. Tears glistened in her eyes as I turned on the cold tap and took her gently by the hand. She was wearing a linen blouse, the cuffs tight around her wrist. 'Here, let me roll up your sleeve for you.'

Without warning, Sammi jerked her arm away forcefully. 'There's no need for that,' she said, thrusting her arm, sleeve and all, under the running water. I watched as the thin fabric quickly became saturated and began to turn see-through. 'Can you pass me a tea towel, please?' she said. I turned away to pull a clean one from the drawer. By the time I turned back, Sammi's wounded arm was drawn up against her chest in an odd, protective gesture.

'How bad is it?' I asked her. 'Don't you want to have a look?'

'It's fine,' she said coldly. 'It was only a splash, it doesn't hurt that much.'

'Well, if you're sure.' I placed the tea towel next to her on the draining board. 'I'd leave it under the water a bit longer if I were you, then it'll be less likely to blister.'

Sammi nodded and turned back to the sink. In that moment, I had the overwhelming sense that she wanted me to go. She was such a creature of contradictions – talkative one moment, reticent the next. Reaching past her, I picked up my half-filled coffee cup. 'I'm going upstairs to get dressed. Give me a shout if you need anything. There's a first aid kit in the bathroom if you're looking for a plaster.'

She looked at me; her eyes were empty. 'Thank you, Chloe, I will.'

As I climbed the stairs, I realised I hadn't asked Sammi if she knew anything about the photo that was missing from my room. Never mind, it couldn't have disappeared into thin air. It was sure to turn up sooner or later.

19

Megan

I smoothed the tips of Pete's chest hair with a hand, so that I could just feel it tickling my palm. His eyes flickered open and he brushed his lips across the slope of my shoulder. I shivered and pressed my body against his, enjoying the feel of his hard torso against my own soft curves.

A couple of hours ago, I'd been in bed, enjoying a long lie-in after the previous night's late shift. I had the day off and I'd been planning to spend it at home, catching up on some reading and generally relaxing. Then Pete had called unexpectedly: he happened to be in the area and did I fancy meeting up? This had been the template for all our encounters thus far: nothing planned in advance, no fore-warning about where or when. Instead I'd get a call or a text, asking if I was free in half an hour – an hour, if I was lucky. Being one of life's natural-born organisers, I did find it a tad frustrating – but also, I must admit, deeply excit-ing. By the time Pete arrived at Bellevue Rise, I was hungry for him, dragging him into the house like a desperate housewife seducing the window cleaner. And now, here we were in my vast bed, enveloped in a blissful, post-coital embrace.

I was just about to ask Pete if he wanted to stay for some food when I heard the sound of a key turning in the front door. I groaned into Pete's left bicep. Chloe was at work and Sammi had left the house at the crack of dawn on another one of her fashionista assignments, so I'd assumed I would have the house to myself. I was already imagining Pete and me browsing the shelves at the deli down the road, before we assembled a light lunch at home, then returned to bed for a second – and possibly even a third – innings.

'Who do you think that is?' Pete asked sleepily, as he raked his hand through my hair.

'Probably my housemate, Sammi,' I replied. 'I wasn't expecting her back so soon.'

We heard the front door slam shut, then the sound of footsteps coming up the stairs. 'Shit,' I muttered.

A moment later, there was a knock at the door. 'Megan, are you in there?' came Chloe's voice.

'Hang on a minute,' I said, springing out of bed and reaching for my robe.

I opened the door a few inches and peered through the gap. It was a few days since I'd seen Chloe and it looked as if she'd lost weight; her face was all sharp angles, still and pale. 'Hey, Chloe, how come you're not at work?'

She stared at me with red-rimmed eyes. 'I wasn't feeling

that great, so I told Richard I'd be working from home for the rest of the day.'

'You do look a bit peaky. What's up with you?'

'Nothing major, just a headache.'

'There's some paracetamol in the bathroom cabinet.'

'Thanks.' Chloe's gaze drifted over my shoulder to where Pete was lying in bed. 'Hi,' she said, raising her hand in greeting.

'Hey there,' he replied. 'I'm Megan's friend, Pete.'

Chloe's lips twitched in amusement. 'Pleased to meet you, Pete.' Her eyes shifted to me. 'Sorry, Meg, I didn't realise you were *indisposed*. I'll grab that paracetamol from the bathroom, then I'll go back downstairs and give you two some privacy.'

'It's OK,' came Pete's voice from behind me. 'I need to get going anyway.'

My head snapped round. 'Do you?'

He grinned sheepishly. 'The kids are coming back from boarding school for the weekend. I'm supposed to be picking them up from Waterloo in half an hour. Sorry, I should have said something sooner.'

Yes, you bloody well should have, you thoughtless bastard, I thought silently.

As soon as I'd seen him out, I went to find Chloe, who was sitting in the back garden. Her laptop lay open on the bistro table, but rather than working, she was staring straight ahead, apparently lost in thought.

'Mind if I join you?' I asked, as I stepped through the back door.

She gave me a wan smile. 'Be my guest – and sorry about earlier. I hope I didn't drive him away.'

'Don't worry about it; like Pete said, he wasn't planning to stick around anyway.'

Chloe licked her lips; I thought she seemed slightly nervous. 'Sammi did say you'd started seeing someone from work. I didn't realise things were moving along so quickly. Pete's a surgeon at the hospital, isn't he?'

'Yeah, orthopaedics.' I sat down next to her. I wasn't surprised that Sammi had blabbed; I got the impression she and Chloe were pretty close these days. 'I actually wanted to tell you myself; I was just waiting for the right opportunity. It seems like we've hardly seen each other recently and I wanted to tell you in person, rather than putting it in a text or an email.'

'I understand,' Chloe said. 'So, how's it going with you two?'

'All right, I suppose.'

She raised her eyebrows. 'Hardly a ringing endorsement.'

I sighed. 'I like him a lot – more than I've liked anyone for quite a while, actually – but I'm trying to play it cool. It's only early days and I haven't got the faintest idea how he feels about me; we don't really talk about stuff like that.'

'So what *do* you talk about?'

I shrugged carelessly. 'Oh, you know, the usual . . . work . . . his kids.'

'He's got children?'

'Yeah, they're eight and thirteen.'

'Really? He doesn't look old enough.'

'I think he and his ex married young.'

'How long has he been divorced?'

I took a deep breath. 'Technically speaking, he's still married . . . in fact, he and his wife still live together. He *is* getting divorced, though.'

'Ah,' Chloe said, nodding slowly. 'What do people at work think about you two getting together?'

'They don't know. Pete doesn't want to tell anyone until it's all finalised; he's worried his wife will try to screw him financially if she finds out he's seeing someone else.'

Chloe pressed her tongue into the side of her cheek as she digested this information. I could feel the disapproval emanating from her in waves. I decided it was time for a swift change of subject. 'Sammi tells me the night terrors are back.'

At the mere mention of them, Chloe's whole body seemed to go limp. 'Yeah, it's been horrible. I think they're actually worse than before.'

'What do you think triggered them this time?'

'Work,' she replied baldly. 'The *Neurosis* set is doing my head in; nothing seems to be going to plan.' She looked down and began rubbing at the skin on the back of her left hand in a compulsive fashion. 'Bryan's constantly on my case about the budget and the tech guys keep throwing all sorts of obstacles in my way. I've come very close to telling them all to fuck off.'

'Oh hon, I'm so sorry I haven't been there for you lately. I've just had so much on. If I'd known you were going through a rough patch, I would've made the time.'

She blinked hard several times. 'That's OK, I'm sure Pete's a much more attractive proposition than me right now.'

'Forget Pete, *you're* my priority now. We need to find a way of channelling that stress. I don't want to see you getting into the same state you did at university.'

'Sammi thinks I should do more yoga.'

Something inside me burned. I was the one who had suggested yoga to Chloe as a form of relaxation, but now it seemed Sammi was keen to take the glory.

Chloe tilted her head to the side and looked at me. 'Did you know Sammi suffers from anxiety?'

'No,' I said, genuinely surprised. 'I didn't think she was the type; she seems positively brimming with confidence to me.' *Too much confidence*, I was tempted to add.

'I think it's more or less under control these days, but when it gets really bad she takes medication for it.'

'What sort of medication?'

'She didn't say. I think she only told me so I didn't feel like I was the only person in the house with a mental illness.'

I made a snorting sound. 'You can hardly class night terrors as a mental illness. It's a sleep disorder, caused by the over-arousal of the central nervous system. Admittedly, it's pretty rare in adults, but that doesn't make you a freak.'

'I certainly *feel* like a freak sometimes,' Chloe mumbled.

'Well, you shouldn't,' I told her. 'And another thing you shouldn't be doing is bottling everything up; that's only going to increase your stress levels. Have you talked to Tom about this?'

'No – and I don't want him to find out.'

'That's entirely your prerogative.' I reached across and patted her knee. 'Do you know what I think would do us both the world of good? A big night out. We could hit the South Bank . . . have dinner, check out a couple of bars, maybe even go dancing afterwards.'

'Oh yes, I'd really like that.' Her face brightened and I caught a glimpse of the old Chloe, the free-spirited, fun-loving, easy-going girl I'd met at university.

I rose to my feet. 'In that case, let me get my phone and we'll put a date in the diary.'

It was the middle of the night and I'd woken with a start. At first I didn't know what had jerked me back to consciousness, but then I realised it was the creak of my bedroom door opening. I opened my eyes and nearly had a heart attack. Chloe was standing just inches away, at the side of my bed. Her eyes were open, but strangely vacant; the cold, indifferent eyes of an animal. Both her arms were outstretched, as if she were looking for a victim to throttle.

'Chloe?' I said experimentally. There was no reaction. I sighed; she was clearly having another one of her episodes. Moving slowly, so as not to startle her into wakefulness, I swung my legs over the side of the bed. I barely had one foot on the floor before she lunged towards me, sending us both toppling backwards on to the bed. Her hands gripped my shoulders with surprising force and the ends of her hair dangled into my face, half-blinding me. I had no idea who – or what – Chloe's fevered imagination thought I was at that precise moment, and I experienced a brief flicker of panic as I wondered if she was capable of harming me. But almost before the thought was complete, I told myself to get a grip, and cool, calm, clear-thinking Megan took control.

I was taller and stronger than Chloe, so it was easy enough to wrench her hands off me and catch her in a bear hug. I held her like that, arms pinned to her sides, until, after a few seconds, she stopped struggling and went limp. Satisfied that the fight had gone out of her, I gently escorted her back to bed, where I laid her down and stroked her hair until her eyes fell shut. As I made my way back to my own bedroom, I thought to myself that these episodes were not one-offs. In fact, I had the strong sense that this was only the beginning. But I wouldn't say anything to Chloe. There was no point worrying her unnecessarily; it was far better that she wake up in the morning with no memory of what had just happened.

20

My head is twisted at a *very* peculiar angle. I don't think
it's meant to go that far back because my neck feels as
if it's about to snap. My legs are twisted too, bent at the
knees and bowed backwards, over my head. The weight of
my feet, dangling off the ends of my ankles in mid-air, is
threatening to make me lose my balance, but I can't . . . I
mustn't . . . my life depends on it. At least I'm not alone;
Anouk is trapped underneath me. She's on all fours like a
cat, and I'm holding on to her back for dear life. She's
breathing very heavily, I do hope she's all right. The
seconds are going by ever so slowly . . . *tick* . . . *tick* . . .
tick. I don't think I can take much more.

'And . . . relax.' As soon as the words are out of Miss
Sullivan's mouth, I let go of Anouk and roll on to the thick
purple mat beside her. My heart's pounding and my ham-
strings are so tight they hurt.

When I look up from my half-sitting, half-lying position, Miss Sullivan is wearing a big smile that shows off
her small, perfect teeth.

'Well done, girls!' she says, sounding like she really

means it. 'That's a very difficult trick, I wasn't sure if you'd be able to do it. But you did and I'm very proud of you.'

I can feel myself going red – but in a nice way; it's not often I do something right. Anouk and I turn to each other at the exact same time and I hold up my hands so we can high-five. I'm so glad Anouk likes gymnastics as much as I do. She didn't do gym at her school in France, but Miss Sullivan says she's a natural. She's super flexible (her front walkover is AMAZING!), and even though she's smaller than me, she's strong . . . strong enough to carry my entire weight on her back. I never used to like doing partner work, mainly because I could never find anybody who wanted to be my partner – but with Anouk it's different. It's almost as if we were born to perform tricks together! We both love gym club and we always try to support each other and do our best. Any minute now, we'll find out whether our best is good enough.

Miss Sullivan claps her hands together and calls everyone over to the mats. 'OK, children,' she says. 'I've had a chance to see everyone perform now. I know you all tried really hard, but unfortunately only one duo can represent St Swithun's at next month's Under-Twelves Acro Championships.'

Anouk's sweaty hand creeps across the mat and finds mine. I grip it tightly and hold my breath.

'And that duo is . . .' Miss Sullivan stops and looks at all of us, like she's a judge on a TV talent show. *For crying out loud, just get on with it!* I scream silently.

Then Miss Sullivan points at Anouk and me and says: '*This* very talented partnership right here!'

I blow out a big puff of air through my lips. My head's gone all swimmy. I feel as if I'm looking through a kaleidoscope; colours shift around the room, making it spin like a merry-go-round. Then Anouk's arms are around my neck and her soft hair is tickling the side of my face. 'We did it!' she says in a high, excited voice.

I hug her back. 'Best Friends Forever?' I whisper in her ear.

'Best Friends Forever,' she repeats. Then she pulls away and gives me a smile that almost stops my heart.

Miss Sullivan is clapping now. 'Come on, everyone,' she says. 'Let's give them both a round of applause; they've certainly earned it.'

People start clapping, a delicious, hot noise that fills my head and sends me floating up to the sky. I look round because I want to see Eleanor Hardy's face (Eleanor's rubbish at gym; she only comes because she likes the spangly leotards). Eleanor is clapping (she has to, Miss Sullivan's watching) but she doesn't look happy and her mouth is sucked into a fishy pout. I catch her eye and give her the evils. *That's right, you stupid, fat, ugly bitch, keep clapping; it's about time you showed me some respect.* Sometimes (like right now) I wish certain people could read my thoughts. I expect it's better that they can't, because if they knew what went on in my head, they'd probably lock me up and throw away the key.

21

Chloe

I'd looked and looked, but I couldn't find it anywhere. I knew where it was supposed to be – where it *always* was – nestling in its velvet-lined case, in the drawer of my dressing table. The case was there, but the necklace had gone.

My grandmother's necklace was one of the most precious items I owned – certainly from a sentimental point of view, and probably in monetary terms as well. I was thirteen when my father's mother died and left me the necklace in her will. It was an eye-catching piece dating from the twenties, a diamond, amethyst and seed pearl pendant, suspended from a delicate rope of white gold. My grandfather, who worked for Rolls-Royce and was quite well off, bought it for his wife on their twenty-fifth wedding anniversary. I didn't wear it very often – it was quite an ostentatious item – but when I did, it always attracted a lot of attention.

I cast my mind back to the last time I'd seen it, several weeks earlier. I'd worn it to the wedding reception of a friend of Tom's and I remember thinking how beautifully it set off my beaded, flapper-style dress. A sudden blade of alarm pierced my gullet; I couldn't have lost it as we danced at that stately home on the Surrey-Hampshire border, could I? No, of course not, I would've realised as soon as we got home. I closed my eyes, trying to recall the sequence of events that evening, after the cab had dropped us off at Bellevue Rise. Tom and I were both fairly drunk, but I distinctly remembered taking the necklace off and placing it carefully back inside the case. At least, I thought I did. I had noticed that, just recently, I got muddled about all sorts of things with frightening ease.

If I *had* lost the necklace – and quite frankly I couldn't see how that could have happened – I would be absolutely devastated. My grandmother had been an eccentric character, prickly at times, but I had been fond of her and she of me. I knew how much the necklace meant to her, especially after Granddad died, and she had entrusted its safekeeping to me. Even as a little girl, I had already made up my mind never to sell it, but to pass it on to *my* children one day.

Realising that I still hadn't checked under the bed, I dropped to my knees and squinted into the narrow space under the divan . . . there was nothing, just a solitary hairclip among the dust balls. As I staggered to my feet, I was forced to steady myself on the headboard. I wasn't feeling too good. It wasn't just my anxiety over the missing necklace; I felt physically unwell. I had shocking heartburn, as if I'd swallowed drain cleaner; everything inside me stung.

I was tired too; I couldn't stop yawning and a scratchy veil of fatigue hung over my eyes. The tattered shreds of last night's dreams were still hung high on the masts of my unconscious, like ragged sails, flapping after a storm.

I resigned myself to picking up the search later on; Tom and Sammi were downstairs, cooking dinner, and would be wondering where I was. Dinner had been Sammi's idea; there was a new lasagne recipe she was keen to try out. Unfortunately, Megan wouldn't be joining us, as she was working another one of her interminable late shifts. Earlier on, I'd helped with the meal prep, chopping onions and tomatoes, while Tom made a white sauce under Sammi's supervision. It's funny, but I hadn't realised Tom was so interested in cooking; whenever I went to his, we always got takeaways. But then Sammi came along and it was as if she'd brought out the latent gastronome in him.

Once the lasagne was safely in the oven, I'd excused myself and popped upstairs to get some Gaviscon for my heartburn. I kept it in my dressing table drawer, and as I moved the jewellery case to one side, I thought it seemed unusually light; that's when I discovered the necklace was missing. With any luck, Tom would be able to shed some light on its disappearance.

I could hear them laughing as I made my way downstairs. I was surprised they'd hit it off so quickly – almost from the first time they met, in fact. I liked Sammi, but she was an acquired taste and I couldn't see that she and Tom had that much in common. I must say, she was looking particularly fetching that evening, in a figure-hugging black bandage dress that very few women over the age of twenty-five could get away with – a bit dressy for a simple supper at home, but I guess if you've got it, why not show it off?

When I reached the bottom of the stairs I hesitated, I don't know why. The lights in the hallway were off, making the scene up ahead, in the well-lit kitchen, appear particularly vivid. I watched from the shadows as Sammi lifted a wooden spoon to Tom's lips, her hand underneath it to catch the drips. She was still laughing about something or other and this was making her hand shake. As Tom took the end of the spoon in his mouth, he had to hold her wrist to steady it, an act that seemed to cause even more merriment between them. In that split second, I had a sudden, sharp feeling that this would be one of those moments that would be forever caught on a loop in my mind . . . a marker on the way to the point of no return. I stood there for perhaps a minute more, before coughing loudly into my fist and walking down the hallway towards them.

'You have *got* to taste Sammi's chocolate ganache,' Tom said when I entered the kitchen. 'It's for the gelato sundaes; they're going to be amazing.' He took the wooden spoon from Sammi's hand and went to dip it back in the saucepan.

'Maybe later,' I said, tasting bile in the back of my throat.

'What were you doing upstairs for so long?' Tom asked me. He walked towards me and I thought he was going to give me a kiss, but he was just reaching for the oven glove that was hanging from a hook on the back of the door.

'I was looking for my necklace, the one my grandmother gave me; I think I've lost it.'

'What do you mean, *lost* it?'

'It's not in my drawer like it usually is. Can you remember seeing me take it off after Amy's wedding reception?'

'What?' he said, looking at me strangely.

I scratched the back of my left hand; it felt itchy and I thought I could see the beginnings of a rash. 'The necklace – do you remember seeing me take it off before I went to bed?'

'No,' he said quickly, like he hadn't even bothered to think about it. 'Now stop stressing, it's bound to turn up sooner or later. Come on, let's eat our starter before it gets cold.'

Behind him, Sammi was carrying a wooden platter loaded with garlic bread over to the table. It smelled delicious, but my appetite seemed to have vanished, along with the necklace.

'You've probably just mislaid it,' Sammi suggested. 'I do stuff like that all the time . . . put something down for a second and then forget where I've left it. I can help you look for it later, if you like.'

'Thanks,' I replied, rubbing my temples to try and get rid of the cotton wool feeling in my head.

Sammi set the platter down and turned to look at me. 'Are you all right, Chloe? Only you seem a bit, I don't know . . . *fraught* this evening.'

I glowered at her. 'You'd be fraught too if you'd just lost a family heirloom.'

'Easy, Chloe,' Tom interjected. 'It isn't Sammi's fault the necklace has gone AWOL.'

I stared at the floor. 'No, I know it isn't . . . sorry, Sammi.'

'It's fine, no offence taken,' she said, her face wreathed in smiles. 'I know you've been under a lot of strain lately, what with work and—'

Suddenly she clapped a hand to her mouth and looked at me with huge, round eyes. I'm sure she was just about to say, 'what with work *and the night terrors . . .*' but then, remembering that Tom didn't know about them, she'd caught herself just in time. Luckily, he was absorbed in wrestling open a bottle of Zinfandel and the whole thing went over his head.

The meal was lovely, but I only ate a few forkfuls of lasagne and I skipped dessert altogether. Sammi was livelier than usual and she and Tom swapped easy banter over the dinner table. I did my best to join in, but I felt strangely detached. It was as if my mind was there, but my body was somewhere else, cool and elevated, the top of a mountain perhaps. There was another thing too . . . something bothering the far corners of my mind, casting a shadow, but I didn't know what.

Eventually, the talk turned to Megan's new romance. I'd mentioned it to Tom a couple of days previously and for some reason he found the idea that Megan was dating a surgeon highly amusing.

'I bet they're not short of inspiration when it comes to role play,' he said, giving us both a suggestive wink. He picked up one of the linen napkins and held it across his mouth and nose. 'Nurse Megan . . . scalpel, please.'

Without missing a beat, Sammi picked up a knife and held it out to him. 'Of course, Doctor Pete, anything you say, Doctor Pete,' she said in a squeaky falsetto that sounded absolutely nothing like Megan.

Tom reached for the knife, before deliberately letting it slip between his fingers. It fell to the slate floor with a loud clatter that plucked at my already taut nerves.

'Oh dear, clumsy me! Would you mind awfully picking that up for me, Nurse Megan?' he continued. 'And while you're down there, can you give me a blow job, strictly in the interests of your professional advancement, of course?' He banged the table with the palm of his hand and began howling with laughter. I know they'd both had a few drinks (I was abstaining), but I must admit I found the whole thing rather juvenile. I think Sammi must have read my mind because, instead of responding in kind to Tom's crude joke, she simply rolled her eyes good-naturedly.

Undeterred, Tom embarked on another double entendre, but before he could finish, we heard the front door slam. I glanced at the clock on the oven: 10.20, I hadn't realised it was so late.

'Meg!' I shouted, looking forward to seeing her. 'We're in the kitchen.'

'Yeah, Megan,' Tom added, slurring her name slightly. 'Come and join the party.'

She must have heard us, but the only reply we got was the sound of her footsteps ascending the stairs.

22

Megan

I studied the piece of paper in my hand. The directions were clear enough: Clindamycin, 225 milligrams orally, three times a day. Clindamycin was an antibiotic, commonly used to treat bacterial infections; I dished it out at the hospital all the time.

My gaze turned to the woman standing in the outpatient dispensary. She looked exhausted and there were black circles under her eyes where her mascara had run. A little boy was sitting astride her hip. His face was pale, one side of it drooping a little, as if he might be about to fall asleep, or possibly burst into tears. According to his prescription, he was a year and a half old. I rubbed my chin; something didn't add up.

'Can you tell me what this is for?' I asked the woman.

'He's got an eye infection,' she replied, resting her chin on top of the boy's head. 'How long will we have to wait for it? We've just spent three hours in A&E and I really need to get him home to bed.'

'I understand. We're pretty quiet at the moment; I can do it straight away.' I reached out and stroked the child's chubby forearm with the back of my hand. His skin was warm to the touch; he was clearly running a temperature. 'Why don't you take a seat? I'll get this made up for you as soon as possible.'

The woman thanked me and turned towards the row of chairs opposite the dispensary. I waited until she was out of earshot before taking the prescription over to Serena, the duty manager. I always enjoyed being on shift with Serena. She was organised and decisive, but kind with it, all great qualities for a pharmacist – and she had a youthful energy that belied her fifty-something years.

'There's something wrong here,' I told her. 'This dosage is too high for an eighteen-month-old.'

Serena took the script from my hand and reached for the glasses that were hanging from a cord around her neck. 'Hmm,' she said, frowning. 'I have to agree with you there.' She peered at the scrawled signature at the bottom of the page. 'You'd better call Doctor Freeman and double-check it.'

A few minutes later, I had the answer. 'It turns out the nurse recorded the wrong weight,' I told Serena, as I printed out a fresh prescription on our electronic system. 'Instead of entering twenty-five *pounds* in the chart, she entered twenty-five kilos.'

'Bloody hell, that's more than double his actual weight – no wonder the doctor over-prescribed,' said Serena.

'Good work, Megan; not every pharmacist would have picked that up.'

'Thanks,' I said, feeling a warm glow of pleasure. The consequences could have been serious if the nurse's unwitting error had gone unnoticed.

'You've taken to hospital pharmacy like a duck to water,' Serena said when I returned from handing over the medication to the boy's grateful mother. 'It must be quite a change from working in the community.'

'It is,' I acknowledged. 'But I much prefer it here; it's great being part of a big team and I love working side-by-side with the consultants.'

'Yeah, we've got some good people here, some of the best doctors in the country, in fact – and, most importantly of all, they know how to let their hair down when they're off duty.' Serena's eyes shone with suppressed laughter. 'I went to a barbecue at Bill McCarthy's house last weekend. Have you met Bill yet . . . orthopaedics registrar . . . black curly hair . . . very chatty?'

I shook my head. 'Doesn't ring any bells.'

'In that case, I'll have to introduce you; Bill's a good guy to know. His wife's a midwife here; they're loads of fun and they throw terrific parties. You should have seen how many people were at this barbecue . . . practically the whole of Orthopaedics and at least half of Obs and Gynae.' She threw her head back, as if visualising the scene. 'Suffice to say, a great deal of alcohol was consumed and by the end of the evening everyone was pretty merry.

Then Bill got out his guitar and began jamming with a couple of friends, while the rest of us sang along. We were making a hell of a racket, I'm surprised the neighbours didn't complain.'

'Sounds like Bill is *definitely* someone I need to meet.' I cleared my throat self-consciously. 'I guess Pete Chambers was there, then.'

'Pete? Why, do you know him?'

I turned towards the nearest shelf and pretended to be looking for something amid the anti-inflammatories. 'Only a little bit. We sit on the Ethics Committee together; he seems like a friendly sort.'

'He certainly is . . . that man could charm the skin off a snake.' Serena smiled as she reached behind me for a paper carrier. 'Yeah, Pete and his wife were there. I didn't realise Fiona was expecting their third.'

In that moment it was as if Serena had swung a wrecking ball into my chest; I almost vomited into my mouth. 'You mean she's pregnant?' I said, in what I hoped was a conversational tone.

'Yes, seven months. They've been trying for another baby for years. Their first two were conceived naturally, but they had to go down the IVF route this time. It took them three goes, but they got there in the end.' She looked at me and grinned. 'Isn't it great?'

'It's wonderful news,' I said, even though it was like regurgitating a jagged chunk of metal. 'Absolutely wonderful.'

*

I honestly don't know how I got through the rest of my shift without punching a wall. The depth of Pete's deceit was breath-taking. No wonder he was available so sporadically – and even then only for brief periods. At her advanced stage of pregnancy, dear Fiona would certainly want her husband close by. The talk of a divorce had clearly been an out-and-out lie because, from what Serena had proceeded to reveal, Pete and Fiona were not only very much together, they were even planning on renewing their wedding vows once the baby was born.

I had realised, all too late, that behind Pete's flattering words and affectionate touches, the wheels of a cool calculation had been turning throughout our brief courtship. But what could I do about it? Report him to the hospital's Ethics Committee? Yeah, right. Tell his wife? I'd have to be one hell of a bitch to do that to a heavily pregnant woman. No, I was going to have to suck up the humiliation and the crushing embarrassment and move on. But I must admit, it hurt, it really fucking hurt – and what hurt most of all was the fact that, because I'd been so wrapped up in that pathetic excuse for a man, I hadn't been there for my best friend when she needed me.

As I opened the front door of Number 46, snatches of animated conversation drifted out from the kitchen. Despite the lateness of the hour, it seemed the dinner party I'd been forced to pass on was still in full swing. I was just about to close the door behind me when I heard Tom say my name. I didn't catch all of it, but there was something about a scalpel. Then Sammi started speaking in a silly, high-pitched voice. My cheeks grew hot when I heard the words 'Doctor Pete' and realised she was imitating me. Then it was back to Tom – or should I say 'Doctor Pete' – for a vulgar quip about 'Nurse Megan' giving him a blow job.

I intertwined my fingers, crushing the knuckles of each hand in a rhythmic squeeze. I wouldn't have told Sammi about Pete – told any of them – if I'd known they were only going to take the piss. I elbowed the door shut rather more forcefully than I'd intended and it rattled in its frame. A second later, Chloe called out to me, then Tom did likewise. I ignored them both and started climbing the stairs. I really wasn't in the mood for socialising.

My mood didn't improve when I got upstairs and found one of the sash windows in my bedroom wide open. The room was chilly, and strewn all over the floor were various bank statements and insurance documents, a rogue breeze having apparently attacked the in-tray on top of my chest of drawers, where I kept important paperwork. Overhead, a couple of flies were swimming in a dreamy, pointless circle and I swiped at them with my hand as I stalked over to the window and slammed it shut. I certainly hadn't left it open; Chloe must have been in my room. I didn't mind if she had; after so many years of friendship, we had no secrets from one another. But if she was going to go round opening windows, I wished she'd damn well make sure she shut them. It was a disappointing end to a very disappointing day.

23

Anouk and I are trying to break the record for the world's longest daisy chain. We've been working on it since one o'clock: thirty-six daisies already and there's still another half an hour of lunch break to go. We're sitting behind the big oak tree on the playing field where no one will bother us. I don't like sharing Anouk with other people; it's best when I have her all to myself. I'm singing '*Frère Jacques*' while I thread another daisy on to my end of the chain. I'm not very good at singing, but they're the only words I know in French. It makes me feel good, knowing I can talk to Anouk in two different languages, even though I don't know what the words to '*Frère Jacques*' mean. We're having such a lovely time, but then, out of the corner of my eye, I spot an ugly grey cloud in the beautiful blue sky. And that cloud is Liam.

When Anouk first started at school and Miss Pickering chose me out of the whole class to look after her, I made it clear to Liam that I didn't have time for him any more. It took quite a bit of ignoring him, but he did eventually get the message – so why is his scabby arse walking over here?

'What are you two doing?' he says when he gets closer. There's something icky on the side of his mouth; it looks like peanut butter. *Yuck!*

'Seriously, Liam?' I say, cutting my eyes at him. 'Are you blind, or what?'

'We're making a daisy chain,' says Anouk. 'We're seeing if we can break the world record.'

'What *is* the world record?' he asks, standing there with his feet turned outwards like a duck.

Anouk looks at me. I don't know the answer, so I say the first thing that comes into my head. 'Sixty-eight. If we don't get any more interruptions, we can probably break the record by the end of break time.'

'Is it OK if I watch?' Liam asks.

'Of course you can,' Anouk says, before I even have a chance to open my mouth.

'You can watch, but you mustn't speak,' I tell him. 'Or else you'll ruin our concentration.'

'OK,' Liam says, smiling his slow, stupid smile. 'If you like, I could pick the daisies for you.'

'Yes!' Anouk squeals, like Liam's just done an amazing magic trick. '*Zat* would be a big help.'

Instantly Liam cheers up. The blood rushes to his cheeks and his eyes get brighter, sharper, the way everyone's do when they're in Anouk's orbit.

I turn towards Anouk. 'It's *that*,' I tell her crossly.

She looks at me, confused. 'What?' she says.

I lean over, so my face is right up in hers. 'You said "zat", instead of "that". If you're going to live in this country you ought to learn to speak the language properly. T-H-A-T . . . *that*! Got it?'

Her long eyelashes flutter. '*Oui*,' she says quietly.

It's extremely annoying having Liam around while we're trying to break the world record. He still hasn't wiped the peanut butter off, and he keeps makes sucking noises with his teeth while he's picking the daisies. I shouldn't be surprised; Liam's so thick he can't even read a book without his mouth making the shape of the words. Anouk doesn't seem bothered, though; if I didn't know better, I'd say she actually *liked* having Liam there. She chats away to him in her perky princess way, asking if he's got any brothers and sisters and whether or not his eczema hurts. *Who cares?!!!* I want to scream, and it takes a big effort to stop the words bursting out. I sometimes think that Anouk needs to grow up a bit . . . be a bit less, well . . . *nice*.

The problem is her life has been too easy; she doesn't know anything outside the bubble of her big house and her piano lessons and her ridiculous collection of china Beatrix Potter figures. If only I could make her realise that there's no point being nice to everyone. I can see that's something I'm going to have to work on with her, but there'll be plenty of time for that later.

Usually, lunch break goes too quickly, but today I'm glad when the dinner lady starts ringing the bell to call us back in, because it means we can finally get rid of Liam. I jump to my feet and go to pick up the daisy chain (I don't think it's long enough yet, so Anouk and I will have to finish it tomorrow). But as I lift it up off the grass, only half the daisy chain comes with me. The other half stays right where it is, because Liam's foot in his stupid clunky shoe is resting on the end.

A giant surge of rage jolts through me, almost robbing me of air. It feels as if a fist is pushing into my windpipe, right at the base of my throat, where my collarbones meet.

'Look what you've done, you stupid idiot!' I shout at Liam. 'You've broken our daisy chain, we'll never beat the world record now.'

'It's OK, we can just join the two halves together,' says Anouk, but because of the rush of blood in my ears, her voice sounds muffled and very far away, so I just ignore her.

'Get up!' I shout. 'Get up, you flipping fuckwit!' When Liam doesn't move a muscle, I grab his skinny, white, scabby arm. He digs his heels into the ground and tries to pull his arm away, but I'm pretty strong for a girl and I don't let go. Instead, I twist his arm up behind his back. A moment later, I hear something snap. *Re-sult!* Liam looks at me with the shocked expression of a cartoon character who's just been flattened by a steamroller. Then he tips back his head, lets out an ear-splitting scream and starts blubbing like the great big cry-baby he is.

Everything goes a bit mad after that. One of the dinner ladies comes running over; she turns white as a ghost when she sees Liam's floppy, useless arm. She turns around and shouts at another dinner lady to call an ambulance. Then Miss Pickering appears out of nowhere and says Anouk and I have to go back to the classroom with her. I don't say anything to Anouk as we walk back across the playing field, but I give her a look that says, *Keep your mouth shut – or else*. I'm sure she gets the message; we are best friends, after all.

Not long after we get to the classroom, we hear a siren. Everyone runs over to the window to watch the ambulance drive into the playground – everyone except Anouk, that is. She's gone really quiet and she looks scared. I don't know why, she isn't the one who's broken their arm. The ambulance men are just getting out when Miss Pickering says she's taking me to Mr Finch's office and Mr Wylie is going to look after the class until she gets back.

I've never been to the headmaster's office before. It's smaller than I thought it would be, and the bin under the desk needs emptying. Mr Finch has a grey beard and greasy hair that's stuck to his forehead. He looks very serious. He tells me to sit down, so I do. Miss Pickering stays standing up, over by the door. Then Mr Finch asks me what happened out on the playing field. I tell the truth; *my* truth – that Liam deliberately broke our daisy chain because he didn't want us to break the world record and that I grabbed his arm, just to frighten him . . . only I must have grabbed it a bit too hard without meaning to.

While I'm talking, Mr Finch sits there nodding, with his fingertips pressed together like a church steeple.

'And how do you feel about the fact that Liam has, in all likelihood, broken his arm?' he asks me.

I look up at the ceiling while I check to see what I'm

feeling: it's nothing, a great big ocean of nothing. Mr Finch is looking at me and waiting. Miss Pickering's waiting too; I can't see her, but I feel her eyes drilling holes into the back of my head.

'I feel horrible,' I say. 'I never meant to hurt Liam; he's my friend.' I bite down hard on the skin inside my lip and manage to squeeze out a tear.

'One of the dinner ladies said she heard you using foul language,' Mr Finch says. 'What was it again, Miss Pickering?'

'Fuckwit,' says Miss Pickering. 'She called him a "flipping fuckwit".'

It's ever so funny hearing Miss Pickering swear, but I know I mustn't laugh; that isn't what Mr Finch wants to hear. I know exactly what Mr Finch wants to hear – like I said before, I'm clever, cleverer than anyone knows – and that's why I'm going to make sure I say all the right things. After all, I don't want to get into trouble now, do I?

24

Chloe

A lump rose in my throat and the room seemed to tilt. Taking a deep, steadying breath, I unfurled my tape measure and checked the measurements again. This couldn't be happening. I would never be so careless . . . *would I?* Swallowing hard, I hurried over to my computer. My hands were sweating as I pulled up the paperwork on the screen. Please God, let it be the contractor's error, not mine. A second later, my worst fears were confirmed. The mistake *was* mine – mine and mine alone.

I sat down quickly in my chair. There was a leaden feeling growing in my bowels that owed nothing to the apple Danish and double espresso I'd wolfed on the train in lieu of breakfast. Bryan was going to go crazy when he found out about what I'd done. Finally, he had concrete proof of my incompetence and over-ambition – and he wouldn't keep the news to himself, that's for sure. Oh no, he would be shouting this one from the rooftops and pretty soon Richard Westlake and everyone else at the theatre would know I was an utter imbecile.

I buried my head in my hands, feeling like a puppet whose strings had been cut. I tried to think of a solution, but my brain had frozen and I couldn't see any way through the great big shitty mess in front of me. I'm not sure how long I'd been sitting there before Jess arrived.

'Morning!' she chirruped as she threw her handbag on her desk.

'Chloe?' she added when she got no reply.

Even just raising my head seemed to take a mammoth effort. 'I've made a major balls-up,' I said, meeting her gaze.

Jess frowned. 'What do you mean?'

'The *Neurosis* mirror, the one the specialist glass company has spent the last six weeks making at huge expense . . . it was delivered this morning.' I paused, reluctant to say the words out loud as if, by not saying them, I could somehow pretend it hadn't happened. I scratched the back of my hand absent-mindedly. The rash was getting worse. My skin was now stippled with dry red lesions; it felt as if a small army of microscopic insects had taken up residence there. I turned my attention back to Jess.

'The minute I unwrapped it, I knew there was something wrong; it was too big – *much* too big. Then, when I checked the paperwork, I realised what had happened: I gave the glass company the wrong measurements.'

Jess winced. 'How bad is it?'

'Thirty centimetres out on the width, forty-five on the height.'

'Ouch.'

'Yup,' I replied gloomily. I stared at the *Neurosis* model box that was sitting on the shelf unit next to my desk. The tiny oval mirror in its decorative Gothic frame seemed to taunt me. *You stupid idiot!*, it shrieked. *You were mad to think you could pull this off*. I smiled bitterly. I *must* be going mad if I believed a piece of silver foil was talking to me. Now wouldn't *that* be ironic . . . me, having a nervous breakdown, while I worked on a play about mental illness?

Jess sat down at her desk. 'How on earth did it happen? You're always so meticulous when it comes to measurements; I've seen the way you check and triple-check everything.'

I let out a low growl of exasperation. 'The mirror – frame and all – has to be a very specific size so it fits perfectly on the hydraulic platform that's going to create the revolving effect. But when I spec-ed it for the glass company, I forgot to deduct the frame measurements.'

'So they ended up cutting a piece of glass to match the platform dimensions – and then added the frame on top of that, meaning the whole thing's now way too big.'

I nodded. 'It's a schoolgirl error and utterly unforgivable. I said the mirror would be ready in time for dress rehearsals next week . . . it'll be a miracle if that happens now.'

'It's annoying, agreed, but surely there's a way round it.

Can't the tech guys just adapt the hydraulic platform to accommodate a bigger mirror?'

'No. Unfortunately, it wouldn't be capable of bearing the additional weight – all that extra glass is pretty heavy, remember. They'd have to build a whole new platform from scratch, and that would never fly with Bryan; there's no money in the budget.'

'Hmm,' Jess said, folding her arms across her chest. 'So, why don't we take the frame off and get the glass re-cut to the correct size?'

'Not an option. If we did that, we'd have to commission a brand-new frame to fit the smaller dimensions – yet again, the cost would be prohibitive.'

'Let's get rid of the frame altogether then.'

'No way, the frame is a fundamental part of the design. I specifically wanted the mirror to have a Gothic feel . . . it reflects the dark nature of the piece.' I threw my hands in the air irritably. 'It's no good, Jess, whatever we do it's going to look like a botch job and I *so* wanted everything on this set to be perfect.'

Jess was quiet for a few seconds, her eyebrows knotted in thought. Then she pushed her chair away from the desk and stood up.

'Can you print off the mirror spec for me?'

'Sure,' I said, turning to my computer screen and looking for the relevant file. 'Why do you need it?' I added, as I hit *print*.

'I've got an idea,' said Jess as the printer on her desk

began whirring. 'Don't make any decisions about this until I come back, OK?'

I achieved very little in the hour-and-a-bit that Jess was gone. I had so much to do, I hardly knew where to start, and on top of everything else I'd developed a splitting headache. I hardly recognised myself; I used to be so capable, so organised, but now everything around me seemed to be falling apart. It was as if some pivot had shifted in my life, some relentless mechanism that had begun to pull the pieces slowly apart. I was certain that my erratic sleeping patterns held the key. I hadn't experienced any night terrors in the past few days (at least none that I could remember), but I'd started waking up at all sorts of strange times in the night, emerging from the scraps of oblivion that passed for sleep, only to lie awake for hours, watching the minutes flick by on my digital clock with a growing sense of desperation. Tiredness was making me short-tempered and as a result my relationship with Tom had become strained. Meanwhile, I was receiving dwindling support from my best friend, the person who had previously been my rock, a situation that was only set to get worse as Megan's romance with her surgeon progressed. Just to round it all off, I still hadn't found my grandmother's necklace, which was a constant source of worry. I didn't dare tell my father; he would be absolutely furious with me.

I'd only managed to make a cup of tea and answer a

few emails when Jess bounded back in, still clutching the spec in her hand.

'OK, so I've just had a lengthy discussion with the props team,' she said as she perched on the end of my desk. 'They're going to take a mould of the frame and then recreate it in papier-mâché, which will obviously be heaps lighter than the original metal frame.' She paused and rested her hand on my arm, a gesture of solidarity, of comfort. 'You know how good those guys are . . . once that papier-mâché's painted it'll look just like the real thing. It's going to take a few days, but they said they don't mind putting in some extra hours to get it done.'

My eyes narrowed in suspicion. The solution couldn't be that simple; surely there had to be a catch. 'It's a nice idea,' I conceded. 'But we're sailing a bit close to the wind if we want to get this done in time for dress rehearsals, aren't we? Don't forget, we still need to send the glass back to the manufacturer's for re-cutting and that's going to take a couple of weeks, minimum.'

'No, we won't,' Jess said, a smile playing around her lips. 'That's the beauty of my idea; the papier-mâché can be stuck over the edge of the *existing* glass.' She waved the spec in the air. 'I've done the calculations and the total weight of the new mirror, frame and all, will be two kilos *less* than the spec-ed version – meaning there'll be no negative impact on the performance of the hydraulic platform.'

I could've kissed her. The relief was like a morphine

rush, my body flooded with its opiates. It was a simple idea, but brilliant at the same time.

'You, Jess, are an absolute genius,' I said. 'Why couldn't I have thought of that?' I was just so cross with myself, cross and disappointed. Jess was extremely talented, but she was only an assistant with barely three years' experience on the job. *I* should've been the one who worked this out.

'Don't be too hard on yourself,' she said generously. 'Even the best stage designers in the world get creative block.'

I shook my head. 'Creative block's one thing, but this is basic problem-solving. Honestly, I don't know what's wrong with me; I seem to find it so hard to focus these days.'

Jess laid the spec down on my desk. 'Actually, I had noticed,' she said softly.

I could feel a blush unfurling. 'What do you mean?'

'Just that you haven't been yourself lately. You seem distracted and a bit . . .' She broke off.

'A bit what? Come on, Jess, whatever it is, I can take it.'

'I think *testy* is probably the best way of describing it,' she said, smiling apologetically. 'It's water off a duck's back for me, because I know that's not the real you, but I think some other people at the theatre are starting to feel that they have to walk on eggshells when they're around you.'

I felt a cold horror prickling my skin. 'Really . . . that's how people see me? I had no idea.'

She fixed me with a look. 'So what's going on with you?'

'I haven't been sleeping very well is all,' I said defensively. 'I just need a few good nights' kip and I'll be back to my normal self.'

'Well, so long as that's all it is.' Jess pointed to my left hand. 'By the way, you need to get some steroid cream on that rash. It looks like psoriasis to me. My nan gets it; it's often brought on by stress.'

I ran a hand across the livid marks. 'I'll do that – and thanks for digging me out of the doo-doo with the mirror, Jess. I owe you one.'

She smiled. 'Any time, boss.'

For the remainder of the day, I tried my hardest to push the mirror debacle to the back of my mind, so I could focus on all the other loose ends that needed tying up on the various productions I was working on. But try as I might, I couldn't shake the sense of inadequacy I felt that I hadn't been able to figure out a solution to the problem myself. There was something else troubling me too. Why, despite the fact Jess had just single-handedly salvaged my professional reputation, was there still a current of foreboding cutting a path from my throat to my belly?

25

Megan

I was going down the escalator at London Bridge station when I did a double take. Standing outside Krispy Kreme on the concourse below was a man in a leather jacket who looked just like Tom: same height, same colour hair, same goatee, except he was too far away to be sure. I contemplated calling Tom's number on my mobile and seeing if the man picked up. Then, on the very perimeter of my field of vision, I saw another familiar figure striding confidently across the concourse: a tall, slim woman with long dark hair that waved in all the right places. She wore a lime-green skirt that swung in precise, geometric movements and a fitted peplum jacket. This time, there was no mistaking who it was. Something swayed and lurched in my gut, making me feel suddenly light-headed; it was just as well I was holding on to the handrail.

As soon as I reached the bottom of the escalator, I walked towards the nearest ticket machine and stood in front of it, pretending to be studying the options, but all the while my eyes continued to track the woman in the green skirt – all the way to Krispy Kreme. When the man saw her, he smiled and stepped forward to deliver a kiss. Whether this was on the woman's lips or her cheek, it was impossible to see from where I was standing, but it seemed to me that their contact lasted a fraction too long for it to be purely platonic.

They chatted for a few brief moments and the man clearly said something the woman found highly amusing because she threw her head back and opened her mouth wide in a show of hilarity. Then they started walking towards the exit that led out on to St Thomas Street, a route that would take them directly past me. As they approached, chatting animatedly to one another, I scuttled round to the other side of the ticket machine so they wouldn't see me. But before I did, I got a good look at the man: it was definitely Tom. But what on earth was he doing meeting Sammi in the middle of the day?

To the best of my knowledge, Tom and Sammi had met half a dozen times at most – their acquaintance limited to shared dinners and snatched conversations over the breakfast table in the kitchen at Bellevue Rise. It was just about conceivable that, finding themselves both at a loose end, they had arranged to do something together – visit a gallery perhaps, or grab a spot of lunch – although, to my mind, this would still have been very odd. Knowing Chloe as I did, she would think the same too. Odder still was the fact that Sammi had failed to mention she was meeting Tom during a conversation we'd had just a few hours earlier.

As I tailed the pair out of the station, careful to maintain a discreet distance, I dredged my memory for the precise details of the encounter. Sammi had been sitting in the living room, eating a toasted bagel and watching breakfast TV, and I had come in looking for my phone. More out of politeness than any genuine interest, I enquired about her plans for the day. I remembered her reply quite distinctly: 'I'm doing a Spin class at the gym,' she said. 'Then I'm going into town to talk to an editor about a commission.' If her rendezvous with Tom was perfectly innocent, surely she would have told me about it. No . . . there was definitely something off about this cosy little meeting, but I was going to have to abandon my covert observation as I couldn't afford to be late for work. I felt a wash of frustration as they turned right on to St Thomas Street and disappeared out of sight, then I turned on my heel and began walking towards the hospital.

A couple of hours later, I was still preoccupied with what I'd seen when a vibration coming from the pocket of my white tunic signalled the arrival of a text message. I was in the middle of ward rounds, so it wasn't until they were over and I was heading towards the staff kitchen to make myself a coffee that I had a chance to check my phone. My heart gave a painful fibrillation when I saw it was from Pete.

Free 2mrw pm if u are x

I pursed my lips and shoved the phone back in my pocket. It was nearly a week since I'd learned Pete and Fiona were expecting another child. Pete had called me twice since then, but both times I'd let it ring out and he hadn't bothered leaving voicemails. I'd seen him once at work as well, in the staff canteen, engrossed in a medical journal and a jacket potato. Before he had a chance to notice me, I'd turned away, wrestling a flaccid sandwich from one of the hospital's temperamental vending machines instead.

I had no appetite for any sort of showdown with Pete. I hated confrontation at the best of times and he wasn't worth the energy. I *had* been very angry in the beginning, but that had now given way to a sort of tired resignation. Being practical by nature, there was only so long that I could permit myself to wallow in emotion. In any case, I was used to disappointment; I experienced it all the time with the men I met online. The pattern was always the same: the initial spark, the pursuit, the sex, followed by the exponential waning of enthusiasm and then, finally, the split. Some guys at least had the decency to tell me they were breaking up with me; others simply vanished from the radar without any kind of explanation.

I thought Pete was different – that here, at last, was somebody I could have a real, grown-up relationship with, but now I knew he was just like the others – an immature, self-serving prick, just out for what he could get.

Unusually, I had the staff kitchen all to myself and I lingered there for a while, drinking my coffee and gathering my thoughts. I always enjoyed the daily ward rounds, as they gave me the opportunity to develop relationships with individual patients and observe their progress first-hand. However, they could be rather draining, especially when, like today, I found myself on the intensive care unit. It was difficult tending to people who were existing on the cusp of life and death and it had certainly given me a deeper appreciation of how incredibly lucky I was to be fit and healthy and in control of my own destiny.

As I rinsed my cup at the sink, my thoughts turned once again to what I'd seen at the station. It was clear that Sammi had already succeeded in winning Chloe over, but for me she had a personality like a rash – itchy, chafing, the kind of woman I just couldn't feel comfortable around. I'd been wary of her right from the beginning and my feelings hadn't changed; there was too much about her I didn't know. She did a very good job of playing Little Miss Perfect, but there was a vulpine curve to her mouth and a hunger in her eyes.

Scowling to myself, I set my mug on the draining board and pulled my phone out of my pocket. I had half a mind to text Chloe there and then and ask her if she knew what Tom was up to right now. But she was already under a lot of stress and I didn't want to drop a bombshell on her while she was at work; it would surely be kinder to tell her in person. I must admit, I would be stunned if it turned out Tom was cheating on Chloe. He just didn't seem the sort – but then again, neither did Pete.

I hesitated for a moment, drumming my fingers on my

mobile phone case – thinking, rationalising, calculating – then I pulled up Pete's text message and began typing a reply.

R u at the hospital? x

His reply pinged through almost immediately:

Yes, off duty at 7 x

Me 2, meet me on my dinner break? x

Er, 2mrw would be better x

Can't wait till 2mrw . . . horny NOW!!

I was cringing as I typed it; sexting had never been my style, but in this case the end justified the means. Pete took a minute or so to reply to this last message and I wondered for one horrible moment if I'd misjudged him, but then . . .

OK, u twisted my arm! When/where? x

Nope, I'd been spot on – Pete Chambers thought with his dick, just like all the others.

East Wing, 2nd floor stairwell. 7.15. Don't be late x

I sent my reply and tucked my phone away. As I made my way back to the dispensary, I found that my mood had suddenly lifted.

I was there before Pete. I knew he'd be anxious about meeting me on hospital premises like this and I wouldn't have been at all surprised if he'd had a last-minute change of heart. But no, he arrived bang on time, smartly dressed in suit trousers and an open-necked shirt. My throat thickened when I saw him, which caused me a certain degree of irritation; I hated knowing he could still have that effect on me, after the cruel way he'd led me up the garden path.

'What's the plan then?' he asked.

'Follow me,' I replied, turning towards the double doors that led to the surgical day unit. I knew exactly where I was headed, having scoped it out earlier; I wasn't about to leave anything to chance.

Most of the unit's staff had already left for the day and the corridors were deserted, but that didn't stop Pete casting around over his shoulder every five seconds, fearful we might be spotted. I didn't know why he was so worried; a surgeon chatting to a pharmacist in a hospital corridor was hardly going to raise any eyebrows. As we rounded the next corner, I stopped outside the staff washroom that served the nearby operating theatres.

Pete looked at me in disbelief. 'You are joking?'

'Where's your sense of danger?' I said teasingly. 'Seriously, though, no one's going to come in here; the operating theatres have shut up shop until tomorrow. But just in case . . .' Reaching into my trouser pocket, I withdrew a piece of paper and stuck it to the washroom door with a strip of surgical tape:

DO NOT ENTER!

SANITISATION IN PROGRESS

Pete grinned wolfishly. 'You little minx.'

He reached for me the second we got inside. As his lips pressed roughly against mine and his hands reached under my tunic, I felt the unmistakeable determination of his intent and the automatic surge of my response. But my resolve stayed firm and I refused to allow myself to be distracted from the task at hand.

'We'll have to be quick,' I whispered huskily. 'I've only got half an hour.'

'That shouldn't be a problem,' he whispered back. 'I've been ready for this ever since I got your text.'

I unzipped Pete's trousers and yanked them to the floor along with his underwear. 'Let's go in there, shall we?' I said, pointing to one of the two shower cubicles. 'Just in case somebody does come in.'

Nodding in agreement, he stepped out of his trousers and boxers. I scooped them up off the floor and tossed them over one of the stainless-steel wall hooks. Then I took off the fleece I was wearing and hung it on top of the trousers.

We both stepped into the shower cubicle and I flipped the catch on the door. Pete began fumbling with the buttons of my tunic, his excitement obvious. Just as he was reaching for the final button, I pushed him away and held up a warning finger. 'Condoms!' I hissed, as if the thought had only just occurred to me. 'I borrowed some from the dispensary; they're in the pocket of my fleece . . . don't go anywhere!'

Ignoring Pete's groan of frustration, I slipped the door

catch and stepped out of the cubicle, pulling the door to behind me. It only took a few seconds to retrieve our clothing from the hook and exit the washroom. Outside, I stopped briefly to pull the notice off the door and stuff it in my pocket, before I began walking briskly back along the corridor towards the stairwell.

'Megan?' I heard Pete say, his voice sounding tinny and distant as it filtered through two closed doors. I carried on walking and didn't look back.

26

It's dark in this airing cupboard, dark and very warm. My hands are pressed over my ears, but I can still hear them. They've been arguing for ages and it's all because of me.

It started with the letter that arrived this morning. It's Saturday today, so Dad's not at work. He picked the letter up off the doormat and opened it as we ate our breakfast together. I could tell straight away it was bad news. The more Dad read, the more his face seemed to sag with the weight of the words. When he got to the bottom of the letter, he laid it down on the table and gave a great big sigh like he'd just run a marathon.

'It's from the school,' he said. 'The headmaster wants to see us; apparently you were involved in a physical alter-cation with another student last week.'

'A physical *what*?'

'A scrap of some sort.'

I stared into the puddle of chocolatey milk at the bottom of my cereal bowl. Stupid, shit-stirring Mr Finch. I thought we'd sorted all that out in his office.

'It says here that the other student sustained a "substantial injury, requiring hospital treatment",' Dad said, drawing bunny ears in the air. 'Do you know what the injury was?'

I rested my elbows on the table and cupped my face in my hands, figuring it would make me look more innocent somehow. 'I think he might have broken his arm, but I didn't mean to do it, I swear.'

Dad's face sagged some more. 'So what happened exactly?'

I told him what I'd told Mr Finch and when I'd finished, Dad took in a large mouthful of air, so his cheeks puffed out. Then he let the air out slowly through his nose. 'You do know I'm going to have to tell Mum about this, don't you?'

I'd been hoping and praying he wasn't going to say that; even just hearing the words made my shoulders shake as a freezing shiver ran up my spine. 'No, Dad,' I said, reaching for his hand across the table. 'You can't tell her; you know what'll happen.'

He smiled sadly. 'I'm sorry, sweetheart, I can't keep something this big from her. In any case, the headmaster wants to see us *both*.'

Right on cue, we heard footsteps above us. Mum had woken up. I looked up at the ceiling.

Dad patted the back of my hand. 'She'll be down in a minute. You know how grumpy she is when she wakes up, so I'll wait until she's had a cup of coffee before I tell her. It's probably best if you make yourself scarce for a bit.

Why don't you go over to Anouk's? I can drop you there in the car if you like.'

I shook my head. 'Anouk's visiting her grandma in the old people's home.'

'One of your other friends?'

'I don't have any other friends.'

Dad turned his head to look out of the kitchen window. It was raining, or I know he would've told me to play outside in the garden. 'You'd better go up to your room, then – and don't come down until I tell you.'

So that's what I did. I don't have loads of things to play with in my room, not like Anouk, but I had my books and my friendship bracelet kit and that was enough. Pretty soon, I heard Mum moving round in the bathroom next door to my room and then the creaking of the stairs. Fifteen minutes went by and then half an hour. It was soon after that that I heard the explosion; it was a series of explosions, actually. First there was a scream, or maybe it was more of a howl, then came the sound of crockery smashing, followed by a loud thump, as if a chair had been knocked over. After that the arguing started. The kitchen is right below my bedroom, so I could hear the words licking up through the floor. It went on and on and on, but these are the bits that stick in my head:

Mum: Why does she do it? Why does she have to torture us like this?

Dad: It was an accident, Janine, just a couple of kids mucking around in the playground.

Mum: What if that boy's parents decide to sue us?

Dad: Stuff like this happens all the time in school; no one's going to sue us over an accident.

Mum: I'm telling you, this was no accident. That child's evil; bad things always happen when she's around. I don't know why we didn't hand her over to Social Services years ago.

Dad: How can you say that about your own flesh and blood? You can't hold it against her forever. She was only a little girl; she didn't know what she was doing. She's *still* a little girl, for heaven's sakes.

Mum [makes that kind of *mmmp* noise when you're just about to puke]: I think she knew *exactly* what she was doing.

Dad: You need to find a way of forgiving her, Janine, or it will end up destroying you . . . destroying all of us.

Mum: My life was destroyed four years ago; our darling daughter made sure of that. And don't tell me what I need, you weak, pathetic excuse for a man. What I *need* is a drink . . .

At that point, I didn't want to hear any more, so I climbed into the airing cupboard, which is at the other end of the landing and as far away from the kitchen as I could get. It smells a bit fusty in here; I wouldn't be surprised if half the towels and duvet covers on the shelves above my head weren't even clean. I've been here for ten minutes now. I can still hear their voices, but not the actual words, which is a relief. Suddenly, the voices stop and I hear big, angry ogre footsteps coming up the stairs.

'Where are you?' Mum shouts. 'Where are you, you little bitch?'

'Janine!' Dad calls from the bottom of the stairs. 'Leave her alone! Let's at least wait until we've seen the headmaster and we know all the facts.'

'I know everything I need to know,' Mum snarls. 'Our daughter broke a boy's arm and now she's going to pay for it.'

I've seen Mum in a bad mood a lot before (when *isn't* she in a bad mood?), but this time it sounds as if she's really on the warpath. I open the airing cupboard door a tiny bit and peer through the crack, just in time to see Mum going into my room.

'It's no good hiding,' she says. 'I'm not going to stop looking until I find you.' I hear my wardrobe door sliding open. 'Come out, come out, wherever you are,' she says nastily like a witch in a fairy tale.

I decide to make a run for it and I push open the airing cupboard door and tear along the landing, past my bedroom door, and down the stairs.

'Sweetheart?' Dad says, as I burst into the kitchen, where he's sitting drinking tea as if his only child wasn't just about to get the hiding of her life. I don't bother answering, there's no time; instead I open the back door and run out into the garden, even though I'm not wearing any shoes. It's stopped raining, but the grass is wet and squishy under my toes. I look around for somewhere to hide, but the shed's got a big padlock on it and there isn't anywhere else, so I run to the garden gate. I don't have a plan, I only know I need to get as far away from Mum as possible. If I stand on my tippy-toes, I can reach the bolt on the gate, but it's big and rusty and you can't just slide it open; you have to work it free by jiggling the bolt up and down. The bolt makes so much noise, I don't hear Mum creeping across the grass. Then all at once her hand slams down on my shoulder.

I try to wriggle away from her, but she grabs me by both arms and pushes me back against the gate. My mouth is very dry, I hardly have any spit, and I can hear my heart hammering in my throat.

'I didn't *mean* to hurt Liam,' I tell her. 'It was an accident.'

'I wasn't born yesterday,' she says. 'Now, how do you think I should punish you?'

'I d-d-d-don't kn-kn-know.' She's squeezing me so hard my teeth are chattering in my head. Then she starts dragging me across the garden towards the shed. Something hard and sharp swims up from my belly and tries to push itself out as a sob.

When we get to the shed, Mum holds my arm with one hand, while her other hand reaches for a metal bucket that's lying on the ground with loads of other junk. She turns it upside down and orders me to stand on top of it. I do what she says, even though it's hard because my legs have turned to jelly. I think I've wet myself too, because my knickers feel a bit damp and I just caught a whiff of pee.

'Are you ready?' she says, grabbing me by the neck. The

next thing I know, she's shoving my head downwards and suddenly I can't breathe. The reason I can't breathe is because my whole head is under water. The water's freezing and my hair's floating over my eyes, so I can't see a thing. I try to lift my head up, but I can't; Mum won't let me. My lungs are thrashing as if they're about to explode and my heart feels like a helium balloon, rising away from my feet. Is this what it feels like to die?

I don't know how long I'm under for, but when Mum yanks my head out of the big green water butt that was full to the top because of all the rain we've had, I gasp and gasp as if I'll never be able to get enough air.

Then I hear Dad's voice from somewhere behind us: 'Janine! That's enough!'

'I don't think so,' Mum says and goes to push my head back under – but before she can, Dad's lifting me up off the bucket and into his arms. I'm dripping water all over his shirt, but he doesn't seem to mind. 'I said, *that's enough*,' he repeats.

Mum shoots him an evil look. 'You two deserve each other,' she says, before she stomps off into the house.

27

Chloe

It was almost like old times: Megan and I ensconced in a Colombian tapas bar, agonising over which cocktail to try first. Small and dimly lit, the bar had only opened a month or so earlier and was barely a ten-minute walk from Belle-vue Rise. I'd been dying to check it out, so I was thrilled when Megan phoned me at work, practically *demanding* we put a date in the diary. It was nearly a week before we both had a free evening, but now here we were at last and I was determined to make the most of this rare time together.

'Thanks for organising this, Meg,' I said, as our first cocktail arrived. 'It's just what the doctor ordered.'

'You're very welcome – and remember, this is my treat.'

'You don't have to do that,' I told her. 'Why don't we just go halves?'

'Because *I* want to pay,' Megan said forcefully. 'It's the least I can do. You've been under a lot of stress lately – the night terrors are evidence of that – and I wasn't there when you needed me. But I'm here for you now, I promise.'

A wave of affection for her rolled over me as I realised how much I'd missed her over the past few weeks. 'I really appreciate you saying that, especially when you've got lots of other demands on your time . . . speaking of which, how *is* the sexy surgeon? Maybe I'll even be able to meet him with his clothes on one of these days.'

Megan's face contracted for a second. 'I'm not seeing Pete any more,' she said tartly. 'Not since I found out from a colleague that his wife's pregnant with child number three.'

I gasped. 'So you mean the divorce—'

'Was a load of old bullshit, designed to sweet-talk me into bed.'

I felt dreadful for Megan. I knew she would never knowingly have targeted a married man; she was far too principled for that. 'I'm so sorry, hon. Are you absolutely gutted?'

She gave a quick shrug. 'I was upset at first, but I'm over it now. In any case, I made sure he got his comeuppance.' She leaned across the table and dropped her voice. 'I lured him into one of the hospital washrooms on the promise of a quick shag, then I did a runner with his trousers and underpants.'

The revelation detonated an explosion of laughter that forced the mouthful of caipirinha I'd just swallowed straight back out through my nose.

Megan grinned back at me. 'A hospital porter found him wandering the corridors of the day unit with a surgical mask clamped over his privates.'

I was now laughing so hard that tears were streaming down my face. 'So what did Pete do then?'

'Sent the poor bewildered porter off in search of some scrubs, so he could at least cycle home without being arrested. Except the porter couldn't find any that were the right size, so Pete had to walk through the hospital looking like a complete twat, in trousers that were three inches too short and tight enough to give him a hernia.'

I dabbed at my eyes with a paper napkin. 'And how do you know all this?'

'Because as Pete was mincing through Reception, trying desperately to salvage whatever was left of his dignity, the porter took a photo on his mobile phone and put it on Facebook, along with his account of how he'd found Pete half-naked. Within twenty-four hours, practically everyone on the hospital staff had seen it.'

'What did Pete tell people had happened?'

Megan leaned back in her chair. 'I don't know, but whatever it is, you can be sure it ain't the truth.'

'Will he face any sort of disciplinary action from the hospital authorities?'

'I shouldn't think so, but yesterday I got an email from the Secretary of the Ethics Committee, informing me that Pete had resigned as Chair. I can't help feeling the two incidents are connected . . . I mean, exposing yourself in a hospital corridor isn't most people's idea of ethical behaviour.' Megan's eyes glittered. 'Believe me, it's going to take Mr Chambers a very long time to live this down.'

I had to give it to Megan – she always kept a cool head

in a crisis; it was one of the things I admired most about her. 'Well, it certainly sounds as if he got what he deserved,' I told her. 'Has he tried to contact you since then?'

'No, and if he's got any sense at all, he's worked out exactly why I did it and he'll stay out of my way.'

She sipped her drink with a mischievous smile. 'Anyway, I haven't brought you here to moan about my disastrous love life. What about you, how are things at work?'

'Nothing much has changed. I'm still tearing my hair out over the *Neurosis* set.'

'What about the night terrors – have you had any lately? I know you don't always remember the details, but you generally have some sort of awareness that they've occurred.'

I hesitated; it was an uncomfortable subject to talk about, even with my best friend, but I trusted Megan implicitly and I knew I wouldn't be doing myself any favours by lying to her. My fingers crept to the collar of my shirt. I undid the top two buttons, pulling the material apart to reveal a purplish bruise, just above my collarbone. Megan sucked air through her teeth when she saw it.

'I did this the night before last,' I said, wincing as I brushed my fingertips across the bruise. 'I dreamed I was walking in the woods with my sister, when she was crushed by a falling tree. I knew she would die if I couldn't get the tree off her.' I paused and took a fierce gulp of my drink. The dream had felt so real; I could still remember the intense panic that had engulfed me when the tree fell. It had been paralysing, a hot white noise in my head that hindered any rational thought process – and yet, realising there was no one to save my sister but me, I had been spurred into action. 'All of a sudden I felt this shooting pain and I woke up to find myself kneeling on the floor in the dark, using my right shoulder to push my bed against the wall – except of course it wasn't going anywhere.'

Megan's mouth opened wide. 'You thought you were trying to shift the tree off your sister.'

I nodded. 'What an idiot, eh?'

'Don't say that, Chloe,' Megan chided me gently. 'It was just your unconscious reacting to a perceived threat. All things considered, I think you got off pretty lightly; you could easily have dislocated your shoulder. I'd get some arnica cream on that bruise if I were you; it'll help speed up the healing.'

'Will do,' I replied, buttoning my shirt. 'There's something else too . . . I've started sleepwalking again. I've twice woken up in the kitchen in the middle of the night, with no memory of how I got there.'

Megan arched her eyebrows. 'You can't go on like this, Chloe; you're going to end up really hurting yourself one of these days. I think it's time you had a chat with your GP.'

I sighed. 'That's what Sammi keeps telling me. She's been so sweet since she found out about my night terrors. She knows I don't have time to make personal calls at work, so she even offered to phone the surgery and make the appointment for me.'

'And did she?'

'She called a few times, but she said the line was constantly engaged. So then I tried my luck with the online booking system, but the next available appointment was three weeks away.' I gave a feeble smile. 'With any luck the night terrors will have died a death by then; I think I'm just going to try and ride it out.'

Megan reached for my hands across the table. 'I hate to see you suffering like this. I just wish there was something I could do to help.'

'You *are* helping – by organising tonight and forcing me to relax for a change.' I swallowed hard. 'Listen, Meg, some other weird stuff has been happening too.'

'What kind of stuff?'

'Things keep going missing from my bedroom. First it was a framed photo of my sister and me. One day it was sitting on my mantelpiece, the next day it was gone. I've looked everywhere, but it's literally vanished into thin air. I know how ridiculous that sounds, but it's the truth. I didn't touch that photo; not even to dust it.' I realised that I was gabbling, the words falling over themselves like dominoes. I paused to catch my breath, while Megan regarded me patiently. 'The next thing to go walkabout was my grandmother's necklace.'

'But you're always so careful with that necklace; you can't have lost it.'

I felt a twinge of irritation. 'That's what I'm trying to tell you, Meg. I haven't *lost* anything. I admit that I wasn't sure about the necklace at first, but I've thought and thought and now I'm absolutely certain that I put it back in its box after the last time I wore it. But now it's disappeared, just like the photo frame.'

As I spoke, Megan's face took on a doubtful look, as if she was analysing the situation and concluding that *things don't just disappear for no good reason.*

'Why are you looking at me like that?' I said. 'You don't believe me, do you? You think I'm going mad.'

'Don't be silly, of course I don't think you're going mad,' she said quickly. 'It's just . . .' Her voice tailed off.

'Just *what*?' I said impatiently.

'Well, some strange things have been happening to me too.'

I looked at her in amazement. 'Your stuff's been disappearing as well?'

'Not *disappearing*,' she said guardedly. 'A couple of weeks ago, I came home from work and made something to eat; then I went upstairs for a shower. I distinctly remember taking my watch off and putting it on the bedside table, the way I always do. But when I came back from the bathroom, my watch was lying on the floor. It was over by the door, miles away from the bedside table; I only just avoided standing on it. There was no logical explanation for how it might have ended up there – but there was no harm done and so I didn't think any more about it . . . until now.'

I waved away the waiter who had come to take our food order. 'Anything else?' I asked.

'Actually, yes. Do you remember when Tom came over the other day and you two cooked dinner with Sammi?'

'Of course I do. You were at work that night and when you got back, you went straight upstairs without even saying hello.'

'Sorry about that,' Megan replied, looking slightly sheepish. 'That was the day I discovered Pete was cheating on me with his own wife.'

'Ah, no wonder you didn't feel like joining in.'

'Quite,' she said with a grimace. 'Anyway, when I got to my room, I found the window was wide open and all the paperwork that had been in my in-tray was scattered all over the floor. It wasn't even windy that day; it didn't make sense. I knew I hadn't opened the window myself; I thought maybe you had.'

I shook my head furiously. 'Absolutely not. I've never gone into your room and opened the window, *never*.' I chewed on my lip, trying to work out how the various events might be connected. 'This can't be just coincidence, can it?'

'I don't know. None of these things are very significant by themselves, but when you put them all together . . .' She gave me a tentative look. 'I'm just wondering if it might have something to do with Sammi. I mean, she's the only one with access to our rooms and she was definitely at home around the time my watch was moved.'

I rubbed the side of my jaw. 'But why would she do it? What's in it for her?'

'That necklace of yours must be worth hundreds.'

'But the photo frame isn't. And what about your watch? Why go to all the effort of moving it from one place to another? Why not just take it if the motivation is money? As for chucking your paperwork around and leaving the window open to make it look as if a rogue gust of wind is to blame . . . I just can't see the point.'

'No, you're probably right.' Megan gave a little chuckle. 'To be honest, I think the most likely explanation is that we're both getting a bit forgetful in our old age. I'm sure your necklace will turn up eventually. It'll be somewhere where you least expect it, you'll see.'

'I hope so.' I looked at Megan thoughtfully. She was a better judge of character than I was and I valued her opinion on people, as I valued her opinion on most things. 'What do you make of her?' I asked.

'Sammi?' she said, sticking out her bottom lip. 'To be honest, I've always thought there was something slightly off about her; I just can't put my finger on it.'

My mind flashed back to the time that Sammi scalded herself in the kitchen and her peculiar behaviour in the immediate aftermath. 'I like her, but she plays her cards very close to her chest,' I conceded. 'I've asked her some pretty basic questions about her family and where she grew up and she's made it quite clear the subject is off limits.'

'I'd love to know the real reason she quit her last flat share,' Megan said. 'She was certainly very cagey when we asked her about it.'

'And don't you think it's odd that she's never once brought any friends back to the house? She must *have* friends in the area; she's lived in London for years – but I've never even seen pictures of them on her phone.'

'Maybe you should ask to see the photo album she keeps under her bed.'

'What photo album?'

'I came across it by accident, the day she moved in. She was downstairs cooking dinner and I decided to have a quick look round her room.' Megan raised her palms in the air. 'I know I shouldn't have done it; it was an invasion of privacy, plain and simple, but what can I say . . . I was curious. While I was in there, I spotted this bright orange photo album lying on the floor, sticking out from under the bed. I thought it might have fallen off the bookshelf, so I picked it up – and, being the nosey cow I am, I couldn't resist checking out Sammi's pictures. Except they weren't just pictures, there was other stuff in there too – letters and old newspaper cuttings. I didn't get a proper look at any of it, but it was stuff she definitely didn't want me to see.'

'How do you know that?'

'Because she caught me in the act and practically wrenched the thing out of my hands. Then, when I tried to apologise, she got very tetchy. It was quite unnerving . . . I almost felt as if I was talking to a completely different person. She hasn't mentioned it since, so I think she's forgiven me, but ever since then I always feel really on edge whenever I'm around her.' She broke off and pulled at her earlobe. 'There's something else I need to tell you; it's about Tom.'

'Oh?' I said, feeling my heart spiral up into my throat.

'Did you know he met up with Sammi at London Bridge yesterday?'

'What?' I said, thinking I must have misheard her.

'It's true. I saw them together on the station concourse when I was on my way to work. It wasn't an accidental meeting, either; Tom was waiting for her outside Krispy Kreme. I followed them as far as St Thomas Street, but I don't know where they went after that. I didn't want to be late for work.'

Suddenly I felt very hot. I could feel sweat clinging to the back of my neck, dampening my hair. 'No,' I said quietly. 'I didn't know.'

'There's probably a perfectly innocent explanation,' Meg said, offering me a reassuring smile. 'They're both freelance . . . I expect they just found themselves at a loose end and decided to meet for a quick coffee. I just thought I should mention it.'

'You're probably right. Tom does get on very well with Sammi.' I absent-mindedly strummed the slender gold chain around my neck. I'd spoken to Tom on the phone yesterday morning and he'd made no mention of Sammi, or a coffee date.

'Actually, Tom and I are going through a bit of a rough patch at the moment,' I said, hating how the words felt in my mouth. 'I've even been wondering if we should take a break, just until I've put the *Neurosis* set to bed.'

'Wow, hon,' Megan said, clearly confounded. 'I had no idea you two were having difficulties. Are you sure a break is what you really want?'

I shrugged. 'I don't know what I want. In fact, I don't seem to be very good at making any sort of decision these days.' I held up my empty glass. 'But one thing I do know is that I could murder another one of these.'

28

I've been at the library in the precinct the entire day. I bought an apple and a banana for my lunch, except the banana was all black and squishy when I peeled it, so I had to throw it away. Usually I spend Saturday afternoons with Anouk. I go to her house, or sometimes we play on the swings at the rec, but she said she was going shopping with her mum today, so I came to the library instead. I love it here. It's warm and quiet and there are so many brilliant books to choose from. When I read, I go to a secret kingdom . . . through a hidden tunnel drilled beneath a castle wall to the furthest and darkest corners of my imagination. But I'm back in the real world now, and I've been sitting on this hard chair for so long that my bum's gone numb.

I check the time on the big clock that hangs above the large-print romances . . . two minutes past four. It will take me twenty minutes to walk to Anouk's (ten if I get the bus) and surely they'll be back from the shops by then. I have to be home by six, so that means I'll have one hour and a bit with Anouk. It's not as long as I'd like, but it's better than nothing and it will keep me going until I can see her again at school on Monday.

I love going to Anouk's house. It's so *clean* and the fridge is always full of food. There are big, fluffy towels in all the bathrooms and when I use the loo, I can't resist burying my face in them because they smell so yummy. Anouk's mum Lucy is the nicest lady I've ever met (except for Miss Pickering, of course). I haven't met Anouk's dad yet because he has a very important job and he's always away on business, but I bet he's nice too.

Sometimes (quite a lot of times) I imagine what it would be like if I moved in to Anouk's house. I might get Anouk to ask Lucy if it would be OK. I won't do it just yet, because that would be weird, but maybe in a month or two. Before the half-term holidays would be perfect.

Lucy answers the intercom straight away, almost as if she was expecting me. A second later, the electric gates open and when I get to the front door Lucy's already there, waiting for me.

'This is a nice surprise,' she says with a big smile. 'Did the birthday party finish early then? Anouk said I shouldn't come to pick her up until five-thirty.'

I'm confused. 'What birthday party?'

'I think Anouk said the girl's name was Kayla; she lives in Cherry Tree Drive.' Then Lucy's face scrunches up; the penny's just dropped and I know she's embarrassed. 'I'm so sorry, darling; I hope I haven't put my foot in it. I just assumed the whole class had been invited.'

Kayla and I aren't friends exactly, but we're not

enemies either. She didn't used to speak to me at all, but she's a lot friendlier since Anouk and I became best friends; most people are. I knew her birthday was coming up because she kept going on about the karaoke machine her parents were getting her, but she didn't say anything about a party – not to me, anyway.

'It's all right,' I say, squeezing out a smile. 'I was busy this afternoon anyway; I've been shopping with my mum.'

'That sounds fun,' Lucy says. 'Did she get you anything nice?'

'Er, some new shoes and . . . um, a jumper.'

'Ooh, how lovely, you'll have to wear them next time you come round. How did you get here, do you need a lift home?'

I shake my head. 'No, thank you.'

'Well, OK then. I'll tell Anouk you popped round.'

Cherry Tree Drive isn't on my way home, but I've got some time to kill, so I don't mind going the long way round. The houses here are lovely – not as big as Anouk's, but big enough. I don't know which number Kayla lives at, but her house is easy enough to spot. It's the one with balloons on the front door and the purple *Happy Birthday* banner. I can hear music and voices coming from round the back, so I think they must be in the garden.

I walk towards the gate at the side of the house. It's made of twisty black metal and there's a piece of wood on the other side to stop people looking in. Luckily, there's a narrow gap next to the hinge and if I put my face up against the gap and tilt my head just so, I can see a group of kids, sitting in a circle on the grass, playing pass-the-parcel. I reckon half the class is there, maybe more. Anouk stands out straight away. She's wearing a dress the colour of a satsuma and her hair is torched into gold by the afternoon sun. Her beauty burns so bright that I almost want to put a pinhole in a paper plate and look at her through it, just like we did when Miss Pickering took us outside to watch the eclipse. Next to Anouk is Liam, with his arm in a plaster cast. Oh . . . my . . . God, I can't believe it, Kayla even invited LIAM!!

The music plays and the parcel goes round and round the circle. I watch as layer after layer comes off, until it eventually stops in the hands of the birthday girl (funny, that). Kayla tears off the last layer to reveal a shiny silver charm bracelet, holding it up so everyone can see just what a lucky girl she is. Then a woman appears and she's carrying a huge pink and white birthday cake. My mouth starts watering straight away; I didn't realise how hungry I was until now. The woman puts the cake down on the table next to the blanket and everybody jumps up, crowding round her as she lights the candles. They all look so happy, especially Anouk. She hasn't learned yet that you can't trust everyone you meet.

Never mind; she'll find out soon enough.

29

Megan

I arrived home from work in the middle of the afternoon. It hadn't been a bad shift, but I felt a bit low, which was unusual for me. A few hours earlier, I'd been on the ICU, visiting a new admission – a female cyclist, roughly my age, who'd been hit by a lorry less than half a mile from the hospital. The notes at the foot of her bed revealed she had suffered a massive head trauma, as well as a ruptured spleen and numerous broken bones. She hadn't regained consciousness since the accident, and from where I was standing the prognosis didn't look good.

Unusually, there was no name or date of birth on her chart, leading me to surmise that she hadn't been carrying any ID at the time of the accident, and no one had yet reported her missing. I queried it with one of the nurses, who confirmed that efforts were still being made to identify the victim and trace her next of kin. It broke my heart to think that somewhere there was a family who had no idea their loved one was lying in a hospital bed, kept alive by a ventilator and an aggressive cocktail of drugs. I spent longer than strictly necessary at her bedside. I don't know why; I suppose I just hated the thought of her being alone.

I don't know if she felt my presence, but if she did I hope she found it comforting. As I left the unit, head bowed and deep in thought, I almost ran straight into Pete, who was walking at the head of a group of bright-eyed medical students. As we passed each other in the corridor, I turned, very deliberately, to look at him, but he avoided any eye contact. Coward.

The house appeared to be empty. The downstairs rooms were deserted, but there was a curious atmosphere, a sort of heaviness in the air. Even though I was gasping for a cup of tea, my first priority was changing out of my work things. Up in my bedroom, I quickly stripped off my uniform tunic and black trousers and pulled on jeans and a loose, thigh-length T-shirt. It was only as I pulled out my hair elastic and tossed it on the bedside table that I noticed the dress that I'd left lying on the bed earlier on. It had slipped off its hanger as I'd dragged a cardigan out of the wardrobe. Given that I was already in serious danger of missing the 7.05 to London Bridge, I'd tossed it on the bed, intending to hang it up later. It was a pale pink wrap dress with a tiered skirt and delicate embroidery on the neckline and sleeves, much more expensive than the things I usually wore. I'd spent three weeks drooling over it on ASOS before finally taking the plunge; I'd only had the chance to wear it once or twice.

When I'd seen it that morning, the dress had been in

pristine condition, but now there was a large black stain on the chiffon top layer. Gasping in disbelief, I went over to the bed, whereupon the source of the stain immediately became apparent. My rose-gold fountain pen – a thirtieth birthday present from Chloe – was lying next to it on the bed. The lid was off and the exposed nib was nestling against the fabric of the dress. I didn't know how long it had been there – evidently long enough to produce a stain roughly five centimetres in diameter. I released a volley of expletives as I jammed the lid back on the pen and tossed it to the floor in disgust. The dress was ruined; I just couldn't see how on earth it had happened. I always kept the fountain pen in the canvas messenger bag I took to work. When I wasn't using it, the bag was more often than not looped over one of the knobs on my wardrobe door – could the pen have rolled out on to the bed as I slung the bag over my shoulder that morning? Possible, but unlikely. I didn't use the pen every day and I tried to remember the last time I'd seen it; it was several days at least, possibly a week. It would have been easy enough for someone to take the pen from my bag without me knowing.

Just then, I heard a noise coming from the ground floor. It must be Sammi, but where on earth had she been hiding? Quickly, before I could lose my nerve, I grabbed the dress and went downstairs. I found Sammi standing in the kitchen, leaning with both hands on the worktop, her head down, her shoulders rigid. She didn't move her body as I entered, but simply rotated her head, like an eagle watching a field mouse. I could feel her silently auditing my flaws: the shine on my unpowdered nose, the bra strap poking out from under my T-shirt, the loose threads hanging from the hem of my jeans.

'Hi, Meg-aaan,' she said. She had a particular way of saying my name, snapping the first syllable against the roof of her mouth and drawing out the second in something akin to a sigh, that made the hairs on my arms bristle.

I offered no greeting, but simply held out the dress. 'Look at this,' I said curtly.

'Look at what?' she replied, her expression all innocence and haughty incomprehension.

I gestured to the ink stain. 'My favourite dress, it's ruined.'

She pinched her face together and studied the stain, her eyes somehow angry and indifferent at the same time.

'Oh my goodness, I see what you mean. How annoying! How did that happen?' Her words sounded hollow, like lines she'd rehearsed so often they'd lost their meaning.

'I've no idea,' I said, smiling sarcastically. 'I thought perhaps you might be able to answer that question.'

'I'm sorry, Megan, I'm not sure what you're getting at.'

I could feel my armpits growing sweaty. I don't know why I felt so jumpy – what could I possibly have to fear from Sammi?

'When I left the house this morning, there was nothing wrong with this dress. I've just come home now to find it covered in ink.'

She flicked her tongue over her incisors. 'Ink?' she repeated.

'It leaked out of my fountain pen,' I said. 'I can't think how it ended up on my bed. Next to the dress. With the lid off.'

Sammi shifted position so that she was now facing me. 'I'm sorry, Megan, but your guess is as good as mine.'

'You didn't *borrow* it from my bag, then – my fountain pen, I mean – and leave it lying on the bed?'

'No, I haven't touched your bag. I've got plenty of pens of my own.' She gave a smile that was as sweet as icing, setting my teeth on edge.

I could feel my earlier conviction wavering. I had no proof, no witnesses, and of course there was always the outside chance the pen had simply slipped out of my bag and on to the bed without me realising. Even if Sammi *were* responsible, she was never going to admit it. The silence revolved around us. Then she held a finger in the air, as if inspiration had suddenly struck. 'I know a specialist dry cleaner's in Shoreditch; they're absolute miracle workers. Loads of fashion editors send their stuff there after it's been trashed on shoots. If anyone can get that stain out, they can. I can give you directions if you like.'

'Thanks, but I think it's a lost cause,' I said as I went over to the swing bin and stuffed the dress inside. As I looked up, Sammi's pale face seemed to glow with a dark victory.

30

Chloe

I was feeling somewhat anxious as I waited outside the theatre. An hour or so earlier, Sammi had pinged me a text, asking if I wanted to meet her for a drink after work. In actual fact, I didn't. I was tired and my recent conversation with Megan about the strange goings-on in the house had unnerved me more than I cared to admit. Half of me was tempted to fob Sammi off with an excuse, but the other half was curious to know what lay behind her invitation. I wondered if there was something in particular she wanted to discuss with me; something she preferred to reveal in a public place, where I would be less likely to make a scene. *Tom doesn't love you any more. He thinks your boobs are too small and he's fed up of listening to you moan about work; he wants to be with me now. Oh, and you know that six-month South America trip . . . the one you two have been talking about ever since you first met, except you know you'll never actually do it because you're so worried about abandoning your precious career? Well, he's doing it with me now, and we're leaving in the morning.*

In my already fragile emotional state, it was difficult not to think the worst. After a couple more cocktails at the Colombian tapas bar, I had extracted more information from Megan about exactly what it was she had witnessed at London Bridge. She had reported a kiss (possibly chaste, possibly not) and had described Tom and Sammi's demeanour as 'upbeat' as they left the station together. It wasn't very much to go on; I needed to know more and there were only two people who could supply that information. Unfortunately, the day after Megan's disclosure, Tom had gone up north to work on a pop concert at one of the big stadiums. He wouldn't be back until the end of next week and, if I was going to have it out with him, I would prefer to do it face-to-face. Actually, part of me was relieved he had gone. I wasn't feeling strong enough for a confrontation; the longer I could put it off, the better. But now, here was Sammi, wanting to meet me, and I doubted very much it was to discuss the Bellevue Rise cleaning rota.

By the time she eventually arrived, a full twelve minutes late, my stomach was in knots and it was all I could do to wring out a smile. Sammi claimed not to know the area very well, so I suggested we head to a pub I knew in Belgravia. En route, she chatted brightly about a reality TV star she'd interviewed that afternoon and whose propensity to gab on was, apparently, the reason for her tardiness. She seemed almost excessively friendly and I wondered if she were simply tenderising me before she went in for the kill.

'This is nice, isn't it?' Sammi remarked, as we carried our drinks to a table by the window, next to a large group of braying men in well-cut suits.

'What is?' I said, unable to keep the accusatory tone out of my voice.

'Us two . . . meeting up like this,' she said. 'I know it's a bit last minute, but I was up in town anyway and I just thought to myself, *Why not text Chloe on the off chance? She can only say no.*' She beamed at me in a way I found inexplicably infuriating. 'But I'm so glad you didn't. I've been meaning to suggest a night out together for ages.'

'I can't stay for the whole evening,' I said peevishly. 'I've got to be at work early tomorrow. There's a technical problem with one of the productions I've been working on, I have to redesign part of the set.'

'I understand, just let me know when you're ready to go.' She grinned again. Her features were almost too expressive, like those of an actress.

I picked up my vodka cranberry and drained a third of it in one go. 'Was there a special reason you wanted to meet up?'

'Not really,' she said, and I could see she was taken aback by my directness. 'I just thought it would be nice to meet away from the house for a change.'

'Megan will be sorry she missed out,' I said, studying Sammi's face carefully, trying to gauge her reaction. 'In fact, why don't I give her a call? She was on an early shift today, so she'll be leaving work soon.'

Sammi reached out and brushed the back of my hand. She had long, delicate fingers and the touch felt almost like a caress. 'I'd rather you didn't. I get the impression Megan's not my biggest fan.'

'Nonsense,' I lied. 'You're just very different personalities, that's all.'

'Then why did she accuse me of damaging her dress when I haven't been anywhere near it?' Sammi said, with a momentary flash of anger.

'Did she?' I said, playing dumb. Megan had told me about the ink-stained dress and her skirmish with Sammi – although from what she'd said, she had stopped short of a direct accusation.

'Yes, I'm not quite sure what she thought had happened, but she seemed to be suggesting I'd borrowed her fountain pen without asking, then put it back on her bed without putting the lid on properly, so it leaked all over her dress. I think she was probably just upset and looking for someone to blame.' Sammi gave a loud sniff. 'We've never really hit it off . . . like you said, we're just too different. But I'd like to think that you and I are friends, Chloe.' The hard edges of her features softened, making her look quite different.

'This is going to sound silly, but I felt a connection with you almost from the moment we met,' she went on. 'I don't have loads of friends; I've always been the sort of person who prefers their own company. I expect it has something to do with the fact that I grew up an only child.'

Her face was unguarded, vulnerable and even a little sad. It was as if for a second a window had flown open and I'd caught a glimpse of something behind the confident façade. Despite my reservations about Sammi, I was flattered to hear her say those things. And if I'm honest, I also felt a connection with her, which was precisely why the thought of her sneaking off to meet Tom behind my back hurt so much.

'I hope we're friends too,' I replied. 'It's such a shame you and Megan haven't gelled; she really is a lovely person when you get to know her. It's not too late, though. I really think that if we all put in a bit more effort, we can make this house share a huge success.' I knew I sounded like an over-jolly scoutmaster trying to coax a reluctant teenager up Scafell Pike.

'Of course,' she said, straightening her back and folding her hands. 'I love living at Bellevue Rise, and please trust me when I say that I want this to work out as much as you do.'

'*Can* I trust you, though?' I blurted out the words almost without thinking.

She laughed uneasily. 'That's a strange thing to say . . . of course you can.' Her face grew more serious. 'Is there something on your mind, Chloe? If there is, you must tell me.'

I took a deep breath to galvanise myself. 'Why did you and Tom meet up at London Bridge station last Wednesday?'

There was a hiatus, like one of those pauses that occur in the theatre, when darkness falls and the stagehands have to hustle to get the props into place for the next scene.

'Why?' she said carefully. 'What has Tom said?'

I drained the rest of my drink. 'He hasn't said anything, because I haven't asked him.' I gave her a hard smile. 'I'm doing my best not to jump to conclusions, but the fact that neither one of you has seen fit to mention it to me up until this point does raise one or two concerns.'

The colour rose on Sammi's neck and cheeks. 'If Tom didn't tell you, how do you know we met?' she said carefully.

I wondered if she was playing for time. 'That's not important,' I lashed out. 'What *is* important is that you tell me the truth; no lies, no bullshit.'

Sammi's gaze drifted to the window. 'Tom and I agreed to keep it between ourselves; we didn't think you'd ever find out.' My heart began thrashing in my chest. It took a considerable effort to keep the swelling tide of emotion off my face.

She turned to face me and our eyes locked together. 'Tom's worried about you, Chloe; we both are. I appreciate that I don't know you very well, but even I can see that you haven't been your usual self lately. Tom asked me to meet him for a coffee so we could discuss it; it seemed more respectful than talking about you in whispers at the house.'

As she spoke, I felt a lessening of pressure, like a belt being loosened, or the removal of an uncomfortable pair of shoes. 'So what exactly did you talk about?'

'Tom's scared you're about to dump him. I did my best to convince him that it was the furthest thing from your mind.' She hesitated and looked at me anxiously. 'That was the right thing to say, wasn't it?'

It was true that I had been considering a temporary split, but just until my sleep sorted itself out and I got my head straight at work – and actually, once I'd had a chance to think it through, I'd realised what a singularly bad idea it was. I was struggling to cope as things were; without Tom in my life, I would probably fall apart.

'Yes, it was the right thing to say,' I reassured her. 'I love Tom, there's no way I want to break up with him.' A sudden, horrible thought hurtled through my mind. 'You didn't tell him about the night terrors, did you?'

'Absolutely not,' Sammi said. 'You told me you didn't want Tom to find out and there's no way I'd break a confidence. I simply said that you were under a lot of stress at work and you were having trouble sleeping.'

I drummed my fingers on the tabletop. 'How did Tom react?'

'He seemed very relieved. He told me he was going away for work for a while and asked me to keep an eye on you while he was gone. And that was it really . . . we were in the café for less than half an hour and then we went our separate ways.'

I narrowed my eyes. 'But why would he talk to you and not Megan? No offence, but she knows me a whole lot better than you do.'

'He didn't think she'd agree to meet him behind your back.' She shrugged. 'Maybe that makes her a better friend than me; I don't know. I'm so sorry, Chloe, I thought I was doing the right thing, but I know how it must look . . . the two of us sneaking round behind your back.'

'Apology accepted,' I said. 'Just one more thing . . . when you said you didn't think I was my usual self, what did you mean exactly?'

'You've lost your sparkle. You seem detached; you're snappy and irritable.'

'Anything else?'

'You look different,' she said.

'Do I?'

'Yes,' she said, flinging her arm at me. 'I mean, just look at you, Chloe . . . you've got bags under your eyes, your skirt needs ironing, there's a hole in your tights – and I don't know if you brushed your hair before you left the house this morning, but it certainly doesn't look like it.'

'Thanks very much,' I muttered, baring my teeth in a parody of a smile.

She bit her lip. 'Shit, Chloe, that sounded awful, didn't it?'

'I've certainly had nicer compliments.' My mouth was twitching at the corners. I glanced at Sammi; her nose was crinkling as if she were trying to ward off a sneeze. Unable to hold back any longer, I started laughing. I laughed with relief and with the sheer pleasure of letting go. Then Sammi started laughing too and in that moment, the tension between us began to evaporate.

31

I've decided it's time I showed Anouk what's what. She acts as if life is a big shiny present she gets to unwrap every day. Well, it isn't; sometimes it's a slimy monster with one eye and a black, rotten heart. I know I'm not very old, but I've been around long enough to know that life will stab you in the back, or put nails under your tyres, or push you over a cliff edge without so much as a backward glance. But if you're smart, like me, you can use life's mean tricks to help you get what you want. So believe me, I'll be doing Anouk a favour. And when she does know what's what, she'll realise what a huge mistake she made going to Kayla's stupid party, and she and I will be tied together forever.

I told her to meet me by the swings at the rec after school. She didn't want to at first, but she changed her mind when I reminded her what had happened to Liam. My heart flutters when I see her walking across the playground towards me, her beautiful hair bouncing with every step; I *knew* she wouldn't let me down. It's only when she gets closer that I see her eyes are red, as if she's been crying.

I think I should probably ask her what's wrong, but I don't, because there's no time to be nice. And anyway, where did being nice ever get anyone?

'Follow me,' I tell her, smiling because of the secret I'm holding inside. Then I lead her to the little path that runs behind the back gardens of the houses in Churchill Close. I've been there quite a lot recently, watching and listening and planning. This is a big day for Anouk and I don't want to leave anything to chance. When we're nearly at the garages, I stop and turn towards a garden that's separated from the path by a wire fence. The fence isn't very high, which is silly really; the people who live here are asking for something like this to happen.

'What are we doing here?' Anouk says in a wobbly voice. 'I know, why don't we go back to my house and play with my Girl's World?'

'No,' I say. 'We're going to do something much more fun.' I put my finger on my lips, the way Miss Pickering does when she's about to read us a story. If Anouk makes too much noise, someone might come out. Then I put my hand in my coat pocket and pull out the slice of salami I took from the fridge at home. After a quick look around to make sure no one's watching, I roll up the salami and push it into one of the diamond-shaped gaps in the wire.

'Here, Barney, Barney, Barney,' I say in a quiet voice. 'Come out, come out, wherever you are.'

Barney's a good dog and we've practised this a few times now, so he comes straight away. I wait for him to jump up and rest his front paws against the fence. The minute he chomps down on the salami, I grab him by the loose skin on the back of his neck and lift him up in the air and over the fence. Then I pop him inside my coat and do the zip up quickly before he has a chance to escape.

Behind me, Anouk makes a noise in the back of her throat, like a cat coughing up a fur ball; she's really going to have to toughen up.

'Come on,' I tell her.

'Where are we going now?' she moans. I wish she'd stop asking so many flipping questions!

'Wait and see,' I tell her. 'Wait and see.'

It doesn't take long to get to the allotments. There's no one else around; there usually isn't at this time of day. In the corner, next to the compost heap, is a big metal dustbin with a chimney thingy sticking out on top. It's for burning leaves and stuff. I know how it works, I've seen people use it. I start walking over to it, my hands wrapped across my tummy like a pregnant lady. Suddenly, I realise Anouk isn't behind me. She's still standing by the gate, looking like a wet weekend. I have to go back and practically drag her by the arm (which isn't very easy when you've got a wriggly dog inside your coat!). I don't know why she's making this so hard; I wish she would just trust me and realise that I'm doing this for her own good.

Once we get to the bin, I lift up the lid and toss it on the ground. Then I unzip my coat and drop Barney inside . . . plop, down he goes, on to the nice big pile of leaves I chucked in there yesterday. He looks up at me with his big, soppy eyes. Poor little thing, he doesn't know what's going on. He will in a minute! I pick up the lid and jam it on top of the bin; now it's time for the good bit.

As soon as Anouk sees the matches, her face goes all crinkly and white, like a piece of paper screwed into a ball and thrown away. 'I want to go home,' she says. I can almost smell her fear, but that's OK, because I was frightened too the first time.

'Stop whining and watch this,' I tell her. As I strike the match, there's a buzzing in my ears, the sound of my own blood pumping in my head. It's a nice feeling; it helps remind me I'm alive. I'm about to drop the burning match down the chimney thingy when a voice rudely interrupts me. I can't believe it, there's someone else here . . . a man, standing next to a shed on the other side of the allotments. He's shouting and waving a walking stick in the air.

'What are you doing?' he says. 'Get away from there.' Then he starts coming towards us, but he can't move very fast because he's got a bad leg. This is REALLY annoying. I've spent ages planning this and now that moron has gone and ruined my best friend's big day!!

I flick the match into a bed of lettuces and turn to Anouk. 'Run,' I tell her. She doesn't move, pale and stiff as a statue. Meanwhile, the man with the stick is getting closer and closer. 'Do it!' I hiss, shoving Anouk in the back. *Then* she starts running. At least she's learned something today: *I* make the rules around here.

32

Megan

I glanced over at Serena. She was still on the phone, her brow crinkled with concentration as she advised one of the hospital's registrars on pain management for a patient with leukaemia. I knew that if I was going to do it, it had to be now. I turned to the vast system of drawers behind me. It filled an entire wall, and would be highly confusing to the uninitiated, but it only took me a few seconds to find what I was looking for. As I pulled open the drawer, a pebble of fear lodged in my throat. If I was caught, it could cost me my job. My hand was shaking as I scooped up a modest quantity of the white tablets and poured them into a small amber bottle. I'd promised Chloe I would do this for her, and I wasn't about to let her down a second time.

She had been in a wretched state when I came across her this morning, sprawled across the chaise in the sitting room, a look of pain collected on her face as if she had some terminal illness. I listened with horror as she told me that she'd woken up some time around three that morning

– not in her own bed, or even within the relative safety of the house, but in Number 46's small front garden. Barefoot and clad only in a short nightie, she was shocked to find herself inexplicably clawing at the loose earth around the rose bushes with her hands. Even more worrying than her scratched arms and broken fingernails was the fact she had absolutely no memory of going downstairs or unlocking the front door. Too unnerved to go back to bed, Chloe spent the rest of the night on the chaise, knowing it was both hard enough and narrow enough to ensure sleep never came.

By the time I found her, she was anxious and weepy and fretting about the important meeting she was supposed to be chairing at work in less than three hours' time. I did what I could to comfort her, but it was clear that words were not enough. 'I'm falling apart,' she told me. 'I don't know how much longer I can go on like this. Please, Meg, isn't there something you can do . . . just to get me through the next couple of weeks, until I can see my GP?'

It was a big ask, but this latest turn of events was very disturbing. Chloe had never gone outdoors during the course of her night terrors before and it was clear to me that they were now entering a new and potentially danger-ous phase. I knew I had to do something, or it was surely only a matter of time before she came to serious harm.

It was late afternoon when I arrived home after my shift and Chloe was still at work, as I knew she would be. I'd arranged to see some former colleagues that evening, who were in town for a pharmaceutical conference. They would be staying the night at a hotel and, knowing what we were like when we all got together, I suspected it would be a late one. I grabbed something to eat and went upstairs to change, hoping Chloe would be back by the time the taxi came to pick me up. If she wasn't, no matter, I could always leave the tablets outside her bedroom door.

The skirt I wanted to wear needed ironing and I had to touch up some chipped polish on my toenails, so it took me longer than expected to get ready. I knew the taxi would be here any minute, so I was rushing as I went downstairs to the kitchen in search of pen and paper, so I could dash off a quick note to Chloe. I was hunched over the kitchen table, writing out the dosage instructions, when I heard a floorboard creak. I hadn't realised anyone else was home and the sound made me jump. When I turned my head towards the open door, I saw Sammi standing in the shadowy hallway. Even though she was the one spying on me, I felt for a moment like a child caught peeking through a forbidden door. She gave me a narrow smile as she stepped across the threshold into the well-lit kitchen.

'Hi Megan, what are you doing?' she said. Her pupils were so dilated I could barely discern the iris and it gave her an unworldly, almost spectral appearance.

None of your damn business, I was tempted to say. 'Leaving a note for Chloe before I go out,' I replied as I added a kiss to the bottom of the note and folded the paper in half.

'What's it about? I can pass on a message if you like.'

'I've got some tablets for her to help her sleep. I think she's reaching the end of her tether with these night terrors.'

'What sort of tablets?'

Jesus, what is this . . . twenty fucking questions?

'Just a mild sedative; it acts on the central nervous system to induce a state of relaxation.'

She gave me a mocking look. 'Do you really think they're going to work?' The tone in her voice suggested she was annoyed with me and I thought I knew the reason why. It was transparently obvious that Sammi had few – if any – friends of her own and for some reason she had become fixated with Chloe. She must have been thrilled when she learned about the night terrors, no doubt viewing it as a golden opportunity to act as chief comforter and confidante to Chloe. But now here *I* was – supporting my best friend in her time of need and providing a practical solution, albeit only a temporary one, to the problem.

'Absolutely,' I said, assuming the calm, quietly assertive attitude I took with difficult patients. 'In addition to its sedative effect, this particular drug also suppresses stage four sleep . . . the phase when dreaming and sleepwalking typically occur – so in fact it should be highly effective in addressing Chloe's problems.'

Sammi's face was defiant. 'Shouldn't a doctor be making those sorts of decisions?'

I sighed. 'Well, yes, in an ideal world they would. But I *am* a fully qualified and highly experienced pharmacist, Sammi. I do know what I'm doing – and anyway, I took

advice from one of the consultants at work, who special-
ises in sleep disorders.' I picked up the amber bottle on the
kitchen table and gave it a little shake. 'This is only a
short-term measure, just until Chloe can get an appointment with her GP.'

Sammi stared at me, unblinking. I got the impression
she didn't believe me, as if she could see it in the air around
me, like a spider spinning a web. 'Well, let's hope you're
right, because I'm just as worried about Chloe as you are.'
She gave me a noxious smile. 'I think it's great that you can
use your medical knowledge to help her; Chloe's very lucky
to have a friend like you.' She was about to say something
else, but she was interrupted by the sound of a horn beep-
ing outside.

'Shit, that's my taxi,' I said, grabbing my handbag off
the kitchen table. I gestured to the note and the tablets. 'Do
me a favour, will you, and put those outside Chloe's bedroom door? That way, she'll see them if she gets home late
and goes straight to bed.'

Sammi gave a small nod. 'No problem at all.'

As the taxi made its way through the rapidly darkening
streets of South London, there was no doubt in my mind
that Sammi would deliver the medication safely to Chloe.
After all, in doing so she would be able to claim some credit
for providing her with the best night's sleep she'd had in
weeks. I didn't blame Sammi for wanting to be friends with
Chloe, for she was certainly a friend worth having. What I
couldn't understand was how she had managed to pull the

wool over Chloe's eyes quite so effectively. Chloe liked to see the best in people, but she was no fool – so why then had she swallowed wholesale Sammi's claim that the reason she'd met Tom in secret was purely out of concern for her wellbeing? It was certainly a plausible defence but, if I were Chloe, I would be asking a lot more questions, rather than simply accepting Sammi's explanation at face value. Why not confront Tom as well, I suggested when Chloe told me what Sammi had said; that way she could identify any possible discrepancies between the pair's accounts. Chloe, however, who was always sensitive to other people's feelings, insisted she wasn't going to say anything to Tom because she didn't want him to feel bad about going behind her back. What's more, Sammi had apparently agreed not to tell Tom that Chloe knew about their meeting. It seemed like a messy, over-complicated resolution to me – but perhaps, in her vulnerable, sleep-deprived state, Chloe simply didn't have the emotional strength to call Tom out on it. Whatever the reason, it was her decision and I had to respect that. At least she hadn't told Sammi that I was the one who'd seen her with Tom at London Bridge. Things were difficult enough between Sammi and me already, and this would only make things worse.

Ever since the incident with the fountain pen, I'd done my best to avoid Sammi – no easy task when we were living under the same roof. Try as I might, I couldn't work her out. Even with my medical background, I had never come across anyone quite like her before. She seemed strangely detached a lot of the time, although she was perfectly capable of turning on the charm when she wanted to. Another thing I'd noticed was her growing sense of entitlement around the house. When she first moved in, she spent most evenings in her bedroom, tiny as it was. And when she did her freelance writing at the kitchen table during the day, she always took care to clear her work things away before Chloe and I came home. But just lately her behaviour had changed. It was little things at first – she'd forget to buy loo roll when it was her turn, or leave her breakfast dishes in the sink unwashed, instead of putting them straight in the dishwasher. But then she grew bolder. She'd start work at the kitchen table, sometimes even before I'd left the house, and leave her things there at the end of the day, so it would be up to me to push her notebook and her laptop and all her other shit out of the way. Later on, in the evening, she'd often commandeer the TV in the sitting room, not even offering to change the channel when someone else came in. It was almost as if it was *her* house, and we were just the lodgers. I wanted to say something, but I knew I'd sound childish and, even though I didn't like to admit it, I was a little bit scared of Sammi, of how she might react. My overriding instinct was that she was up to something; I just didn't know what.

But right now, I told myself as the cab pulled up outside the hotel where my friends were staying, I wasn't going to worry about Sammi. Tonight, I was going to relax and enjoy myself.

33

Chloe

I could have cried with relief when I saw the small amber pill bottle sitting outside my bedroom door. Megan had come through for me, just like I knew she would. Despite my shitty mood, I couldn't help smiling as I read her note:

> *Hey Hon,*
> *These should do the trick. Take one at bedtime and*
> *<u>avoid alcohol</u>! Sweet dreams* 😴
> *M x*

I knew what a risk Megan had taken getting the tablets for me, and as soon as the fog that was smothering my brain had lifted, I would find a way to show her how grateful I was. But, after another challenging (and that was putting it politely) day at work, all I wanted to do right now was sleep. Not the scrappy, fussy, burrowing in the dark I'd endured for weeks, but deep, dreamless sleep – the kind that left me feeling refreshed and ready to tackle whatever the day threw at me. I swallowed one of the pills, changed into my night things and fell into bed.

I remembered nothing more until I heard the distant, continual buzzing of what sounded like an angry insect. It sounded impossibly far away and it seemed to take me forever to reach it. Finally, I surfaced into consciousness and realised that it wasn't an insect after all, but the sound of my alarm clock going off. I silenced it, then lay there for a minute or two, gathering my thoughts. I didn't feel tired, just a little spaced out. I couldn't remember having any dreams – good or bad – in the night, and when I raised myself up on to my elbows and looked around, nothing in my room appeared to have been disturbed. My bedroom door, meanwhile, was firmly shut, just the way I had left it. The pills, it seemed, had done their job.

I'd set my alarm rather earlier than usual. I had some work to do before I left for the theatre and it was easier to concentrate at home where there were fewer distractions. To my immense frustration, another problem had arisen with the *Neurosis* set – this one relating to the trap door I had designed. Known as a 'vampire' trap, it consisted of two sprung leaves that parted under pressure and immediately reclosed. Placed in the stage wall, it was supposed to give the impression that a figure was passing through solid matter. The problem was that since my initial specification, the costume department had made significant alterations to an elaborate headdress, worn by the principal actress in the final scene. The upshot was that the headdress was now too big to pass through the trap doors without snagging. With dress rehearsals less than two weeks away, it was down to me to find a solution.

When I got home last night, I'd spent several hours in front of my laptop, using specialist software to modify my original design. I was now confident that the trap door's sprung leaves could be re-calibrated so that they retracted more fully, thus allowing actress and headdress to pass through unhindered. I figured that another half an hour's work ought to do it and then the modifications would be ready to present to Bryan and the set builders at the emergency meeting we'd scheduled for ten that morning.

As I descended the stairs, still in my PJs, my legs felt strangely leaden, and when I entered the kitchen the bright sunlight flooding the room made me blink like a cave dweller. I put the kettle on and fired up my laptop, which I'd left recharging on the kitchen table. A couple of minutes later, I was sitting in front of it, coffee mug in hand, as I scanned the contents of the folder titled 'Neurosis' that sat on my desktop. I couldn't immediately see what I was looking for, so I rearranged the files in date order. The document I needed – the one that contained all my calculations and the drawings I had painstakingly prepared – should have been at the top of the list, but for some reason it wasn't. I stared at the screen, chewing my thumbnail; I must have saved the document in a different folder by mistake. I searched for it by name. It didn't exist; perhaps I'd called it something else.

I tried a keyword search for 'vampire trap'. A couple of files popped up, but they were old ones, relating to the original spec. Could I have dragged the file into the trash by mistake? A moment later the glimmer of hope faded . . . I could see from the icon on my taskbar that the trashcan was empty, which struck me as odd because I hadn't touched the trash for several weeks. But then I remembered that Jess had been using my laptop at work the previous day; she must have emptied it.

I felt a lurching, sick-to-the-stomach sense of helplessness. All the work I'd done last night had disappeared. I was certain I'd saved it before I went to bed, so how could this be? I closed my eyes and brought my hand to my chest, trying to press my heart back to its normal rhythm. My emotions were a terrible mix of impotent anger, disbelief and fear . . . fear that some hideous metamorphosis was taking place inside me, the kind that made me forget stuff and imagine things that weren't there. Feeling a sob rise up in my throat, I drew in a couple of deep breaths in an attempt to calm myself.

The rest of the day passed in a blur. There was no way I could recreate my modified design before ten a.m., so I was forced to ad-lib my way through the meeting. It was clear from his body language that Bryan was appalled by my apparent lack of preparation and my mortification was complete when, halfway through proceedings, Richard Westlake joined us unexpectedly. As I spoke, I could feel the weight of his gaze on me, and everything seemed to be happening in slow motion, as if I were underwater.

It took me the rest of the day to reproduce the work I

had done in just three hours the night before. Stress had made me woolly-headed and a little disoriented, and from lunchtime onwards I was counting the hours until I could pop another one of Megan's magic pills and slip into blissful unconsciousness. I managed to leave work more or less on time for once, and on the way home I treated myself to a gin and tonic from the trolley service on board the train. As I plodded up the gentle hill to Bellevue Rise, I thought that I would probably have another before dinner, but when I got to the front door and reached into my coat pocket, my keys were gone. Frantically, I checked all my other pockets, and then my handbag, upending it on to the front lawn, but the keys were nowhere to be found. I jammed my fists into my temples. This could *not* be happening, not today of all days when so much else had already gone wrong. I always kept the door keys in my coat pocket and I remembered putting them back there after letting myself in the previous night.

Sighing, I pushed the doorbell. I knew Megan was on a late shift, but Sammi should be home; she rarely went out in the evening, unless it was to some work-related event. When she didn't come to the door straight away, I rang the bell again, listening as the chimes rang out in the hall. A few minutes went by and then I pushed open the flap of the letterbox and shouted Sammi's name: still no response. I looked up at the house; all the windows were closed. I went round to the side and rattled the gate that led to the back garden, but it was firmly padlocked on the other side.

Tears started in my eyes. I brushed them away angrily

and told myself not to be such a baby. What was wrong with me? I was locked out of the house, that was all, but I could feel a kind of panic blooming in me, as if I were about to faint or start screaming my head off. I walked back round to the front of the house and retrieved my phone, which was still lying on the grass with the other spilled contents of my handbag. I called Sammi, releasing a breath of irritation as it went straight to voicemail, and left a curt message, urging her to call me as soon as she got home. Then I stuffed my things back into my handbag and started walking to the nearest pub, where I ordered a second G and T, this one a double.

Half an hour went by and Sammi still hadn't returned my call, so I sent Megan a text, outlining my dilemma. She replied almost immediately, saying she wouldn't be home for another couple of hours. I would've cut my losses and gone to Tom's, but he was still up north, so my best option was to stay in the pub and wait for Sammi to call me. I drank my gin, then I bought some nuts and a Diet Coke and played around on my phone for a bit. I kept trying Sammi's number, but she didn't pick up. Finally, I texted Megan again and asked her to collect me from the pub on her way home from the station. She was full of apologies when she eventually arrived, even though none of this was her fault.

'Sorry, Chloe, I got here as fast as I could,' she said. 'Did you just forget to take your keys out with you this morning?'

I shook my head. 'No, I definitely had them with me. I

think they must have fallen out of my coat pocket. I'll check the studio when I get into work tomorrow and if I can't find them I'll just have to get another set cut.'

'I wonder why Sammi isn't answering her phone,' Megan muttered. 'Where the hell is she anyway? It's not like she's got any friends to go out with.'

I shrugged weakly as I followed her out of the pub. 'I don't know and I don't care. All I want to do now is go to bed; I feel absolutely shattered.'

Megan looked over her shoulder at me. 'Did you take one of the tablets last night? I asked Sammi to leave them outside your bedroom door.'

'Yeah, thanks for that, Meg, I feel like I slept a lot better, although I did wake up feeling a bit groggy.'

She gave me an understanding smile. 'It's one of the side effects, unfortunately, although you should notice it less and less as your body gets used to the drug. Have you made an appointment to see your GP yet?'

I shook my head.

'Well, make sure you do,' she said gently. 'Because I won't be able to get you any more tablets; you need a proper prescription.'

'I know, I know, I'll do it in the morning, I swear,' I said, knowing it was a promise I wouldn't keep.

When I stepped into the dark house and flicked the light switch in the hall, the first thing I saw were my keys. They were lying on top of the spindly console table; I knew they were mine because they were attached to the silver key ring

Tom had bought me at Camden Market on our very first date. I gave a quick shake of my head, unable to believe my own eyes. Not for the first time that day, I had the disconcerting sense that I was losing my mind.

'I don't understand . . .' I said, looking at Megan. 'I didn't leave my keys on the table; I *know* I didn't. They were in my coat pocket, just like they always are.'

Megan batted her hand in front of her face as she walked down the hall to the kitchen. 'Don't sweat it, Chloe. You've found them now, that's all that matters.'

'I suppose so,' I said gruffly as I turned towards the stairs. 'I'm going straight to bed, see you tomorrow.'

All I could think of was sleep, but when I reached the landing, I froze. I could hear a strange noise, or rather a collection of strange noises; an unearthly collection of moans and cries that seemed to reach deep inside me. I bashed my right ear with the heel of my hand, thinking I was hearing things. I wasn't. The noises were definitely there and they were emanating from Sammi's room. I walked up to her closed door and said her name. When there was no reply, I checked my watch. It was just coming up to nine-thirty. Surely she couldn't be in bed already, and if she was at home, why hadn't she returned any of my calls?

Slowly, I turned the doorknob and pushed open the door. The noises were louder now and sounded even more unearthly. As I looked around the room, something rippled in the narrow bed. The unexpected movement made me jump. 'Who's there?' I said in a quavering voice.

The shape in the bed shifted again. 'It's me, Chloe,' came Sammi's voice out of the darkness. 'Who else would it be?'

I squinted, trying to find her face in the gloom. 'I heard some horrible noises; I thought I'd better investigate.' I jabbed my finger in the air as a particularly piercing note rang out. '*Those* noises.'

Sammi laughed softly. 'That's just my iPod, silly. They're whale sounds, they help me relax. I've had it on repeat for hours.'

'Oh,' I said, taken aback. 'Have you been here for a while?'

'I haven't left the house all day.'

'Right,' I said tightly. 'Only I came home from work and realised I didn't have my keys. I've been calling your mobile for the past two hours.'

'Oh my God, Chloe, I'm so sorry. Where have you been all this time?'

'In the pub, waiting for Megan to get back from work. I left you loads of messages.'

'I put my phone on silent,' Sammi explained. 'I had a migraine; I've been in bed since six-thirty.'

I felt my fingers clench. 'Didn't you hear me ringing the doorbell?'

'No, sorry. I guess I must've dozed off.'

I had to get out of there as the whales were driving me mad. 'OK . . . well, sorry for disturbing you. I'm going to bed myself now.'

'Shall I turn my iPod off in case it keeps you awake?'

'No, don't worry. I doubt I'll even be able to hear it from my room.'

As I closed Sammi's door, I couldn't help thinking how perky she sounded for someone who'd been suffering from a migraine all evening.

I knew I wasn't supposed to take the tablets with alcohol, but I'd only had a couple of drinks, so I figured it would be all right. As I plummeted into unconsciousness, for a moment I thought I could hear a woman's voice, very close, whispering in my ear.

34

No one's supposed to be in the classroom during morning break, but I went up to one of the teachers in the playground and said I had to use the toilet. I didn't, though – instead I came here to the classroom and went straight to the cupboard in the corner, where we all store our lunchboxes until break time.

Hunger is clawing at my stomach like an angry bear. There was no milk for my cereal again and I haven't eaten since last night (and even that was only half a tin of tomato soup). I'm so hungry I could eat a hippopotamus, never mind a horse! I've got my usual cheese and pickle sandwiches, but if I eat them now I'll have nothing left for lunch.

I slide open the cupboard door. The brightly coloured lunchboxes look so pretty all lined up. Seeing them makes me feel ashamed of my old paper bag that's tatty and grease-stained from being used so many times. I reach towards the pink My Little Pony lunchbox that's nearest to me and unhook the catch. When the lid flips open I see two sandwiches, neatly cut into triangles (ham, by the look of them), a packet of pickled onion Monster Munch and a fat piece of Swiss roll. It's a difficult choice, but I grab the Swiss roll and cram it in my mouth with both hands. It's sweet and soft and spongy and my head goes all woozy from the sugar. Before I've even finished eating it, I'm opening the next lunchbox. This one's red and it's got racing cars all over it. The sandwiches inside are a bit stinky (that's egg for you!), but the mini pork pie looks yummy. As I bite into it, I think that it's possibly the most delicious thing I've ever tasted; the pastry is buttery and the meat is so *meaty*. I know I should stop at that, but I can't; I'm like an addict, hooked on food. One more lunchbox, I tell myself, just one more. The next one belongs to Liam. I know that because his name is written in magic marker on the lid. I haven't even had a chance to see what's inside when I hear a loud, cross voice that sounds just like Mum.

'What do you think you're doing?'

I whip round and there's Miss Pickering standing in the doorway with her hands on her hips. I see in her face that's usually so smooth and sunny, a big scribble of disappointment.

'Nothing,' I say, wondering if I've got any pork pie crumbs around my mouth.

'It doesn't look like nothing to me.' Miss Pickering points to the cupboard, where Liam's lunchbox is lying open. 'It looks very much to me as if you were just about to help yourself to something from that lunchbox.'

'Oh that,' I say. 'Liam was hungry and he asked me to get him a snack.'

'*Really?*' Miss Pickering says. Her voice sounds jagged and angry.

'Yes,' I say, staring her right in the eyes. 'His plaster cast makes it hard for him to do stuff and, seeing as it's my fault he had to have the cast in the first place, I thought it was only fair I help him out.'

Miss Pickering's hand goes up to her chin. 'So you and Liam are friends again, are you?'

'That's right.'

Miss Pickering sighs and shakes her head. 'Please don't lie to me.'

'I'm not lying.'

She takes a couple of steps towards me. 'Yes, you are, because I've just spent the last five minutes watching you through the glass.' She points to the little window in the top half of the classroom door and my heart dives down into my shoes.

'You were stealing from your classmates' lunchboxes. You do know that stealing's wrong, don't you?'

My mind flashes back to a cop show Dad and I watched on TV the other night, after Mum went upstairs. It was way past my bedtime, but Dad doesn't care about that sort of stuff. 'No comment,' I say. If I say nothing, it's up to them to prove it and it will be Miss Pickering's word against mine.

'Is that really all you've got to say for yourself?'

'No comment.'

Miss Pickering's mouth is all twisted, like she's chewing on something sour. 'First Liam's arm and now this. I don't know what's happened to you lately. You used to be such a sweet girl.'

No, Miss, I'm not sweet, I'm just very good at pretending. 'No comment.'

'If you won't speak to me, perhaps you'll speak to Mr Finch.'

As I follow her down the corridor to the headmaster's office, there is something growing inside me. I can feel it in my stomach, hard and smooth, about the size of a tennis ball. It draws the air out of my lungs and sucks the blood from my veins.

35

Megan

I was sitting on a blue leather banquette, champagne flute in hand, observing Sammi as she worked the room. I had to admit she was good. *Very* good. There was a light in her eyes I hadn't seen before as she approached a tall, tanned man of indeterminate middle age dressed all in black. She touched him lightly on the back and he spun round, clearly delighted to see her, and immediately enveloped her in a hug. Throughout their lively conversation – one that involved lots of gesticulating and hair tossing on Sammi's part – the man stared at her with an expression almost of wonder, as if she were a rare butterfly he'd come across on a fence post.

Just then, a waitress passed by with a tray of canapés. I took the serviette she was offering and helped myself to a filo tartlet. To my surprise, I was having quite a pleasant evening, despite feeling a long way out of my comfort zone. The only launches I'd been to were for pharmaceutical products and they had all been spectacularly dull affairs. This launch party, for a diffusion line of handbags by a designer I'd never heard of, was in a different league altogether. Held in an exclusive private members' club, it was full of immaculately accessorised people making excited conversation in high, glassy voices, and it was clear that Sammi fitted in to this milieu perfectly.

I had been nothing short of stunned by her invitation, which had come just twenty-four hours earlier, as I relaxed in the sitting room with a low-calorie hot chocolate and a late-night talk show.

'I'm going to a fashion launch in Soho tomorrow night,' she said, as she perched on the arm of a chair. 'There'll be loads of free booze and food.'

'That'll be nice for you,' I said, irritated by the interruption.

'I was wondering if you wanted to come with me.'

I almost choked on my hot chocolate. 'Are you serious?' I asked.

'Of course I am, I think it'll be fun,' she said in a measured tone. 'I know the PR really well; I can easily get you on the guest list.'

My first instinct was to decline politely. Why on earth would I want to spend an entire evening with someone I didn't trust, or even particularly like? But then I thought better of it. After all, what is it they say? *Keep your friends close and your enemies closer.* And what's more I was intrigued to see Sammi in her natural habitat. Would she be as awkward around her colleagues as she appeared to be with me?

The answer, I knew now, was a resounding *no*. For the past half an hour I'd watched as she had air-kissed, flirted and generally charmed her way around the room, clearly in her element. It didn't do any harm that she looked hot as hell in a thigh-skimming purple dress that she'd teamed with stiletto heel ankle boots and an array of colourful beaded jewellery. As she introduced me to a succession of fashion editors, photographers and even a model or two, I felt like her underdressed hillbilly cousin, down in the big city from my home in the sticks. It wasn't long before I started to feel I was cramping her style; besides which, the shoes I was wearing weren't doing my bunion any favours. Despite Sammi's protestations, I assured her that I would be perfectly happy sitting on the sidelines for a while, drinking my fizz and people-watching.

As I watched her flitting from person to person with consummate ease, I wondered how many of these people were bona fide friends and how many were mere business contacts, people who could be picked up and dropped again at any moment, depending on their usefulness. Having disengaged herself from the man in black, I saw that Sammi was momentarily alone. She turned in a slow circle to scan the room quite shamelessly, as if sizing up her potential prey. There was a shaft of light from an overhead spot, illuminating the space behind her. It was so bright that she appeared to be nothing but a figure, faceless, expressionless.

The next moment, a passing waitress bearing a tray laden with empty glasses nudged her arm. The sudden movement caused Sammi to spill some champagne from her own glass down the front of her dress. It was clearly an accident, but Sammi glared at the waitress as if she'd just slapped her across the face. A moment later, she spotted someone across the room she wanted to talk to and all of a sudden her smile was back in place.

I was on my third glass of champagne when Sammi drifted back over to me. 'How are you doing, Megan – getting bored yet?' she asked. 'I'm pretty much done here, so we can go whenever you like.'

'I've had a great time, thanks,' I said. 'Was it a worthwhile evening for you?'

She rocked her hand from side to side. 'So-so. I don't enjoy these things all that much, to be honest. Unfortunately, kissing arse is just part of being a freelancer.'

'Well, you certainly seem to be very good at it.' I eyed the large stain on the front of her dress. 'It's such a shame that waitress made you spill your drink.'

'Isn't it just?' she said, plucking at the damp fabric. 'This dress isn't even mine, I borrowed it from the fashion cupboard at *Marie Claire*.'

'You'll have to take it to that specialist dry cleaner's – you know, the one in Shoreditch?' There was a mocking tone in my voice, I couldn't resist it. Sammi looked at me for a long moment, as if she were trying to work me out.

'Why did you invite me here, Sammi?' I said, emboldened by the two and a half glasses of champagne I'd drunk.

She stared at me so intently I could see the stripes of

gold alternating with the brown in her eyes like spokes of a wheel.

'I thought it would be nice if we got to know each other a bit better.'

I nodded slowly. 'Only, I wondered if perhaps you had an ulterior motive.'

Her eyes widened innocently. 'Such as?'

I licked my lips. 'Perhaps you thought it would be a good way to ingratiate yourself with Chloe – you know, if you appeared to be making a big effort with me.'

She didn't even flinch. 'I know you don't like me, Megan, and here's the thing – I don't like you much either.'

I was shocked not so much by this statement as by the calm with which she delivered it. I shrugged, trying to give off an air of indifference, but inside my chest my heart was beating wildly. 'I think it's fair to say we don't have much in common.'

'Except for Chloe.'

'Yes,' I agreed, holding her gaze. 'Except for Chloe.'

She regarded me coolly. 'Not that it makes any difference, because I can see you've already made up your mind about me – but, for your information, I invited you because I wanted to offer an olive branch. I know we're never going to be friends, but I thought it would be better for all of us, Chloe included, if we could at least get along. Now I know I was wrong.' A sliver of steel had entered her tone. 'But if you think you're going to drive me out of my own home, you can think again. Living at Bellevue Rise suits me very well and I can assure you that I have no intention of moving out, not until I'm good and ready. There's only one person who can make me go, and that's the landlord – and, so long as I keep paying my rent on time, I don't think he'll have any problems with me staying.' She folded her arms and gave me a 'so fuck you' look.

Unfortunately for me, she was right. Although it had been our decision to get a third person in, strictly speaking Chloe and I weren't sub-letting to Sammi. Her tenancy agreement was with the landlord, so only he could give her notice to quit.

Sammi leaned towards me. I could smell her perfume, something musky and assertive. 'Of course, Megan, if you find living with me so uncomfortable, there's nothing stopping *you* from moving out. I'm sure Chloe and I can easily find someone to replace you.'

Her words were like a blade running under my ribs, making me almost gasp for breath. There was no pretence about Sammi now; her fake charm had left the room with the waitress and her tray of canapés. She smiled, but it was a sharp, hostile smile, as though acknowledging a problem . . . and the problem was me.

36

I can feel the rage whizzing through my body, tiny, cold marbles that shoot around my skeleton and rattle behind my eyes. After a whole week of 'thinking very hard about it', Finch has finally come up with a 'suitable' punishment and it's not BLOODY FAIR!! I won't be representing St Swithun's in the Under-Twelves Acro Championships with Anouk after all. All I did was help myself to a bit of cake and a manky old pork pie; it's hardly the crime of the century. And anyway, I was starving; I needed that food a lot more than those other kids did.

I've just told Anouk the bad news and she wasn't as upset as I thought she'd be. I expect she *is* upset; she's just pretending not to be, so I won't feel so bad about letting her down. Although . . . I have noticed that she's been kinda quiet just lately. She looks a bit out of sorts too; I hope she isn't coming down with something. We haven't seen each other much outside of school either. Last Saturday, she was doing stuff with her mum (AGAIN!), and the Saturday before she said she was going horse riding with one of her cousins; I didn't even know she had any cousins.

Anyway, you won't believe who Miss Sullivan has picked to replace me in the competition – only Eleanor flipping Hardy! She's not half as good as me; she can't even do a proper Arabian handspring. *And* she looks disgusting in her leotard with her big fat thighs that rub together at the top. That stupid bitch is never going to let me hear the end of this.

Miss Pickering's a stupid bitch too. It's bad enough that she grassed me up to Finch, but ever since that thing with the lunchboxes she's been acting all funny. She told me not to bother watering the plants on her desk any more and when I came in to school early the other day, she said she didn't need any help getting the classroom ready and I should wait outside until the bell rang. I don't understand why she's being so mean to me. I used to be her favourite, her Special Little Helper, but now it's as if she's ripped out my heart and stomped all over it. Don't worry, she's not going to get away with it. I'm going to make her pay. I'm not quite sure how just yet, but it won't be long before I come up with a plan. I'm good at making plans and I have a feeling that this one's going to be my best plan EVER!

37

Chloe

My eyes flickered open. I felt empty and tender inside, as if I had been exposed to a mild contagion, but otherwise perfectly calm. As I lay there, bits and pieces of the previous night drifted back to me.

A naked, sub-human creature with a bald, over-sized head like a baby's and toxic breath, was squatting on my chest, his mouth so close that his spittle peppered me with hot, foul shrapnel. That, thankfully, was the extent of my memory. I knew of course that this visitor wasn't real, that he was merely a figment of my imagination, a hallucination from the transitional phase that lay between wakefulness and sleep. But none of that prevented it from scaring the shit out of me; the memory alone made me recoil in disgust. As I threw back the duvet, despondency rolled over me. Could the tablets be losing their effect already?

I got out of bed, catching sight of myself in the dressing table mirror as I crossed the room. It gave back such a faint reflection of myself, it was as if the glass was reluctant to admit that I was there. And then, just behind me, through the open door, I saw a shape, just a shadow, a flicker of movement on the landing. I wheeled around, but there was nothing there. I was sure I'd shut my bedroom door before I went to bed last night, which meant that either someone had entered while I was sleeping or, much more likely, I had gone walkabout in the night. As I looked about the room, I had the overwhelming feeling that every object – every single ornament, book and article of clothing – had been picked up, examined and put back. The air felt disturbed, though I couldn't identify any specific item that had actually changed position. I massaged my eyes with my fingertips. There was no time to brood over it now; I had to get to work.

If I'd known what was going to happen, I would have stayed in bed. Less than three hours later, I was getting a bollocking from Richard. It turned out that my revisions for the vampire trap had been way off the mark. The set builders had followed the new spec I'd provided, only to find that the newly calibrated sprung leaves still didn't retract fully enough to allow the headdress to pass through cleanly. The only alternative was to build a new trap door from scratch and there was no time – or money – for that. There was an icy cast in Richard's voice as he informed me that the costume department had reluctantly agreed to rework the headdress, even though the new, smaller version wouldn't have nearly the same impact as the original.

'I don't understand how you could let this happen,'

Richard berated me in his office. 'Dress rehearsals start on Thursday; you knew there was no room for error. The costume department are going to have to work round the clock to redo the headpiece . . . I don't mind telling you that you're not their favourite person right now.'

'I can assure you, Richard, that I didn't "let" anything happen,' I insisted. 'I did the calculations, I thought it would work; it was an honest mistake.'

His jaw muscles flexed. 'Unfortunately, this isn't the only mistake you've made recently, Chloe, is it?'

'I'm not sure I know what you're referring to,' I said defensively.

'Then let me refresh your memory. The revolving mirror – I believe your calculations were also inaccurate on that occasion.'

Jess was the only one who knew about my mistake with the mirror; I never thought she'd tell Richard. How could she throw me under the bus like that?

'Oh, yes . . . the mirror,' I said, feeling perspiration blooming at the armholes of my dress. 'I *was* slightly adrift on the measurements, but it's been sorted now.'

Richard studied me over the top of his dark-rimmed glasses. '*Slightly* adrift? That's not what I heard.'

I started to remonstrate, but he put up a hand to silence me. 'Please, Chloe, I'm really not interested in splitting hairs at this stage. I need to understand what's going on in your head. This isn't like you at all; you're usually so meticulous.'

I drew my hand wearily across my forehead. 'It's just a

blip. I've been having trouble sleeping lately, and when I'm tired I find it hard to concentrate and that's when I make silly mistakes. But I'm trying to find a solution, I promise you. I'm taking some new medication; I'll be back on top of my game in no time, you'll see.'

'Fair enough,' he replied. 'But I want you to take some time off, just so you can recharge your batteries.'

'Honestly, Richard, that's really not necess—'

His hand went up again. 'No arguments. I want you to take the rest of the week off. Hopefully, you'll come back fully refreshed on Monday and ready for the next challenge.'

My face fell. 'But that means I'll miss the start of dress rehearsals. What if adjustments need to be made to the set?'

'You don't need to worry about that. I've already spoken to Jess and she's willing to step into the breach temporarily. I know she's not as experienced as you, but she knows the set inside out and Bryan has agreed to give her any additional support that's required.'

I felt as if something was covering my mouth and nose, gripping me like a vice. I tried to breathe, but despite the relentless heaving of my diaphragm, I couldn't seem to get enough oxygen into my lungs. I had a horrible feeling I was going to suffocate right there in Richard's office.

'You may as well take off now,' he continued, seemingly oblivious to my mounting anxiety. 'If there are any loose ends that need tying up, Jess can always drop you an email.'

He was sitting just a few feet away, but he looked hopelessly, impossibly remote, like someone you can just make out distantly, a dark silhouette in the middle of a snowstorm. I knew then that they were all conspiring against me: Richard, Bryan, the costume department . . . but it was Jess's betrayal that hurt the most. I always knew she was ambitious, but I never thought she'd stoop this low. No doubt she'd been whispering behind my back for ages, trying to discredit me, so she could step smoothly into my shoes.

I fought a manic, nervous urge to laugh. 'Whatever you think is best, Richard,' I managed to squeeze out.

I didn't go straight home. Instead I went to the river and flopped down on a bench, staring at the murky Thames as it ebbed and flowed. I'm not sure how long I sat there, for a kind of emotional hypothermia blurred the passage of time. After a little while, I started to feel chilly – I'd left the theatre in such a rush, I'd forgotten my jacket. Unable to face the humiliation of returning for it, I decided I might as well go home. During the train journey, I thought about texting Megan, or Tom, but when I checked my handbag, my phone wasn't there.

Sammi was surprised to see me when I walked into the kitchen, where she was hard at work on her latest commission. I told her I'd left work early because I wasn't feeling well, eliciting appropriate noises of sympathy. Eager to locate my phone, I asked if she'd seen it anywhere. She said she hadn't and suggested I might have left it at work. I knew that couldn't be the case because I hadn't used it all day and the last time I'd seen it was at home, the previous evening. Sammi picked up her own phone then and used it to call mine, but instead of ringing out it just went straight to voicemail, indicating that the battery had probably died.

I went upstairs to my bedroom and looked everywhere the phone could possibly be – in drawers, on shelves, under furniture. I was starting to feel panicky. My whole life was on that phone, I'd be lost without it. Having exhausted every possible hiding place, I decided to try the sitting room. As I was feeling down the back of the sofa, Sammi's voice drifted out from the kitchen.

'Have you found it yet?'

'No,' I said, flinging a cushion bad-temperedly across the room.

A few minutes later, Sammi appeared in the doorway. 'I've checked the kitchen; it's definitely not there. Where was the last place you used it?'

'In my bedroom, but I've already turned the place upside down.'

'Why don't I go upstairs and have another look for you – fresh pair of eyes and all that?' When I didn't answer straight away, she added: 'Would that be OK . . . me going in your room?'

I acknowledged her offer with a fluttering hand. 'Yes, yes, be my guest.'

Having drawn a blank in the sitting room, I had convinced myself that a thief must have stolen the phone from my bag during my journey to work that morning when I heard Sammi's footsteps pounding down the stairs.

'I've found it!' she cried as she burst into the room, holding my iPhone triumphantly aloft.

I groaned in relief. 'Where was it?'

'Under your bed,' she said, as she handed me the phone. 'Trapped between the headboard and the wall.'

I stared at her, my face slack and stupid. 'It can't have been; I looked under the bed.'

She shrugged. 'I guess you just didn't look hard enough.'

'I can assure you that I looked very hard indeed.' My voice sounded high and thin, like the note of a violin string about to snap. 'If the phone was under the bed, there's no way I could have missed it.'

Sammi gave me a look of manufactured patience. 'Just answer me this: were you using your phone in bed last night?'

I nodded grudgingly.

'Well then, that explains it; the phone must have slipped down the back of the bed without you realising.'

'I'm not disputing that, Sammi, I'm just saying that I *checked* under the bed just now and the phone definitely wasn't there,' I snapped, feeling the colour rising to my cheeks.

She looked into my eyes as if searching for something, the way a doctor might look to see if there was any hope in the brain of a madwoman. 'I can't help noticing that you seem to be losing quite a lot of stuff just lately,' she said in an emollient voice. 'Then there's all the other stuff . . . the not sleeping and the night terrors and so on.'

'What are you saying?'

'Just that I'm worried about you and I think you need help. As I've said before, your GP would be a good starting point and then perhaps he could refer you to a psychologist or counsellor if he thought it was necessary.'

There was a dull pain unravelling in my stomach. 'Why would I want to see a psychologist? Do you think I'm losing the plot?'

'I think you're in a very vulnerable state of mind, Chloe, and I don't want to see you reach breaking point. Lots of people have mental health problems, it's nothing to be ashamed of.'

She spoke very slowly and carefully, as if I were a child. A sharp tang of dislike flooded my mouth, souring my saliva. I couldn't bear to look at her concerned expression any more so I turned away. The world around me had become indecipherable, some kind of obscure charade conducted over my head and behind my back.

38

The school nurse looks at the little glass stick in her hand. 'Well, your temperature's normal, lovie, which is a very good sign.'

I make my eyes go big and round. 'But I don't feel well.'

The nurse sits down next to me on the hard sick bay bed. 'So tell me again, where does it hurt?' she says, with one of those tooth-achey looks that adults get when they think you're lying.

I wrap my arms around my body. 'All over.'

She puts her hand on the back of my head, moving it all the way down the slippery slope of my hair to my shoulders. I want to smile because it feels nice, but I know I mustn't.

She thinks about it for a couple of seconds. Then she says, 'Do you know what I think would be a really good idea?'

I shake my head.

'I think you should go back to the class and join in with whatever the others are doing. That'll help take your mind off it and then you'll feel better.'

As she goes to stand up, I grab the bottom of her cardigan. 'Please don't make me go back to Miss Pickering's class. I'm scared something bad will happen.'

The nurse gives a little laugh. 'Don't be silly, Miss Pickering won't make you do anything you don't want to.'

Very gently she lifts my hand from her cardigan and goes to put the temperature thingy on the side. I wait, just long enough. *One . . . two . . . three . . . four . . . five.* 'Oh yes, she will,' I say, almost under my breath, but not quite.

The nurse turns round and gives me a laser beam look. She's worried now. Excellent!

'What do you mean?' she asks me.

'Nothing,' I say, then I give a little sigh and stare at the floor.

'Has Miss Pickering made you do things you didn't want to before?'

I don't answer and carry on staring at the floor. I wonder if I'll be able to squeeze out a few tears. Not this time, worst luck.

The nurse sits down next to me again. She smells of washing powder mixed with antiseptic. 'It's OK, lovie,' she says. 'Whatever it is you can tell me.'

'I can't. Miss Pickering said something bad would happen to me if I told.'

She looks VERY worried now! 'An adult should never ask a child to keep a secret,' she says, putting her arm around me. It feels so lovely, the soft wool of her cardigan tickling the back of my neck, that I almost melt into a puddle, right there on the sick bay floor.

'But Miss Pickering *said* . . .'

'Don't you worry about Miss Pickering, nothing bad is going to happen to you, I promise.'

I feel sad for real then, knowing this is a promise she can't keep. I wipe some pretend snot away from my nose.

'Miss Pickering makes me come in early in the morning, before the bell. She says it's so we can spend time together.' I stop and count to five again in my head. '*Alone.*'

'And what do you do with Miss Pickering when you come in early?'

'We talk.'

'About what?'

'All sorts of things, but mainly books. Miss Pickering likes reading as much as I do.'

The nurse doesn't look quite as bothered as I hoped she would at this point, so I add, 'And when we talk, Miss Pickering likes me to sit on her knee. But I don't like it, it makes me feel funny.'

The nurse's hand goes up to her cheek. 'Does Miss Pickering do anything else that makes you feel funny?'

'She takes pictures of me with her camera – *and* she gave me the money to go on the school trip out of her own purse. She made me lie to the school secretary and say that my parents had given it to me.'

The nurse's eyes have gone all googly, as if she can't believe what's she's hearing, but I don't stop. Instead, I play my trump card. '*And* she gave me this. She said I have to kiss it every night before I go to bed and think of her.' I reach into the pocket of my skirt and pull out the hankie

Miss Pickering lent me ages ago, the one that I've been keeping in my box of treasures. 'See, it's even got her initials in the corner: *Harriet Jane Pickering.*'

The nurse looks as if she might be about to puke. 'I'm going to have to tell Mr Finch about this. You do understand why, don't you?'

I nod my head and blink back make-believe tears. What a brave girl I am.

39

Megan

It's an awful thing to feel uncomfortable in your own home. Whenever I was in the house with Sammi, especially when it was just the two of us, my nerves were stretched so tightly that my toes clenched in my shoes. I did my best to keep out of her way, but sometimes our paths crossed unavoidably – outside the bathroom, or in the kitchen at meal times. She was always nice as pie; it amazed me how she could do that – act as if nothing had happened. 'Good morning, Megan,' she would say, or 'Hope you had a fun day at work.' But every time she spoke to me, it was with a smirking defiance.

Something else that struck me as unusual was the fact there was barely a trace of Sammi on the internet. I'd searched and searched – not just on social media, but everywhere – and there was nothing beyond her LinkedIn profile, a few references to some women's magazine articles she'd written and a couple of photos taken at a charity gala two years ago. It just wasn't normal for someone of our age, especially a journo.

I hadn't said anything to Chloe; I didn't want to worry her. She was fragile enough, what with all the problems at work and being forced to take time off, which she wasn't very happy about. The last thing she needed was me adding to her stress levels. I wished Tom were here, instead of hundreds of miles away in Newcastle. Just like me, he'd do anything in his power to protect Chloe from harm, and I knew he'd be horrified to see the state she was in right now.

I thought Chloe's innate kindness was probably what had made her vulnerable to a predatory individual like Sammi. Right from the start, Sammi seemed to sense that Chloe was a softer and more pliable personality than me, and she homed in on that, almost as if she had a kind of feral instinct, a nose for weakness. It was becoming increasingly obvious that Sammi had hidden motives, befriending Chloe in the ruthlessly efficient way she had. Unfortunately, I didn't know what her end game was and that was what worried me the most.

I needed to work out my next move. I knew one thing: I couldn't go on living in this toxic environment, wondering what Sammi was going to do next, forever casting furtive glances at her, the way you might try to catch a glimpse of a grisly car accident while you were trying to keep your eyes on the road. Reluctant as I was, I figured I should probably start looking for another place to live, because Sammi had made it quite clear that she was going nowhere. I just hoped I would be able to convince Chloe to come with me, because there was no way I was leaving her alone in the house with that woman.

Whatever was fuelling Sammi's behaviour – be it loneliness, spite, or some sort of personality disorder – it all added up to one thing: she had power, and power could be dangerous. I had a cold, sick feeling deep down inside. I felt as if something bad was about to happen. I didn't want it to, but I wasn't sure I would be able to stop it.

40

Chloe

I was glad that my enforced sick leave was nearly over. Just one more day to go and then I'd be back at the theatre, the place where I felt most at home. Richard phoned me yesterday to see how I was doing. I found his concern hugely reassuring; when I saw his number on my phone, I thought for one terrible moment he was calling to sack me. Jess had been in touch too. She sent a sweet email on Thursday, saying how much she missed me and letting me know that the first day of dress rehearsals had gone smoothly.

I did wonder if I'd ever be able to trust Jess again, having convinced myself that she was the back-stabber who'd told Richard about my error with the mirror. After which she'd gaily offered to take my place at dress rehearsals, intent on proving that she could do my job just as well – if not better – than me. But, thanks to Megan, I saw things a bit differently now.

Megan, it must be said, was well acquainted with me and my trust issues, which had their roots in my childhood and my parents' ugly divorce. Consequently, she knew just how to handle me whenever I got a bit paranoid. Gently and tactfully, she reminded me there was no evidence that Jess was the one who told Richard about my fuck-up, pointing out that it could just as easily have been a member of the props department, who had worked on the replacement mirror frame. It was a possibility I hadn't considered, even though it was a really rather obvious one. I did that sometimes when I was stressed – made assumptions, failed to see what was right under my nose. Megan, by contrast, had always been good at seeing situations from multiple perspectives – analysing the data, working out the likely probabilities – no matter how much pressure she was under.

It was also Megan who suggested that, by agreeing to oversee the *Neurosis* dress rehearsals in my stead, Jess wasn't undermining me; rather she was protecting my interests, ensuring that the stage design achieved my vision and met the high standards she knew I'd set. Once I'd talked things through with Megan, I felt bad that I'd jumped to conclusions so quickly and when I got back on Monday, I was going to take Jess out to lunch and properly clear the air between us. We'd had a brilliant working relationship thus far and I didn't want misunderstandings or petty jealousies to spoil that.

Adding to my more positive frame of mind was the fact that Tom would be home in a few days' time. It felt like he'd been gone for ages and I'd missed him more than I thought I would. We'd been in touch every day since he'd been gone and I got the impression he was missing me too. I was touched that he had reached out to Sammi to discuss his concerns about me and I hoped that when he returned, he would be able to see that I was almost back to my normal self.

My sleep, meanwhile, was much improved. I'd discovered that taking two tablets before I went to bed, instead of just one, propelled me into a deep and dreamless state of unconsciousness. On the down side, I always woke up feeling rather muzzy and disoriented – sometimes even a little nauseous – but all in all, it seemed like a small price to pay.

Megan was quite cross when she found out I'd been experimenting with the dosage, but in the end she acknowledged that, if two tablets worked better for me than one, there was no harm in continuing with it. She was also mollified by the fact I had finally booked an appointment to see my GP. It wasn't for another couple of weeks, however, and I just hoped I would be able to eke out the remaining tablets until then.

For the first time in weeks, I actually looked forward to going to bed and, as I slipped between the sheets that night, I had no sense of foreboding. I opened my book and started to read, but I only managed four pages before my eyelids began to droop.

I woke with a start and knew immediately that something was out of kilter. I'd slept well enough, but my vision was slightly blurred, as if I'd turned my head too quickly and the room hadn't quite settled into place. The white light filtering through the curtains told me it was morning, but there was an eerie quiet in the air. I lifted my head to see the time on my alarm clock: five-thirty, far too early to get up, especially on a Sunday. My head was halfway back to the pillow when I noticed that the top edge of the pale duvet cover was streaked with dark stains. Thinking it must be a trick of the light, or something to do with my hazy vision, I clicked on the bedside lamp. As its soft glow illuminated the bed, I felt a shuddering sensation in my chest, something breaking open inside me. The duvet cover was covered in blood.

It was like leaning against an electric fence. A jolt went through me, knocking me back against the padded headboard. Gasping in horror, I kicked the duvet cover away from my body. With my arms now exposed, I noticed something else: both my hands were covered in blood. It was dark and gummy, coating my palms and filling my nail beds.

For a few seconds, all I could do was stare at my hands, holding them up to the light, just to be sure I wasn't mistaken. It didn't make any sense. I remembered nothing about the night's events, but I had a growing sense of trepidation, a feeling of having been overpowered, engulfed by something savage and shaming. I glanced at the door, which was shut, just as it had been when I went to sleep. I jumped out of bed and tore off my nightie, convinced I must have sustained some injury in the night without realising. I stood in front of the dressing table mirror, twisting and turning as I scrutinised every inch of my body, stopping only once I was satisfied that the blood definitely wasn't mine. The big question then was: whose blood was it?

I pulled on my dressing gown and cautiously opened the bedroom door. As I stepped out on to the landing, I don't know what I was expecting to see, but it certainly wasn't the chain of bloody handprints that extended the full length of the banister. My heart was thudding as I followed the handprints down the stairs. I felt like the girl in the fairy tale, following a trail of breadcrumbs, not knowing what I would find when they ran out.

When I reached the bottom of the stairs, I saw that there was another bloody imprint on the back of the front door, close to the latch. I hesitated, wondering if I should wake Megan up, but then thought better of it. There was a pair of Sammi's trainers by the door and I shoved my feet into them, not bothering to do up the laces. The pressure on my skull felt immense, as if my brow might explode at any minute. I didn't want to open the door, but I needed to know what lay beyond it.

Outside, the air was cold and fragile. I walked down the garden path and stood on the pavement, looking up and down the deserted street. It had rained in the night and pungent spirals of scent were rising from the gardens. A sudden gust of wind caught some sheets of newspaper lying in the road. But then another movement caught my eye. A fur stole was draped over the next-door neighbour's picket fence, the fur stirring as the breeze snatched at it.

The Housemate

Then I realised with a cold, hard shock that it wasn't a stole, but an animal, a tortoiseshell cat. I gripped my dressing gown tightly around my throat and moved a few steps closer. The cat's head was a caved-in mess, sticky and oozing, filling the air with a sickening ferrous smell. Its two front legs were spread wide and wedged in the gaps between the pickets, so it hung in a bizarre crucifixion pose, the matted, blood-stained fur of its belly exposed.

My stomach seized and I gagged violently. The houses opposite were swaying alarmingly and I knew I was hyper-ventilating, so I took a few deep gulps of fresh air. The houses lurched back into position and the blood surged to my head, and with it, a sense of utter revulsion.

I turned my head to the side and squeezed my eyes tight shut, but still the questions pressed in, closing my nostrils, filling my mouth. Inside my head, fear and embarrassment were swelling, leaving no room for anything else. I knew that it was me; there was no doubt in my mind about it. What I didn't understand was how I could have done something so appalling, so *perverted*, without remember-ing a thing about it. As I stood there, dry-retching over a drain cover, I felt a small but insistent voice calling from the furthest corners of my consciousness, warning me in a whisper so faint that I couldn't make out the words.

Shaking my head briskly, I walked back to the house. There was no time to stand there, agonising over how my unconscious mind had allowed this to happen; I had work to do. First, I had to get rid of the poor creature before anyone else saw it, then I had to clean the bloody handprints from the house before the others woke up. I couldn't risk anyone finding out about this; they'd think I was sick in the head – and they'd probably be correct in that assumption.

As I marched up the garden path, one more gruesome surprise awaited me, something I'd failed to notice earlier: a blood-stained brick lying in the earth around one of the rose bushes. I didn't know where it had come from, but I could guess what it had been used for. I bent down and picked it up, holding it gingerly at one end, as if I were a scenes-of-crime officer, and tossed it with a shudder into our wheelie bin.

I had thought I was getting better, but that had been naïve. My life was a china teacup, already well on its way from my delicate grip to a marble floor.

41

When I woke up on my seventh birthday, I had no idea that from that moment on, there would be a *before* and an *after*, a *was* and a *will be*. And that I would never again be quite the same girl I was before.

If I close my eyes now, I can still see the pale blue morning sky on the insides of my eyelids and smell the big lavender bush that took up most of the flowerbed in our front garden. It was the last day of school before we broke up for the summer holidays. Dad had already left and Mum was going to drop Emmie and me off on her way to work, just like she usually did – me at St Swithun's, Emmie at nursery. I'd already opened two of my presents – a Tamagotchi and some face paints – and Mum had promised there would be others when I got home. I never did get those presents and I don't know where they went. After what happened later, it didn't seem a very good idea to ask.

Even though it was a long time ago, I can remember exactly what my little sister was wearing that day: pink dungarees and her favourite purple shoes with the cut-out flower shapes on the toes. She liked to wear her hair a different way every single day, and that day she'd asked Mum to put it in two bunches, tied with bright yellow ribbons. Emmie was much prettier than me, with her blond hair and freckles and her smile that was like the sun popping out from behind a cloud. She was Mum's favourite, I knew that from the beginning, but I didn't mind and that's the God's honest truth.

It was just me and Emmie in the house because Mum had gone to get the car out of the garage. She always did that because it was easier to strap Emmie into her booster seat once the car was on the drive. We were a bit late that morning because I'd been opening my presents and Mum was in a rush, worried that she'd be late for work. When she went out to the garage, she left the front door open and told me to look after Emmie, who was three and a half at the time.

It's funny, because even though everything else about that day is burned on my brain, I can't remember what it was that made me take my eyes off Emmie. It might have been something on the telly, or maybe I was looking at my new Tamagotchi. I turned my back, only for a moment, but that was enough.

I didn't realise Emmie wasn't there until I heard a horrible clonk. It was loud enough for me to get a sick feeling in my tummy and go running outside. That's when I saw my little sister lying on the drive, underneath Mum's car. There was blood coming out of her ear. And just like that I was an only child again.

It took me a long time to understand what death

meant. Emmie's toys were still on the shelves in her bedroom, her pillow still had a dip where her head had been, and her photo still smiled down from the windowsill in the living room, but Emmie had gone. And then it hit me: death is forever. A hole in the ground; a small body clutching her favourite stuffed elephant, the one she never left home without, lying like Sleeping Beauty inside a tiny white coffin. Except this Sleeping Beauty was never going to wake up.

After that, I just had to carry on the best way I could. Mum and Dad were too busy making *arrangements* and going to dead kid support groups to pay any attention to me. I remember the long, achey silences around the table at dinnertime; the way Mum stared over the top of my head as if I wasn't even there. Then there were the whispers behind my back at school and the scared looks from the teachers who didn't know what to say to me. From that moment on, I felt as if I was on a different wavelength, out of radio contact with the rest of the world and waving at it from another galaxy.

I didn't know it at the time, but if things could have stayed that way, it would have been so much better for me. But they didn't, because after a little while, Mum started to pay *too much* attention to me. It started with the odd smack on the back of the legs (not because I'd been naughty or anything, just because Mum felt like it). The smacks soon turned to shoves and slaps. There was other stuff too, like twisting my arm behind my back and pulling my hair; once she held my arm over the spout of the kettle while it boiled. There was name-calling as well – she started to use nasty swear words, words that mums aren't even supposed to know.

But the worst thing by far was the endless waiting . . . trying to read Mum's face to see what sort of mood she was in. I'd look for clues in the sound she made as she walked upstairs; I'd watch every muscle of her body to try and work out if she was about to take a swing at me. I know it's a funny thing to say, but even when I was expecting it, it always came as a shock.

In the beginning Dad would tell her off for doing stuff to me, but it happened so many times that after a while he gave up. He used to be so big and strong, but after Emmie's accident he became a thin grey shadow and stopped bothering – about everything. He didn't care about Mum hurting me, or if she shouted at him, or drank wine every night, or let the house turn into a pigsty, or lost her job at the bank. As time went on and things at home got worse and worse, I felt everything inside me shrinking and shrivelling until my heart felt as small and dead as a dried pea.

I had nightmares too. Nightmares about falling down a well and not being able to get back out. Nightmares about wolves with foam around their mouths chasing me through the woods. I'd wake up in the middle of the night with my heart going a hundred miles an hour and the sheets in a tangle, not knowing where I was. Sometimes I'd even wet the bed.

I know Mum blames me for The Bad Thing. I bet Dad does too, even though he makes out he doesn't. They're right to blame me as well, because it was All My Fault (even if Mum should have looked in her mirror before she reversed out of the garage).

I only took my eye off Emmie for a second, I swear. Or maybe it was ten seconds. OK then, two minutes . . . absolute tops.

42

Megan

Chloe was waiting for me when I got home. She looked anxious; it was an expression she seemed to be wearing more and more these days. She claimed to be sleeping much better since upping the dosage on the tablets I'd given her. But I couldn't help noticing that one of her eyelids was twitching and her face had a greyish pallor. She'd gone back to work on Monday and, while things seemed to be going OK, I did worry that she might have returned too soon. To my mind, she was still in a very delicate state and her ashen appearance only lent weight to that view.

It had been a long, tough day for me too. My ICU patient, the cyclist who'd been hit by a lorry, had died that afternoon without ever regaining consciousness. Thankfully, the police had managed to ID her, and her family had been at her bedside as she slipped away. As I watched them clinging to each other in the relatives' room afterwards, it was yet another painful reminder that life was such a flimsy thing and could be snatched away when we least expect it.

I'd been looking forward to a quiet evening in with a ready meal and some mindless reality TV, but Chloe clearly had something on her mind and wanted to talk.

'I think Sammi's planning to move out,' she announced breathlessly, before I had even closed the front door behind me. On hearing her news, my mood instantly brightened.

'I didn't see that one coming,' I said, as I dumped my bag at the bottom of the stairs. 'What's she said, then?'

'She hasn't said anything,' Chloe replied, tailing me into the sitting room. 'But I've got the evidence right here.'

She waved a sheaf of papers at me, most of them torn and teabag-stained. I recognised them straight away – estate agents' details of properties to let.

'They were in the kitchen bin,' she explained. 'I only found them because the bin bag split while I was emptying it. God knows when she was planning on telling us. If she isn't happy living here you'd think she'd at least have the decency to let us know.'

I sat down on the sofa. 'Would you really be that upset if Sammi moved out?'

'It would certainly be inconvenient,' Chloe admitted, sitting down next to me. 'We'd have to re-advertise the room and set up loads of interviews and all the rest of it, but do you know what? I don't think I'd really miss Sammi that much.'

'I thought you two were friends.'

Chloe rubbed her bare arms as if she had a sudden case

of goosebumps. 'I know, but to be honest with you she's starting to give me the creeps.'

Had Chloe finally twigged that Sammi wasn't quite who she appeared to be? I gave her a searching look. 'Why, what's happened?'

'Nothing really, it's more of a feeling. She's just so intense and she's always giving me advice, even when I haven't asked for it. I didn't mind at first, but now it's starting to get on my nerves. It's almost as if she sees herself as some sort of big sister, which is a bit bloody much when she's only one year older than me and we hardly know each other. Then there's my stuff that keeps going missing. I know I've got no proof, but it has crossed my mind that Sammi might have something to do with it.'

She crooked one side of her mouth into an embarrassed smile. 'I know you've had reservations about her for a while; maybe I should have listened to you sooner.'

Then it was my turn to look awkward. 'Look, hon, there's something I need to tell you.' I pointed to the property details on her lap. 'It isn't Sammi who's looking to move out, it's me.' As Chloe opened her mouth to protest, I held up my hand. 'But it's not what you think. I'm wondering if maybe we should *both* move out, because Sammi does more than give me the creeps; she's actually starting to scare me.'

Chloe stared at me, her eyes huge and horrified. 'Are you serious, Megan? Why didn't you say something before?'

'Because I didn't want to worry you for no good reason.

In the beginning, I thought it was just a case of me not really clicking with Sammi, which hardly makes her a bad person. I could see how well you two were getting on and I didn't want to start slagging her off to you when I didn't have any real justification.'

'But now you do?'

There was a muscle ticking in Chloe's jaw. I deliberated for a few seconds, unsure if I should be sharing my concerns when she was clearly under strain. But what if I kept quiet and then something bad happened? Surely it was better for Chloe to be prepared.

I opened my mouth and the words came tumbling out, all the odd things I'd noticed about Sammi since she moved in – her emotional flatness, her superficial charm, the effortless way she switched from one personality to another in the space of a few seconds – worries and doubts that had been cemented when she confronted me so shockingly at the fashion launch.

Chloe stayed silent throughout my monologue and when I had finished, she put a hand to her forehead. I felt a rush of protectiveness towards her. She looked so small and helpless, bundled up in her oversized jumper.

'I'm really shocked she said that stuff to you about not moving out,' Chloe said, looking slightly dazed.

I nodded. 'And it was the *way* she said it that was so disturbing; it almost sounded like she was laying down the gauntlet. Now you know why I decided to take a look around and see what other rentals were available.'

Chloe looked utterly forlorn. 'I've been so stupid,' she said. 'I should have known Sammi was too good to be true.'

'Don't be too hard on yourself. She's a smooth operator. You should've seen how she worked the room at that fashion launch; she had everyone there eating out of her hand.' I reached across the sofa and squeezed Chloe's arm. 'There's something else you should know. I have to stress that it's just a theory; I might be barking up the wrong tree completely.'

'Go on,' Chloe said.

I faltered, feeling as if I was about to breach a massive confidence, even though I wasn't, because Sammi had never confided in me about anything, except of course her determination to remain at Bellevue Rise until the landlord evicted her, or hell froze over, whichever one came first.

I took a shallow breath. 'I think Sammi might have tried to commit suicide at some point in the past.'

Chloe's hands flew to her mouth. 'What makes you say that?' she asked.

'Have you noticed that she always wears long sleeves, and I mean *always*, even during that stinking hot weather we had last month?'

Chloe nodded. 'Now you come to mention it – yes, I have, actually.'

'Well, when we used the ladies' loos together at this party the other week, one of Sammi's sleeves rode up while she was washing her hands and I couldn't help noticing that there was a great big scar, right across her wrist, just here.' I pointed to my own arm, indicating the position. The scar had been pale and puckered and impossible to miss. As soon as Sammi realised I'd seen it, she'd tugged her sleeve down quickly and turned towards the hand driers. 'Of course, it's perfectly possible Sammi got the scar by some innocent means,' I said, trying to reassure Chloe. 'But if she's mentally unstable, we need to tread very carefully around her. I've dealt with enough psych patients to know they can be unpredictable.'

'Sammi did say she suffered from anxiety attacks, not that I've seen any evidence of that so far,' Chloe murmured. 'Do you think she could have been playing them down and that her condition's more serious than she's been letting on?'

I shrugged. 'I suppose it's possible.'

'Jesus, Megan, you don't think she would try to harm us physically, do you?'

'I shouldn't think so,' I said, sounding more confident than I felt. 'I'm just saying we should be on our guard, that's all.'

Chloe shuddered. 'It's going to be hard acting normal with Sammi, knowing what I know now.' She glanced at the pile of estate agents' details. 'Did you get as far as arranging a viewing on any of these?'

I shook my head. 'There was no point; it's all way out of our price range. Everything seems much more expensive compared to the last time we looked. And even if we could afford them, nothing I saw was a patch on Bellevue Rise.'

'Bugger,' Chloe muttered. 'Maybe this has been Sammi's plan all along – convincing us to move out, so she can have the house all to herself.'

I gave a dry laugh. 'I'm sure Sammi would be more than happy to see the back of *me*, but I'm not so sure about you . . . in case you hadn't noticed, she seems to have formed quite an attachment.'

Chloe scrunched up her face. 'You know what, Meg, I really don't see why we should be the ones to move. *We* found this place and as far as I'm concerned it's *our* house, not hers.'

'I agree with you completely.'

'So what are we going to do about it?'

Before I could answer, the doorbell rang. 'That'll be Tom,' Chloe said, springing to her feet. 'His train was due in half an hour ago; he said he was going to come straight here from the station.'

She disappeared from the room and a few seconds later I heard a squeal of excitement as she and Tom were reunited. After that there was a long silence, during which I imagined they were falling into each other's arms. I felt a twinge of envy. I'd only been truly in love once in my life – with a graphic designer I met during the six months I spent in Southeast Asia, the year after I finished my Masters. Once we both returned to our respective homes, the relationship quickly fell apart; he lived in Toronto, so it would have taken a superhuman effort to keep it going. I could still remember the way I felt when he touched me – like a sunflower turning towards the light. And when we kissed, only my mouth existed in that moment, only my hands on his skin were real. I'd give anything to feel that way again; if only Pete hadn't turned out to be such a shit. I tried not to think about him too much, but it was hard when I kept seeing him around the hospital.

My thoughts were interrupted by Chloe's reappearance. Her eyes were sparkling and her cheeks were flushed as she came into the room with Tom.

'Hey, stranger, great to see you,' I said, standing up and giving Tom a hug. 'How was Newcastle?'

'Good, thanks,' he said, slipping off his bulging ruck-sack and letting it drop to the floor. 'I was ready to come home, though.' He glanced at Chloe and she smiled back at him.

'Can I get you a tea or coffee?'

'I got a cappuccino from the kiosk at the station, so I'm OK for the minute, thanks, Megan. Anyway, how are things with you?'

I sat back down again. 'Not bad; we are having a few issues with Sammi, but I won't bore you with all that.'

Tom looked surprised. 'Really?'

Chloe nodded. 'We were just talking about it before you arrived.'

'I thought everything was working out really well with Sammi.'

'It was, but lately weird things keep happening, like stuff going missing, and we don't feel comfortable around her any more.'

Now Tom looked faintly amused. 'You're not still going

on about that necklace, are you, Chloe? You were careless and you lost it. Why can't you just accept that?'

'Because that's not what happened,' Chloe said in a low voice. 'Anyway, it's not just the necklace – quite a few things have disappeared or been moved – and Megan thinks Sammi deliberately ruined a dress of hers the other week.'

'She was very rude to me the other evening as well,' I added.

'There's other stuff too,' Chloe went on. 'Like the fact Sammi doesn't seem to have a single friend, and every time I ask about her family, she always brushes me off without ever actually answering the question.'

Tom drew his hand over his face. 'I seriously think you two are over-reacting. I appreciate that I don't know Sammi as well as you do, but I've spent quite a bit of time with her and nothing I've seen so far makes me think that she's anything other than a nice, honest, decent person.'

'The fact is, Tom, none of us really knows anything about her at all,' I said. 'Other than what she's chosen to tell us.'

'I bet that scrapbook you found would give us some useful background information,' said Chloe, turning to me. 'How about we go upstairs right now and see if we can find it? At least then we'll know who we're dealing with.'

'What are you talking about, Chloe? What scrapbook?' Tom asked.

'Megan saw a photo album full of documents and old

newspaper cuttings in Sammi's room when she first moved in. Sammi completely freaked out when she saw Megan looking through it.'

'I'm not surprised; I'd be pissed off if I found my house-mate looking through my personal stuff,' Tom retaliated. 'The poor woman is entitled to a bit of privacy, you know.'

'Not if she poses a threat to us,' Chloe shot back.

Tom laughed. 'Just listen to yourself, Chloe. Are you completely paranoid or what? You haven't got a shred of evidence that Sammi's a threat in any way, shape or form. I think you two both need to get a grip and grow up a bit.'

'Just because you've had a few dinners with Sammi and cosy chats over cups of coffee, you think you know her,' Chloe snapped. 'But let me tell you something, you haven't got the faintest idea what she's really like.'

Tom took a step back, clearly startled by the severity of Chloe's tone. '*Cosy chats over cups of coffee?* What's that supposed to mean?'

Chloe snared her bottom lip in her teeth. I got the impression she hadn't meant to let the cat out of the bag like that. 'I know you and Sammi met up behind my back a couple of weeks ago,' she said, blinking hard.

Tom opened his mouth to reply, but the words seemed to shrivel in his throat because no sound came out.

'And don't even think about denying it, because Megan saw you at London Bridge station,' Chloe spat.

Tom glared at me. I glared right back; there was no way he was going to make me feel guilty for sharing that with my best friend.

'We met up to talk about *you*, Chloe,' he said, spreading his arms wide. 'I thought you were behaving in a way that was out of character and I was worried about you.'

'Did you honestly think that *Sammi* would have more knowledge of the inner workings of my mind than my best friend of the past twelve years?' Chloe said in a clipped voice. 'I suppose the fact she's rather easy on the eye didn't hurt, did it?'

Tom gave a hollow laugh. 'Please don't tell me you think I had any sort of ulterior motive in meeting up with Sammi.'

'I don't know what to think any more, Tom. You're supposed to be on my side, but instead you're treating me and Megan like a pair of silly schoolgirls picking on someone in the playground.'

'Well, that's exactly what you sound like,' Tom grunted.

Chloe's expression darkened. 'If that's the way you feel, you may as well leave right now, because Megan and I are going to look for that scrapbook and I'd hate for you to be party to anything that made you feel uncomfortable.'

'Fine with me,' Tom said, picking up his rucksack. 'Give me a call when you come to your senses.'

Chloe didn't say a word as Tom stalked out of the room. A moment later, we heard the front door slam shut.

'Don't you think you should go after him?' I asked her.

'Absolutely not,' she said. She walked towards the door, stopping at the threshold to look over her shoulder. 'Are you coming, then? Sammi's at the gym, she won't be back for at least half an hour – plenty of time to search her room.'

Sammi's room was just as spartan as I remembered. I felt bad about going through her things, but if we were going to work out the best way to deal with the situation, we needed information.

'Try not to move anything or she'll know we've been in here,' I said, as I got down on my hands and knees to look under the bed.

'Can you see anything?' Chloe asked, brushing her fingers along the spines of Sammi's magazine collection.

I sat back on my heels. 'Nope, but this was where it was before, so she's obviously found a better hiding place. It's pretty big, so there aren't many places it could be.'

I went to the chest of drawers and pulled out the first drawer. It contained a collection of silky underwear – most of it designer by the look of it – and I found myself wondering how Sammi could afford stuff like that on a freelance journalist's salary. The second drawer held gym wear, all of it painstakingly folded – leggings on one side, tops on the other. The third drawer yielded something altogether more interesting: a bottle of what looked like prescription medication, nestling beside a pile of pyjamas. Having made a mental note of its exact position, I picked it up for a closer look. The label bore Sammi's name, alongside that of a chain of chemists; it wasn't a local branch, I observed – the address was all the way over in Fulham.

'What is it?' Chloe asked, coming up behind me.

'Lurasipine,' I said slowly, as my brain began to compute. 'It works by blocking the receptors for various neurotransmitters.'

'What are neurotransmitters when they're at home?'

'Chemicals that nerves use to communicate with each other.'

'It must be what Sammi takes for her anxiety attacks,' Chloe said.

'It is sometimes used to treat anxiety disorders but only in extreme cases. The side effects can be quite significant – drowsiness, dizziness, memory loss, visual disturbances. That's why doctors usually only prescribe it for anxiety where other drug treatments have failed. It is quite commonly used to treat another condition, however.'

'What condition's that?'

I scratched the side of my face. There was no way to break it to Chloe gently. 'It's an anti-psychotic; it's usually prescribed to schizophrenics.'

'My God!' Chloe shrieked. 'Are you trying to tell me we're living with someone psychotic?'

'Let's not get ahead of ourselves,' I said. I was trying to sound calm, but I could feel a vein throbbing at my temple. 'I know Sammi's an oddball, but it's a big leap from that to schizophrenia – and as I said, if her anxiety's severe enough, her GP might well have prescribed this.'

'I don't like this one little bit,' Chloe said, going over to the wardrobe and wrenching open the door. 'We've got to find that photo album. I need to know what she's hiding from us.'

She reached up and began patting the shelf above the hanging rail, dislodging a stack of towels in the process.

'Be careful, Chloe. We can't leave any sign that we've been here, we need to leave everything exactly as we found it.'

She made an impatient noise as she pushed the towels back into position. 'The scrapbook has to be here somewhere; it's the only place we haven't looked.'

'Hey, what's that?' I said, pointing to a large metal box nestling among the shoeboxes under the hanging rail. It definitely hadn't been there the last time I looked in Sammi's wardrobe.

Chloe looked down. 'Looks like one of those cash boxes.' She nudged it with her toe, before bending down for a closer examination. 'It *is* a cash box – look, it's got a keyhole.' She tried the lid. 'Fuck it, she's locked it.' She lifted it up and gave it a little shake. There was a dull rattling sound. 'There's definitely something in there and, whatever it is, it's quite heavy.' She put the box back and looked up at me, her face split in a wide, deranged smile that made the tendons in her throat stand out. 'It has to be the album, doesn't it?' Her eyes began frantically casting around the room. 'Where do you think Sammi might have hidden the key? Come on, Megan, don't just stand there – *think*!'

I didn't have time to offer a suggestion, because just then I heard a noise from downstairs, a kind of dragging sound like a chair leg scraping across a floor. I frowned at Chloe. 'Did you hear the front door open?'

'No,' she mouthed silently.

'Hey, guys, are you up there?' Sammi's voice called out from somewhere downstairs. 'I'm making a cup of tea, does anyone want one?'

Chloe closed the wardrobe door softly and lunged for the door. I was one step behind her.

43

I can't remember what brought me down here, to the scrubby patch of woodland on the edge of the Common. Was it the way the light was trickling so prettily through the trees, or was it the sound of laughing? It doesn't much matter either way. The point is I'm here now.

I went round to Anouk's house earlier on. Although she hadn't invited me, I thought it would be a nice surprise for her – but when Lucy answered my call on the intercom, she told me Anouk was out.

'Out where?' I asked.

'She's not available, all right?' Lucy said. Then the intercom went dead and the electric gates stayed shut. I think I must have done something to upset her, but I don't know what it is.

Afterwards, I went down to the allotments, but there were too many people around, all beavering away on their scabby little plots of earth. At least the old man with the walking stick wasn't there. I'm pretty sure he got Barney out of the leaf burner after me and Anouk ran away that time, because I saw Barney the other day, out for a walk with his owner. He growled as I walked by, so I guess he recognised me. I'm going to come back later, when it's quiet, and pull up that old man's stupid cabbages. That'll show him.

When I left the allotments, I still wasn't ready to go home. I didn't fancy the library, so I decided to head to the Common, just for a change. The Common isn't that exciting; it's a triangle of grass in between the shops and the rec, where people go to play football and walk their dogs. The woods are OK, though; you can find some interesting stuff in there, like old pram wheels and pages from mucky magazines. I once found a nest of baby mice, all curled up together, so tiny and weak. Their mummy wasn't there; I think she must have run away and left them, so I decided to put them out of their misery. The way I saw it, I was doing them a favour.

As I get closer to the woods, I can hear voices and giggling. That's annoying, because I like it best when I have the woods to myself. I don't want them to know I'm here, so I hide behind a big tree and look around. That's when I see them: Anouk and that fat pig Eleanor Hardy. They're sitting on the fallen tree trunk where I like to sit sometimes.

I'm really confused; I don't understand what they're doing here, *together*, when they're not even friends. As I watch them, my thoughts are like fluffy dandelion clocks, coming apart in the wind; I can't seem to catch them. *Why is Anouk plaiting Eleanor's hair?* It's horrid hair, thin and stringy, like rats' tails. And: *Why isn't Anouk wearing the friendship bracelet I made her when she said she was never going to take it off?*

They're talking to each other, but I'm not close enough to hear what they're saying. Very slowly and quietly I tiptoe over to the next tree. Then the next one. And then one more. *Now* I can hear them.

'What are you going to wear to Tara's party?' Eleanor says.

Tara's having a party? Nobody told me.

'Probably something new,' Anouk answers. 'I'm going shopping with Mum next weekend.'

I can't believe Anouk's going shopping *again*. She's already got enough party dresses to fill my entire bedroom. I wish she'd bung a few of her old dresses my way!

Anouk has finished plaiting Eleanor's hair now. I think she's pleased with how it's turned out because she's smiling as she ties a scrunchy around the end. Then her smile melts away. '*She* hasn't been invited to Tara's party, has she?' she says suddenly.

'Don't be silly, Noukie,' Eleanor says. '*Nobody* wants her at their party, she'd stink the whole house out for one thing.' She pinches the end of her nose and gives a catty little laugh. 'Seriously, I don't know how you put up with the smell for so long; I don't think her mum even knows what a washing machine is.'

Anouk shivers. 'The smell wasn't the worst thing.'

'So what was, then?' Eleanor says, pulling the plait over her shoulder and stroking the end like it was some sort of pet.

'Her personality; she's a complete psycho.'

Eleanor claps her hands together like Anouk's just said the funniest thing she's ever heard. 'Love it, Noukie! That's what I'm going to call her from now on: *psycho girl*.'

Something drops deep inside of me, as if a plug has been pulled and all my dreams have drained away. It's me; *I'm* psycho girl. They've been talking about me.

At first, I want to run – very fast and very far, to get away from their stuck-up smiles and their stupid snarky comments. But then I feel rage, like a wave, begin deep behind my ribcage and grow, filling every artery and vein, until my eyeballs swell with it. I want to plunge my fingernails into her face, to pull open the seams of her pretty smile and cut angry, crescent-shaped lines into her cheeks. I want her to scream, to writhe, to bleed. I want her pain to last forever.

44

Chloe

Megan was working a late shift and wouldn't be home for several hours. In the meantime, I was on my own with Sammi. I could feel the malevolence quivering and turning in the air of the old house, the way dust turns in a beam of sunlight.

It was forty-eight hours since our failed attempt to find the photo album. I was desperate to get my hands on it, convinced it held the answers to the many questions we had about our enigmatic housemate. So many things about Sammi didn't add up – the lack of social media presence, the dearth of friends and family, the way she kept trying to ingratiate herself with me, while simultaneously shutting Megan out.

And what about the fact that practically everything she wore was designer? She was clearly earning good money, so why would she rent a room the size of a shoebox, in a shared house that was miles from the nearest Tube station?

Then there was that creepy business with my missing

door keys and the work that had mysteriously vanished from my laptop. The more I thought about it, the more certain I was that Sammi, who would, after all, have had ample opportunity, had done those things to mess with my head. She had succeeded too – and what's more, I was convinced that her behaviour had contributed to my night terrors, making them more frequent and terrifying than any I'd experienced before.

Megan and I both loved living at Bellevue Rise and, after just a few months, it already felt more like home than any place I'd lived since leaving university. Neither of us were willing to let it go without a fight; one way or another, we were going to get rid of her. After discussing the various options, Megan and I had decided against any direct confrontation. Instead, we would freeze Sammi out, in the hope that she would leave the house of her own accord. This meant keeping contact with her to a bare minimum and generally making life at Number 46 as uncomfortable for her as possible. Megan felt that the success, or otherwise, of this tactic would be largely down to me. It was her belief that once Sammi realised she hadn't got her hooks into me after all, she would admit defeat, pack her bags and go. Not wanting to let my best friend down, I was determined to play my part. With any luck, Sammi would get the message sooner rather than later – and if she didn't, we would just have to come up with a Plan B.

I'd been giving Sammi the cold shoulder for the past two days, addressing her only when strictly necessary and brushing off her attempts to engage me in conversation. Earlier that evening, I'd been watching TV in the sitting room when she returned home, slamming the front door noisily behind her. I don't know where she'd been, but I assumed it was to some work-related event. As she sat down next to me on the sofa, I caught a whiff of alcohol on her breath.

'What are you watching?' she asked me.

'Nothing very interesting,' I replied. 'Actually, I was just about to go up to my room.'

I stood up abruptly and thrust the remote control into her hands.

She gave a little laugh. 'Was it something I said?'

'I'm just tired, that's all,' I said, studiously avoiding any eye contact.

Before heading upstairs, I went to the kitchen to make myself a cup of hot chocolate. As I threw the empty milk container in the bin, I made a horrible discovery – the missing photo of my sister and me, now viciously torn in half and placed on top of the trash in plain sight. It felt as if a rock was lodged in my throat as I picked up the two pieces and tucked them in the pocket of my dress. Sammi really was a nasty piece of work. What sort of sick person did a thing like that and didn't even try to hide their cruel handiwork? The sooner that woman was out of our lives, the better.

I'd spent the rest of the evening in my bedroom, reading a book – or at least *trying* to read. Intrusive thoughts kept popping into my head. Megan had assured me that Sammi was unlikely to pose a physical threat – but, even with her superior medical knowledge, how could she, how could *anyone*, know what our housemate was really capable of?

A little while ago, I heard Sammi making her way upstairs. I listened in a state of hyper alertness as she prepared for bed, brushing her teeth, flushing the loo, clicking off the light switch on the landing.

'Sleep well, Chloe,' she said in a soft voice that was almost a whisper as she passed my bedroom door. I didn't give her the satisfaction of a response.

It was probably time I turned in too. I had a busy day at work tomorrow and I needed a good night's sleep. I reached instinctively for the amber pill bottle on my bedside table. As I unscrewed the cap, my mind began turning over, assembling various scraps of information, the pieces cohering slowly at first. Somewhere in the back of my mind, a dangling fragment was on the point of meeting its target, and then . . . bullseye! I knew what Sammi had done: swapped her own medication for mine.

It all made perfect sense. The tablets had certainly improved my quality of sleep but, ever since I'd started taking them, I'd also experienced episodes of dizziness, blurred vision and memory blanks – all side effects of the anti-psychotic, whose name I couldn't remember, that Sammi had been prescribed.

The realisation came as something of a relief . . . *that* was why I'd murdered the poor cat, whose remains now lay inside a bin bag in a skip two streets away. I wasn't a monster; I'd simply been experiencing one of my night terrors. However, the drugs in my system had made me act out of character, which was why I'd responded to a perceived threat, i.e. the cat, with unnatural violence. It didn't make what I'd done all right – God knows, I'd spent hours wondering what sort of agonies the creature's poor owners were going through after it failed to return home – but at least now there was an explanation for my behaviour.

It would have been easy enough for Sammi to make the switch, when Megan asked her to leave the tablets outside my bedroom door. The only question that remained was *why*? What possible motivation could she have for drugging me? To make me more compliant, more in need of support, more dependent on her, perhaps? I could only hazard a guess about what went on inside that twisted mind of hers.

The thought of what she'd done made me feel quite sick. How could I ever have considered this person – this *interloper* – a friend? I shuddered involuntarily and made a mental note to speak to Megan in the morning and ask her what, if any, permanent ill effects I might have suffered from ingesting the anti-psychotic. I'd only been taking them for a couple of weeks, so hopefully once they were out of my system, I'd be back to my normal self.

I got up and went over to the door, still clutching the pill bottle. Outside, the landing lay in darkness and there was no glimmer of light under Sammi's bedroom door. As I flushed the tablets down the toilet and embarked on my own night-time rituals, a single question revolved in my head. Who was Samantha Charlesworth (if that was even her real name) and what did she want?

It was dark and I was cold, colder than I'd ever been before. In the distance, a bell was tolling, its peals deep and resonant. I knew instantly that it was a signal, a warning of imminent danger. I had to get as far away from here as possible, even if it meant crossing frozen wastelands and negotiating treacherous ravines. I knew my life was in grievous danger, but my legs felt heavy, as if they were encased in armour; just putting one foot in front of the other took a huge effort.

Finally, I reached the door and, after groping and fumbling, found the handle and yanked it open. To my horror, the way out was barred by a wraith in a long cloak. As the cloak swished, I thought I caught the glint of a knife and knew instinctively what was coming: a smothering hand to my mouth, a flick left, a slit right, a final upward stroke to split the ribs and penetrate the heart. I turned quickly, trying to go back the way I had come, but the door was no longer there. Desperate to escape, I stepped to the side, my arms outstretched in the darkness, trying to feel my way. My hands briefly made contact with something soft and warm and all at once, the air split open in a scream.

Suddenly, there was a flare of light. Everything around me seemed to be collapsing. The reality I had inhabited just a few seconds earlier began to shrivel and deflate. I turned towards the light and saw a woman standing in a doorway.

Her skin appeared almost translucent in the half-light, as if she were beginning to dissolve from the inside out.

'Chloe?' the woman said. 'Are you OK? I thought I heard someone scream.'

My head was spinning. My thoughts were in havoc, a jumble of images that made no sense. The woman came towards me and put her arm around my shoulders.

'Megan?' I said blearily, feeling myself break into full consciousness.

She smiled. 'Don't worry, hon; it was just a dream. Come on, let's get you back to bed.'

Just then, something caught her eye. 'What the . . .?' she said, squinting into the darkness at the bottom of the stairs.

I followed the direction of her gaze. There was a shape on the hall floor, just behind the front door. I thought at first it was a heap of things that had fallen off the coat stand. For a moment or two, Megan and I just looked at each other in bewilderment. Then I turned back to the shape and realised that it was in fact a person – and they weren't moving. Megan flicked the light switch on the landing and I saw to my horror that Sammi's bedroom door was wide open, the bed beyond it empty.

I was seized by a numbing shock. I felt as if all the blood were draining out of me, to be replaced by an icy nausea.

'Sammi?' I shrieked. 'Sammi, are you all right?'

Megan began bolting down the stairs, almost falling over in her haste. I followed her, but much more slowly, gripping the banister as I went.

By the time I reached the bottom, Megan was on her knees next to our unconscious flatmate. Sammi's face was ghoulishly white and she was bleeding from a nasty head wound, her pyjama top already stained with crimson.

'What did you do, Chloe?' Megan asked hoarsely.

'I d-d-don't know,' I stuttered. 'Everything happened so quickly.'

Megan's face was rigid as she held two fingers to the side of Sammi's neck.

'Is she going to be OK?' I asked.

Megan turned towards me with a stricken expression. 'Call an ambulance,' she said. When I didn't react immediately, she shouted at me: 'CALL A FUCKING AMBULANCE, CHLOE – NOW!'

Shocked into action, I hurried to the phone on the console table, my hand shaking as I punched in the numbers. My head felt like it was swelling, overheated, humming with cross-wired currents of panic and confusion. I could barely remember my own address when the operator asked me.

By the time I put down the handset, Megan had already begun CPR. I sank to the floor and began rocking back and forth on my haunches as I watched her pressing down on Sammi's chest with surprising force. I could feel myself coming apart inside, growing ragged, bits flailing around.

'I didn't mean to do it,' I said, and I began to cry, great choking tears of fear and guilt.

45

Megan

I could tell right away she was dead. The probability was she'd either fractured her skull or broken her neck. Even though I knew CPR was a waste of time, I felt I had to do something; I couldn't just stand there. I'd only attempted resuscitation once before, when a patient went into cardiac arrest at the doctor's surgery where I managed the dispensary. But it was quite different working on someone I actually knew. Meanwhile, Chloe was falling apart. She kept repeating that she hadn't meant to hurt Sammi, insisting that she'd been acting in self-defence, convinced our housemate was some sort of assassin who'd come to hurt her.

Performing CPR for a prolonged period requires a considerable amount of stamina and I soon became exhausted. When Sammi's lips began to turn purple, I stopped fighting a lost cause and slumped back against the bottom stair. Chloe began hyperventilating.

'I've killed her, haven't I?' she wailed, tears running

down her cheeks. 'I pushed Sammi down the stairs and killed her.'

'You were asleep, you didn't know what you were doing. You can't be held responsible for your actions,' I said.

'They're going to arrest me for murder, aren't they?' Chloe said, scrabbling at her throat as if she were suffocating.

'Breathe, Chloe,' I said. 'Nice and deep . . . come on, do it with me.' I began exhaling and inhaling, slowly and deeply, until Chloe got into my rhythm.

'Now listen,' I told her, gripping her wrists. 'Any minute now, the emergency services are going to be here and we need to get our stories straight.'

'I can't go to prison, Meg, I can't!' she sobbed.

In the distance, I could hear sirens. I closed my eyes for a few seconds, trying to think. 'You could always say you were in bed when it happened; I'd back you up.'

'What?' Chloe said, looking at me as if I was speaking another language.

'You could tell them you were asleep in your room when you heard a loud noise. You thought it might be a burglar, so you came and woke me up. We went to investigate and that's when we found Sammi at the bottom of the stairs. We have no idea how she got there, but we can only assume she tripped and fell.'

Chloe gave a convulsive gasp. 'Do you really think they'd believe us?'

'I don't know, but look at it this way: what evidence is

there to prove she was pushed?' The sirens were getting nearer; the paramedics would be here any minute now, followed, no doubt, by the police.

'It's your call, Chloe; I can't make the decision for you.'

She looked at me and there was such an expression of terror on her face that I felt my insides crumple.

46

I really thought Anouk was different. I did *everything* for her. I looked after her when she didn't know anybody at school. I taught her how to play cat's cradle and showed her where the best blackberry bushes were, behind the scout hut. I told her how pretty she was all the time and pretended not to be bored when she went on and on about her precious *Papa* and how much she missed him. I wish I hadn't bothered now because unfortunately, she turned out to be mean and spiteful, just like all the other kids at school. *Unfortunately* for me, of course – but *double unfortunately* for Anouk.

I knew that teaching her a lesson wasn't going to be easy. But if it was easy, it wouldn't be so much fun, now would it? The tricky part was always going to be getting into her house, something that would take massive amounts of brains and bravery. Luckily, I've got both of those.

Anouk has been ignoring me for weeks, ever since I took her down to the allotments. It's pretty unfair of her to take it out on me, when it wasn't *my* fault our game with Barney was ruined; it was that stupid old man.

Nowadays, Anouk spends every breaktime with Eleanor and those cackling airheads she hangs around with. I have to watch them, prancing around the playground with their matching high ponytails, acting like they're the Queens of St Swithun's. Meanwhile, there's me, eating my cheese and pickle sandwiches all alone like a total loser. Nobody wants to be my friend any more, not even Liam.

I don't let it get to me, though. I stay focused, keeping my eyes sharp and my ears open. I'm in the changing rooms after PE when I hear Anouk and Eleanor talking on the other side of the wooden divide.

'Do you want to come to my house on Saturday?' Eleanor asks Anouk. 'My mum says she'll take us swimming.'

'Sorry, I can't. My dad's coming back from Germany on Saturday,' Anouk tells her. 'He's been away for ages this time, nearly three weeks. Mum's picking him up from the airport.'

'Will he bring you back a present?'

Anouk giggles. 'Of course.'

'Are you going to the airport as well?'

'No, I wish I was, but Mum doesn't want me missing my piano lesson on Saturday morning. I'm taking my Grade Two exam in a couple of weeks, so I need all the practice I can get.'

'You're so clever, Noukie, I wish I could play an instrument.'

I can hear the cat-who-got-the-cream tone in Anouk's voice as she tells Eleanor: 'My piano teacher says I've got real talent, and she knows what she's talking about; Mum says she's one of the best teachers in the whole county.'

After that, they start talking about which boy in our class has the coolest hair. That's when I tune out; I already have all the information I need.

It's Saturday now and here I am, in Anouk's front garden, hiding behind a big green bush, whose leaves are so shiny they look as if they're made out of plastic. It was easy enough to slip in through the electric gates when Lucy drove out, on her way to the airport. There's a small blue car on the driveway, which I'm guessing belongs to Anouk's piano teacher. I'll have to wait for her to leave before I can put my plan into action.

Forty-five minutes go by and I've got pins and needles in both my feet. I stand up and start stamping them on the ground, but then Anouk's front door opens and I have to duck back down behind the bush. I watch through the leaves as a tall lady comes out and gets into the blue car. She spends a few minutes flipping through a notebook on her lap, then she drives off.

As soon as the electric gates close behind her, I leave my hiding place, walk up to the front door and ring the bell.

'Did you forget something?' Anouk says as she opens the door. As soon as she realises it's me, not her piano teacher, her face closes like a clam shell. 'Oh, it's you,' she says. 'What do you want?'

'My friendship bracelet,' I tell her.

'Your *what*?' she says snootily.

'The friendship bracelet I made you; I want it back.'

She flicks her eyes to the side and looks fed up. 'I don't know where it is.'

'Don't worry, I'll help you look for it,' I say, stepping through the door and pushing right past her.

'Hey, you can't just come in my house without being invited,' she yaps like an annoying little Chihuahua.

'I already did,' I say, as I head for the staircase. 'Come on, the sooner we find it, the sooner I'll be outta here.'

She makes a huffing noise, then she shuts the front door and follows me upstairs.

'So where do you think it's likely to be?' I ask her, rubbing my hands together as I look around the prissy pink bedroom I know so well.

She shrugs. 'Could be anywhere.'

I go over to the big storage unit that's stacked with white-painted wooden boxes filled with toys, most of which Anouk is far too old to be playing with. 'I'll start here, then. Why don't you have a look in your drawers?'

I can tell she's not happy, but she does it anyway.

After just a couple of minutes, I start fanning my face with my hand. 'Phew, it's stuffy in here,' I say. 'Is it OK if we let some air in?'

Anouk is smart enough to do what I tell her and pushes the bottom half of the window up. The edge of her pink curtains moves in the breeze.

'So, how are things with you?' I ask her as I turn a box full of stuffed animals upside down.

'Fine,' she says lamely.

'Are you having fun with Eleanor?'

'Mmm-hmm.'

'I bet you two had a lovely time at Tara's party the other week, didn't you?'

Anouk stops what she's doing and turns round to face me. 'Look, I'm sorry if you feel left out,' she says. 'But you did some really weird stuff and I don't want to hang around with you any more.'

'What stuff?' I say, wondering what she's talking about.

She gives me a dirty look. 'You know . . . breaking Liam's arm and trying to set that dog on fire.'

'Oh, *that* stuff.' I pick a Bugs Bunny up off the floor and begin spinning him round by one of his legs. 'Did you say something to your mum? Is that why she was so rude to me when I called round to see you the other week?'

Anouk shakes her head. 'I didn't say anything, I promise. I think she just picked up on a vibe.'

I cock my head to one side. 'What sort of vibe?'

She sighs. 'Let's just forget it, OK?'

'Perhaps you mean a *psycho girl* vibe.' As I say the word 'psycho', a spray of spit comes flying out of my mouth. 'That *is* what you and your New Best Friend Eleanor call me, isn't it?'

Anouk's face goes heart attack red. 'I don't know what you mean,' she says, lying through her straight white teeth.

'Oh, I think you do.' I toss Bugs over my shoulder and start moving slowly towards her. She backs away towards the window, her eyes bulging with fear.

'You need to go now,' she says in a strange voice as if

she's swallowed a sharp object and can't get it all the way down. 'Mum will be back any minute.'

'I doubt it,' I say. 'It's a long drive to the airport.'

She's shaking now and judging by the way she's panting, she's having difficulty breathing too. The backs of her legs are right up against the window seat; she's got nowhere else to go. I reach out an arm and Anouk steps backwards, up on to the window seat, so now she's standing above me. The only trouble is, poor Anouk doesn't know what's coming next. No idea, that is, until I lunge towards her, pushing her in the stomach as hard as I can. A ripple of shock passes over her rosebud face as she topples backwards, straight through the open window. One minute she's there, the next minute she's gone. Then, a second or two later, I hear the satisfying crunch of her body smacking into the paving slabs below. And just like that the bitter taste in my mouth is replaced by a sudden, soaring rush of joy.

As I turn to go, I spot the friendship bracelet, nestling in a jumble of bangles and hair accessories that are scattered across the top of a chest of drawers. 'Best friends forever,' I whisper, as I pick up the friendship bracelet and push it into my jeans pocket.

I like to write things down. It makes me feel good, seeing how much I've achieved. I'm going to keep this notebook in the biscuit tin under my bed with all my other treasures until I'm old enough to leave home. After that, well, who knows? Maybe I'll take the notebook with me. Or maybe

I'll dig a hole in the ground and bury it where no one will ever find it. Maybe I'll forget all about it, get on with my life, find a good job, buy a beautiful house, get married and have children of my own. Let's face it, with brains like mine, I can do anything I want.

47

Chloe

It was three months since Sammi died and the events of that night still seemed horribly surreal. I'd been trying to get on with my life, but it hadn't been easy. There were days when I felt overwhelmed by the knowledge of what I'd done, cornered, as if I was trapped inside the boot of a speeding car that was heading straight for a brick wall.

Sammi's death had impacted my life in so many ways. I'd given up my job at the theatre; I just couldn't cope with the stress of it all on top of everything else that was going on. Richard generously offered me a month-long sabbatical so I could sort my head out. It was a nice gesture, but I knew that no matter how long he gave me, I would never be the person I was before. I work for a graphic design company now. The job's a lot less pressurised – but also a lot less rewarding. The people seem nice enough, though, and it will certainly do for now.

My relationship with Tom was another casualty. We limped along for a little while after Sammi's death, but the strain of keeping such a huge secret from him was too much and eventually I ended it. I think it will be a long while before I'm ready for another relationship; I'm too busy trying to take care of myself. Sammi's funeral was our last public outing as a couple. I'd been dreading that day, especially the thought of coming face-to-face with Sammi's family. As it happened, none of her family attended, which I found odd and also incredibly sad. But I did meet a woman called Alison, who introduced herself as Sammi's foster mother. We only spoke for a few moments and she didn't stay very long at the wake; I could see how upset she was.

Obviously, I had no idea that Sammi had grown up in foster care. But then, I suppose, there was so little I *did* know about her. Nor did I learn much from the other funeral guests, who seemed to consist mainly of people Sammi knew through work. At the wake, I got chatting to a couple of women who had been on the same journalism course as her at college. However, they admitted that they'd lost touch with her years ago and had only come to the funeral after reading about her death on Facebook.

But there *had* been one positive change in my life. I was having cognitive behavioural therapy for my night terrors. It was Megan's idea; she did some research and found a therapist in Putney who specialised in sleep disorders. I decided to go private because Megan said it would take forever to get a referral from my GP and I wanted to get myself fixed as soon as possible; God forbid that history ever had a chance to repeat itself. I'd had half a dozen sessions so far and fingers crossed, it seemed to be working. There was no doubt the therapy had dredged up some painful memories, but it had been really interesting too – talking about my childhood and trying to pinpoint where it all began.

Megan and I were still at Bellevue Rise. Initially, neither of us thought we'd have the heart to go on living there, but then the landlord offered us a sizeable rent reduction. I think he knew he'd struggle to find new tenants, after the *Evening Standard* ran a piece about the accident. Megan and I realised we'd be fools to turn his offer down and actually, it's not as bad as I thought it would be. I didn't go in Sammi's old room any more than necessary, but I was sure it would be better once all her stuff was gone. I was in there the other day, shooing a wasp out of the window, and I could have sworn I heard those whale noises she used to listen to on her iPod. It was probably just my imagination playing tricks, but it was unsettling all the same.

The inquest was held last week. I didn't want to attend, but Megan said we should, otherwise it might look suspicious. The hardest thing was listening to the results of the post-mortem. The cause of death was given as 'intracerebral haemorrhage, caused by skull fracture'. The pathologist told the inquest it was one of the worst skull fractures he'd ever seen; I felt sick to my stomach when I heard that. And his report suggested one more contributing factor – alcohol intoxication. A fellow journalist who'd been with Sammi at the magazine awards ceremony she'd attended that night testified that he'd seen her drink at least three glasses of wine. As he recorded a verdict of accidental death, the coroner commented that the alcohol level in Sammi's blood was 'not insignificant' and would certainly have impaired her judgement and coordination. He concluded that Sammi most likely fell to her death after becoming disorientated while trying to find the bathroom. Her bladder had been full at the time of her death, lending weight to this theory.

There were no members of Sammi's family at the inquest. Her foster mother also failed to attend, but a day or two later she made contact via her solicitor and asked if she could arrange a convenient time to pick up Sammi's belongings. She was due any minute and I wasn't looking forward to it, praying that she didn't ask any awkward questions. I wished Megan was here for moral support. She'd be much better at dealing with Alison than I would, but unfortunately, she had to work and wouldn't be back till the evening.

The first thing she did when she arrived was ask to see the exact spot where Sammi died. I wasn't prepared for that and my tongue felt clumsy in my mouth as I explained the position of the body and pointed to the cheap, fringed rug at the bottom of the stairs. The floorboards beneath the rug were covered in dried blood that no amount of scrubbing would get out; I didn't think Alison needed to see that. She stood there for a long while, not saying anything, just staring at the rug. It made me so uncomfortable that I walked away, telling her to join me in the kitchen whenever she was ready.

When she eventually appeared in the doorway, her eyes were glistening and she was dabbing at her nose with a tissue. I hadn't been planning to offer any refreshments, not wanting to encourage her to linger, but it seemed callous not to. I invited her to sit at the table and began to prepare a cafetière of coffee.

'Thank you for agreeing to see me, Chloe,' Alison said, as I poured milk into a jug. 'How have you been? It must have been dreadful for you two, finding Sammi at the bottom of the stairs, so badly injured.'

'Oh, you know . . .' I replied ambiguously. 'Good days and bad days. How about you?'

She sighed. 'The same; I still can't believe she's gone. I hadn't seen her since my husband and I moved to Northumberland eighteen months ago, but we Skyped each other regularly.'

I placed the cafetière on the table and went to get mugs. 'I had no idea Sammi was fostered. Did you look after her for a long time?'

'Four years; she came to me just after she'd turned fifteen and stayed until she moved to London to do her journalism training.'

'What happened to her birth parents?'

'Her father had a mental breakdown. He walked out on the family when Sammi was eleven or twelve and, to the best of my knowledge, she didn't have any contact with him after that. Her mother had been unwell for some time and after her father left, Sammi had to step into the role of carer.' Alison shook her head sadly. 'It must have been an incredibly difficult time for her. From what I understand, she didn't have any support at all and I think her schoolwork really suffered as a result. Then, less than two years after her father left, her mother died of pneumonia and that's when Sammi went into care. She'd been through quite a few foster families before she came to me – passed from pillar to post like an unwanted puppy.'

'How awful,' I said quietly. 'Sammi seemed like quite a sensitive person; all those changes in her life must have affected her very deeply.'

Alison nodded. 'Oh, they did. Sammi was suffering; I could see that right away. When she first came to live with me, she was quite a handful. She was rude and she'd fly off the handle at the slightest little thing. She self-harmed too. I think it was her way of exerting control over some small part of her life. Her arms were covered in scars, I don't know if you noticed.'

'*I* didn't, but Megan saw them once,' I replied, as I pushed the plunger on the cafetière. So it wasn't a suicide attempt, just a young girl, desperate for love.

'She needed a huge amount of reassurance and support,' Alison continued as I poured the coffee. 'It wasn't an overnight fix and I had to work very hard to gain her trust, but we got there in the end.'

'Did she have any brothers or sisters?'

'No, Sammi was an only child. Her grandparents are long dead and her two uncles both live overseas, so really I'm the only family she's got.'

I felt a rush of sympathy for Sammi. I knew there had to be some reason she'd turned out the way she had. After everything she'd been through, was it any wonder she was mentally unstable? I thought about asking if Sammi had ever been diagnosed with schizophrenia but decided there was no point. She couldn't hurt us now, so what did it matter either way?

'Poor thing, it sounds as if she had an appalling start in life,' I said, placing a mug of coffee in front of Alison. 'I wonder why she never said anything to Megan and me.'

'She was worried that people would judge her if they knew she'd grown up in care; at least that was the impression I got. She kept it all bottled up inside her, but perhaps that was a mistake. I certainly think she'd have found it easier to make friends if she'd been more open with people.'

I pushed the milk and sugar towards her. 'You must have been pleased that she went on to have such a successful career. Megan and I thought Sammi's work sounded impossibly glamorous; we used to love hearing about all the people she'd interviewed.'

Alison pinched the end of her nose, as if she might be about to cry. 'Yes, I was very proud of her. She was a bright girl and I know there was so much more she wanted to do with her life.' She paused and reached for the tissue that was tucked in her sleeve. 'I was quite worried about her when she first moved to London. She suffered with anxiety and I thought she might find a big city overwhelming. I was afraid she'd struggle with communal living as well. Sammi liked everything just so and I know she locked horns a few times with various housemates over the years.' She gave a lopsided smile. 'But she was happy living here.'

'How do you know that?'

'Because she told me so, on more than one occasion. She spoke particularly fondly of you, Chloe. I know Sammi seemed confident on the outside, but she was an introvert at heart. She had lots of acquaintances, but not many real friends.' Alison looked up at me and we made eye contact. 'I think she regarded *you* as a friend, though.'

All at once, I felt as if I was in a big black box and gradually all the oxygen was being sucked out of it. I picked up my mug and turned towards the door. 'Let's take our coffee upstairs, shall we, and I can show you Sammi's things?'

Just as I had feared, Alison took her time looking around Sammi's room, not that there was much to see. The bed had been stripped and Megan and I had spent the previous evening packing Sammi's things in cardboard boxes we got from the supermarket.

'I'll help you carry everything to your car,' I said, in a bid to hurry things along.

Alison gave me a grateful look. 'Thank you, Chloe. I really appreciate you doing this; it can't have been an easy task.'

'Do you know what you're going to do with it all?'

'I'm not sure; I'll decide when I get back to Northumberland. I expect I'll give most of it to charity; I'd like to keep a few things, though.' She ran a hand over the top of a soft mohair scarf that was sitting on top of one of the boxes. Then she noticed the cash box that was tucked underneath it. 'What's in here?'

I felt my cheeks reddening. 'I don't know; it's locked.'

'Is there a key?'

'Megan and I did find a key inside an empty jar of lip balm that's about the right size. I popped it in Sammi's make-up bag for safekeeping.'

Alison picked up the mohair scarf carefully, almost reverentially, and laid it down on the bed. Then she lifted the cash box and gave it a gentle shake. Whatever was inside made a dull thud.

'It's quite heavy, isn't it?' I said.

Alison smiled sadly. 'I think I know what this is. Where did you say the key was?'

I poked around in a few more boxes until I found Sammi's make-up bag. I unzipped it and handed the small silver key to Alison, watching as she fitted it into the lock. She gave the key a half turn and the cash box sprung open to reveal a worn orange photo album.

My heart was racing; it was Sammi's scrapbook, just as we'd suspected. I'd wanted to try the key in the cash box as soon as we found it, but Megan persuaded me not to, saying it would be disrespectful.

'My hunch was right,' Alison said. 'This is Sammi's

book of memories; it was one of her most treasured possessions.' She sat down on the bed and placed it on her lap. 'Sammi once told me that when she first went into care and was being shunted from one foster home to the next, she felt as if she didn't exist – or if she did, it was only on the periphery of other people's lives. So she decided to start this book, as a way of proving to herself that she was real. It was never intended for public viewing and she was very protective over it; I think I'm one of the few people she ever showed it to. But I want you to see it, Chloe, because I know you meant a lot to her.' She patted the bed beside her. 'Come on, let's look at it together.'

I gritted my teeth. Yes, I'd wanted to see the secrets that the scrapbook held, but not like this, not in front of Sammi's nearest and dearest. But I could hardly refuse. I sat down next to Alison, as she began to turn the pages.

For the next half an hour, Sammi's messy childhood was laid bare. I felt like the worst kind of voyeur as I studied the album's contents and listened to Alison's commentary. There were photographs of Sammi with her various foster parents, important letters from Social Services, newspaper cuttings of her modest achievements – shaving off her hair for a leukaemia charity, runner-up in an inter-schools swimming gala. Despite my discomfort, I was moved by it. As Alison turned to the final page, a tear fell from my eye and landed on the plastic pocket, behind which a teen-aged Sammi grinned toothily over the top of a lit birthday cake. Alison put her arm around my shoulders. I wish she hadn't; it took every fibre of my being not to break down and admit what I'd done.

'Here,' she said, easing the photograph out of its pocket. 'Why don't you keep this, to remember her by?'

I made a gulping noise. 'Thank you,' I said. 'And Alison, I'm so very sorry for your loss.'

She looked at me and the pain in her eyes was raw. I felt a shaft of pity for her, deep and immediate, like a blow to the solar plexus. Whatever Samantha Charlesworth had or hadn't been, she was loved, and that made me feel even worse than I already did. I knew I wasn't a bad person, but I had done a very bad thing. It didn't matter that I'd been semi-conscious when I pushed Sammi down the stairs. Or that she had done some vile things to Megan and me. The fact remained that I had killed another human being and I was going to have to live with that for the rest of my life. The only trouble was, I didn't know if I could.

48

Megan

Ever since I pushed Anouk out of that window, I've been waiting for two things. Waiting to get caught and waiting to feel bad. Neither has happened yet and I know that neither will.

For some reason, Anouk's been on my mind a lot lately. Sometimes, I even fantasise about reaching out to her. She lives in a lakeside home on the French-Swiss border these days, with her financier husband and their adorable twin boys. It's an affluent area and a beautiful place to bring up children, judging by the pictures she posted on Facebook (she really ought to think about adjusting those privacy settings). But in reality, there's not much point contacting her, because she won't have a clue who I am.

The gap in Anouk's memory is due to more than just the passage of time. She sustained various physical injuries in the fall, including two broken legs and a shattered elbow. Her brain was damaged too and as a result she has no memory of the incident itself, or of any part of her life before it. According to what I heard, she didn't even recognise her own parents when she regained consciousness.

To be honest, I was surprised Anouk survived, especially when it was so long before they found her. Her father's flight was delayed, as flights often are, and by the time an ambulance was called, Anouk had already been lying unconscious on those unforgiving patio slabs for several hours. By which time I, of course, was long gone.

In an article I read in the local newspaper, shortly after the event, both Anouk's parents and the doctor who treated her concluded that her injuries were the result of an unfortunate accident. The consensus was that she had been standing on the window seat in her bedroom – perhaps to look at something in the garden that had caught her eye – when she overbalanced and toppled out of the window; I guess it's easily done. She spent a number of weeks recovering in hospital and then, almost as soon as she was discharged, her family left the UK and returned to France, where her rehabilitation continued in an expensive private clinic. Most people assumed that Anouk's parents couldn't bear to go on living in a home that held so many bad memories – and who can blame them?

But that was all a very long time ago and since then I've turned my life around. I worked hard at secondary school, then sixth form college, and ended up winning a bursary, which paid for my university education and got me the hell away from home. Why did I settle on a career in pharmacy? Forget all that crap about wanting to help people and volunteering for Médecins Sans Frontières. Why should I help others when nobody has ever lifted a finger to help me? Everything I've achieved, I did on my own, and I'm very proud of the fact. No, I chose pharmacy because I like the feeling of power it gives me . . . dishing out little white pills that can save a life – or snuff it out. What could be more satisfying than that?

I'm good at my job, I know that, and it frustrates me no end when my fellow professionals fall short of the mark. Take the A&E nurse who mucked up that prescription for Clindamycin. I know she'd probably say she was tired and overworked, but really there's no excuse for making such a basic error. I was tempted to pretend I hadn't noticed the discrepancy . . . to follow the instructions on the prescription to the letter and let that little boy's mother go ahead and give him an overdose. It might have caused nothing more than an upset stomach, but the worst-case scenario doesn't bear thinking about. Still, at least then, I thought to myself that day in the out-patient dispensary, the nurse in question would be held accountable for her error and, hopefully, learn a useful lesson in the process. But then I came to my senses; here, after all, was a golden opportunity to demonstrate my superior abilities to Serena and I would be foolish to throw it away.

I always knew the sky was the limit, but I am surprised at how well I've taken to my chosen profession, especially as I've never been much of a people person. Over the years I've learned how to be sociable, how to win people's trust, how to blend in with the crowd. At first, it required a conscious effort on my part, but I've been doing it so long now it's practically second nature. Sometimes, I forget what a fucking weirdo I was as a kid. That's why I like to read my old notebook every now and then, to help remind me what a long way I've come. But occasionally, usually when I'm least expecting it, I'll catch a glimpse of my former self. I'll look in the mirror and see an eleven-year-old girl with disappointment in her eyes and a heart that's been crushed so many times, it's a wonder it's still beating.

It would be nice if I had some photographs to look at, but precious few exist from the latter part of my childhood. I have my annual school photo, of course, and the odd snap taken by my paternal grandmother. But the picture I treasure the most was taken by my teacher at St Swithun's, just before we set off on a school trip to the seaside. I'm holding hands with Anouk and, despite the ridiculous homemade shorts I'm wearing (what on earth was I thinking?!), I look impossibly happy. That photograph not only reminds me of the blissful times I spent with Anouk, but also of my teacher, Miss Pickering, and how kind she was to me. She didn't know what life was like for me at home – *nobody* did – but she could see how much I struggled to fit in and she did her best to make my life at school as pleasant as possible. It's a shame she betrayed me in the end, just like Anouk did, but I try not to be bitter. The last I heard, Harriet Jane Pickering was working as a receptionist at a shipping company. After the very serious allegations against her, she was certainly never going to work with children again. Nothing was ever proven, of course, but there was enough circumstantial evidence to force her resignation.

Schooldays are supposed to be the happiest years of one's life, but for me, it's been the last decade or so. Until I found Chloe, I didn't know what it was to have a best friend – a *real* best friend, someone who's always there for you and who will *never* let you down. The very first time I met her, I felt as if a film were sliding off me, a murky slick of grime that had clung to me for years, and I emerged all clean and shiny and new. On the face of it, I'm the stronger half of our partnership. I'm the decisive one, the one who shrugs off disappointments and setbacks, the one who can deal with any crisis and figure out a solution to every problem. But the truth is I've always needed Chloe more than she needs me; I just hope she never manages to figure that out. I don't think she will; most of the time, she's too wrapped up in herself to see any further than the end of her cute little nose.

I was convinced that moving in together would mark a new stage in our relationship, an intensifying of the deep bond we already shared. Unfortunately, I didn't reckon on Samantha Charlesworth barging in and upsetting the beautiful equilibrium I'd painstakingly created. There were so many times I felt like sticking a knife between that silly, hair-swishing harpy's shoulder blades; in the circumstances, I think I showed amazing restraint. It was utterly shameless, the way she tried to worm her way into Chloe's affections, offering her a shoulder to cry on, trying to drive a wedge between us. Just because she didn't have a best friend of her own – or *any* friends, for that matter – Sammi thought she would go right ahead and steal mine. Big Mistake.

Chloe's the closest thing I've got to family and I'd die before I'd let her walk out of my life. I cut off all contact with Mum and Dad as soon as I left for university. I don't even know if they're still alive; they've certainly made no attempt to track me down and I really wouldn't be that difficult to find. Everyone in my social circle thinks my parents are living the dream in Oz, alongside my imaginary pilot brother. Despite being on the other side of the world, my 'doting' parents never forget a single birthday or Christmas and I've got a stack of cards and presents to prove it. Chloe doesn't seem to have noticed how similar my mother's handwriting is to mine, but then again she's never been particularly observant.

To be fair, it's partly my fault Chloe gravitated towards Sammi. I left the door wide open when I allowed myself to be distracted by that arsehole Pete Chambers. Chloe's always been on the needy side, so when I wasn't there to pick up the pieces as her flimsy little life started falling apart at the seams, she was forced to look for someone else's sleeve to snivel into.

I always knew Sammi was going to be a tough adversary. I could tell from the way she carried herself that she was damaged goods (well, they do say it takes one to know one), but she had an inner steel. And there was something in her manner – some knowingness or unwarranted curiosity – that told me she might, just *might*, recognise me for what I really am. I was prepared to risk that; what I wasn't prepared to risk was the chance that she might turn Chloe against me. Not when I'd spent twelve long years building the perfect friendship.

I suspected that if she sensed a direct threat from me, Sammi was more likely to dig her heels in than simply roll over, the way most people would. That's why I had to focus on Chloe instead – and convincing her that Sammi was really a devious, manipulative, housemate-from-hell was going to require a considerable amount of creativity.

People are always surprised to learn that scientists have a creative side. They assume that science is all about facts, but most scientific breakthroughs would never have happened without a hefty dose of imagination. Science relies on flights of fancy and inspired guesswork as much as it does on hard evidence and objective analysis. Look at how I got my revenge on Pete. Pretty ingenious, huh? I heard on the grapevine that he's applied for a job at a private hospital in Highgate. Good riddance, I say. Seriously, that man doesn't know how lucky he is. The last man who fucked with me got a dose of Colchicine, blended with his breakfast smoothie. It's used for treating gout, but in healthy people it causes cramping and severe diarrhoea. Too high a dose can trigger organ failure and eventually death. But don't worry, I'm not that sadistic, the projectile shitting was good enough for me.

Anyway, I digress. At first, I toyed with Chloe in subtle ways – items disappearing from her room, keys vanishing from her coat pocket, vital work being deleted from her laptop. I knew she wouldn't think for one nanosecond that straight-as-a-die, member-of-the-hospital-Ethics-Committee Megan might be responsible. The finger of blame would therefore point firmly in Sammi's direction – and, just to grease the wheels of suspicion, I claimed that weird stuff had been happening to me too.

In the interests of honesty, I should point out that I unfairly blamed Sammi for a couple of things. I realised, some time after the event, that it was actually me who left my bedroom window open, so that my room ended up being decorated with the contents of my in-tray. The night before, I'd been burning a Crabtree & Evelyn candle I bought from a charity shop and when I woke up the next morning, my room smelled like a spinster aunt's front parlour. Before I left for work, I opened the window to air the room out, and then promptly forgot I'd done so. As for my ASOS dress . . . with hindsight, I do recall taking my pen out of my bag to fill out a dental insurance claim form and then carelessly tossing it down somewhere in my room. It's funny how these little things slip your mind at the time.

Of course, I was well aware that certain drugs would increase Chloe's sense of disorientation and paranoia, thereby bringing my scheme to fruition more speedily. I'd actually been working on a way to medicate her by stealth – but then, in a delicious irony, she made things so much easier by asking me if I could get my hands on something to help her sleep. Naturally, I was only too happy to oblige.

My special prescription was a non-benzodiazepine sedative, which, in the dose I recommended, not only induces a deep sleep, but also impairs thinking and slows down cognitive functioning. The effects only intensified when Chloe, rather rashly, took it upon herself to up the dosage – but who was I to stand in her way? No wonder the silly thing got herself into such a pickle over the *Neurosis* set; from the sound of it, she was lucky she didn't get herself fired. To be honest, I think it's no bad thing that she fell foul of Richard Westlake. She hero-worshipped that man; it made me sick, listening to the fawning things she used to say about him. Suffice to say, I don't think she has quite such a high opinion of him these days.

I suppose I could've stopped there, but frankly, I was having too much fun. In any case, I wanted to teach Chloe a lesson for having the gall to play besties with someone she'd known for all of two seconds, especially after everything I've done for her over the past twelve years. Ungrateful bitch. Hence the poor little kitty cat, who nobly sacrificed its life for the greater good. After dispatching the creature (humanely, with a single blow to the head, I should add), I collected some of its blood for the next stage of my plan. Knocked out cold by a double dose of pills, Chloe's eyelids barely flickered as I daubed her hands with claret, before creating a trail down the stairs with my own bloody handprints. All that remained was to pose the animal's body for maximum impact and wake Chloe up a short while later by throwing stones at her bedroom window. Then I took up a suitable vantage point behind a neighbour's 4x4, and waited for the show to begin. And what a show it was. I must confess I was slightly disappointed that Chloe never breathed a word to me about her grisly discovery, as I had been looking forward to dispensing words of reassurance and comfort. I guess she was so disgusted by what she thought she'd done that she couldn't bear to confide in anyone, not even her best friend.

Then, a few days later, I had a massive stroke of luck when I stumbled across Sammi's medication while Chloe and I were looking for the photo album; it was an opportunity that was too good to miss. Just for the record, *Lurasipine* doesn't exist; I made the name up on the spur of the moment. If Chloe had had the common sense to read the label on Sammi's pill bottle for herself, she might have realised it contained nothing more than a mild anti-depressant – certainly not the amnesia-inducing anti-psychotic I made it out to be. I knew she wouldn't, though; that's always been Chloe's trouble: she's far too trusting. She's highly suggestible too, the way emotional people tend to be. That's why I was fairly confident that, given a little time, she would eventually reach the wholly inaccurate conclusion that Sammi had tampered with her medication. It's also the reason Chloe believes she's a murderer. But she wasn't the one who pushed Sammi down the stairs. I was.

I didn't have to plan a thing; Chloe did all the hard work for me. I was asleep when the sound of the squeaky floorboard outside her bedroom door woke me up. *Here we go again*, I thought to myself. Another one of Chloe's tedious night terrors. I had half a mind to go back to sleep and let her get on with it, but I needed the loo and anyway, I thought it might be amusing to see what ridiculous pantomime she'd cast herself in this time. I got out of bed and walked towards the door. Out on the landing, I could hear Chloe moving around and muttering to herself. Then, to my surprise, I heard another voice: Sammi's. Chloe must have woken her up too.

'Is that you, Chloe?' I heard her say. 'What are you doing out there?'

Slowly and quietly, I opened my bedroom door. There was just enough light on the landing for me to make out two figures. Although their features were indistinct, I could tell straight away which one was Sammi because of her height. She was standing at the top of the stairs, staring at Chloe, whose arms were curiously outstretched like a zombie.

I've always had the ability to think on my feet and I acted reflexively, charging out on to the landing, straight past Chloe. Before Sammi had a chance to think, let alone react, I was pushing her in the chest with both hands, as hard as I could. For a split second, our eyes met and, in that moment, I almost felt sorry for her. She let out a high-pitched scream as she toppled backwards, hands clawing the empty air in desperation. There was a dull thud and then silence.

I looked back at Chloe, who was tottering around in confusion, clearly still asleep. All I had to do was tiptoe back to my room, turn on the bedside light and step back out on to the landing, acting as if I'd only just woken up. Chloe's imagination did the rest.

I'm glad we've got the house back to ourselves; we should never have let anyone else in. And there's no doubt that Chloe now knows what a real best friend is. However, if she shows any signs of straying again, I shall have no hesitation in threatening to reveal what she did to poor Sammi. I mustn't be too hard on her, though; Chloe's brought me a lot of happiness over the years, the kind of happiness I didn't think was possible for a person like me. And more than that, she reminds me of someone, someone who I loved very much. I can see her now, a ghost child waiting patiently on the edge of my memory; a little girl with yellow ribbons in her hair. I keep trying to reach her, but every time I get near, she dissolves to a fuzzy outline, like the sky at the end of a lovely day, when the sun has disappeared and only its aura remains.

Acknowledgements

Writing is a solitary pursuit, but publishing is definitely a team event and I am indebted to Mari Evans and the hugely talented gang at Headline. A heartfelt thank you to everyone involved, but especially to my editors Sara Adams and Toby Jones for their wonderful, insightful ideas and constant encouragement.